Cover Her Body
— A Singular Village Mystery —

Cover Her Body

— A Singular Village Mystery —

Eleanor Sullivan

YESTERYEAR
PRESS

Cover Her Body

by Eleanor Sullivan

This is a work of fiction. All of the characters, organizations, and events portrayed in this novel are either products of the author's imagination or are used fictitiously.

Book design by Nehmen-Kodner: www.n-kcreative.com
Author photo by Pamela Mougin
Printed in the United States of America

Published by: Yesteryear Press, an imprint of Wyatt-MacKenzie
www.yesteryearpress.com
www.eleanorsullivan.com

First Edition
ISBN: 978-1-936214-55-6
Library of Congress Control Number: 2011935684

*This book is dedicated to my grandmother,
Alice Ruth Ricker Reed Clore,
who instilled in me the love of Zoar.*

My soul has grown deep like the rivers.

—Langston Hughes

Do not squander time, for that is what life is made of.

—Benjamin Franklin

He served God so faithfully and well.
That now he sees him, face to face, in Hell.

—Hilaire Belloc, Epitaph on a Puritan

Acknowledgements

I am indebted to Kathleen Fernandez, former site manager at the Zoar Village State Memorial, who answered countless questions about how the Separatists lived and worked. No detail was too small nor insignificant for her to recall.

Maternity nurse Shirley Martin supplied minute details about births gone wrong, Joan Lynaugh, nurse historian, steered me to obscure resources, and Luci Zahray, the poison lady, suggested deadly herbs and their actions.

Lorin Oberweger, editor extraordinaire, challenged me over and over to create a better story. Nancy Cleary, at Wyatt-MacKenzie Publishing, shepherded this book to print.

The fine people who keep the Zoar Community Association vibrant and thriving were invaluable with information and hospitality.

I thank, too, the Alphas, the Arch Criminals, my Sisters in Crime, and fellow Mystery Writers of America. You all did more than you know to encourage and support me.

Most of all, I thank those courageous settlers who left their home and country to create a new life in a new land. You make us better people by your example.

—Eleanor Sullivan

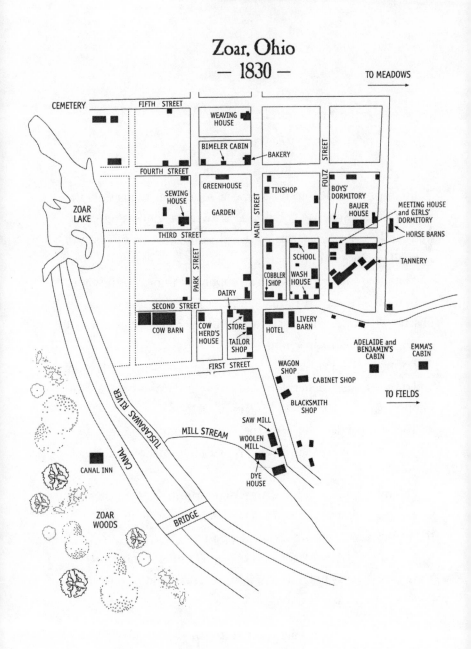

— One —

03 May 1833 — Zoar, Ohio

Ropes creaked as Adelaide slid off the bed and waited, clutching herself in the cold. In the cradle next to the bed, her infant puckered her lips and let out a sigh before sinking back into sleep. Benjamin's side of the bed remained empty. Had he even returned during the night?

Adelaide grabbed her dress from the hook on the wall, pulled it over her head, and moved on stocking feet through the cabin, her hem whispering across the wood plank floor. With a glance up the stairs where her sister slept, she bent to button her shoes, then snatched her shawl off a peg and slipped outside.

The air hung heavy with moisture from last night's storm. Apple blossoms littered the ground by the door, their scent cloying. Nothing stirred. Good. If she hurried she might have just enough time to herself before the workday began.

A fleeting sensation of guilt washed over her. No good Separatist would sneak out for an unsanctioned outing.

With a shrug, she looped her shawl across her chest, grasped her skirts, and plunged down the hill, her feet moving silently over the rough cinders. She hurried past Benjamin's cabinet shop and the blacksmith shop next to it, around the store and dairy, continuing on the path into the woods. She didn't need the moonlight nor a lantern to guide her way. The sound of rushing water hidden below the hill drew her to a favored spot.

She skidded to a stop.

The willow tree—her tree—lay sprawled in the water, its branches flailing about in the raging water. She sank onto a boulder to the side and shut her eyes against the image. No longer would the tree shield her from the prying eyes of her community. Only naked spikes of its stump remained.

A cock crowed in the distance.

The river roared downstream and splattered foam on the boulder. Adelaide tucked her skirt around her ankles, hugged her knees to her chest, and rocked back and forth. The quarrel she'd had with Benjamin the night before lingered in her mouth like the taste of an unripe persimmon.

Her eyes wandered over the surface of the water, pausing on a white object bobbing in the darkness. Blue fabric trailed in the current. Her mind worked to make sense of the sight until horror plunged through her, tightening her throat.

It was a hand. A girl's hand.

A wave splashed over the body and twisted it loose to bob beneath the water and spring up again. Only a strand of tangled hair tethered to a branch kept her from plummeting downstream. If she left to get someone, the girl might be gone. She couldn't let the river take her.

Adelaide hiked up her skirts and plunged into the water, the cold sucking her breath. She struggled for a few steps, but her shoes filled with water, and she tumbled forward. The panic she'd felt all those years ago when the boys had tossed her into the river came back with a rush. She flailed about, gulping dirt-choked water, her arms splashing uselessly.

At last her feet touched bottom. She pushed against it, sprang to the surface, and grabbed onto the body, its buoyancy keeping them both afloat. She spit out muddy water and jerked the girl's hair loose from its tangle. Her churning legs steered them forward until the girl's head bumped into the bank.

She slipped off the corpse and stood in the waist-high water, shivering as a gust of wind rose from the river. Her sodden clothing clung to her small frame, the wet-wool smell of her shawl tangled around her neck, choking her. Adelaide bent down and turned the body toward her.

Johanna. She stared at the open eyes of her friends' beloved daughter as water washed over the girl's face. Her knees buckled as a vision of her own precious baby rose in her mind. She clutched Johanna to her breast and rocked back and forth, the chill forgotten. Whatever would Helga do when she learned of another daughter's death?

The wind picked up, and a wave splattered them. Joanna's lifeless arms flapped about, slapping her with icy hands. *She's so cold, poor child. I have to get her out.* She groaned as she lifted the water-logged body farther up onto the bank. A whoosh of air escaped from Johanna's lips.

Air? No water?

She tugged again. Only a dribble escaped the girl's lips. Puzzled, she rolled Johanna over gently. The skin on the girl's colorless face seemed as if it had been molded out of paraffin. Adelaide reached over and closed her eyes.

A voice from above cut through her. *"Was machst Du?"*

Benjamin ran his hand across the top of the wooden chest with practiced precision, trusting his fingers to tell him if the surface was smooth enough. The lantern pegged on the wall yielded scant light, and wispy haze clogged the view through the cabinet shop's one window. Dissatisfied, he took up a plane and scraped it across the top, tendrils of wood curling in its wake. The reassuring scent of fresh shavings lingered in the crisp air. Once again he examined his work, fingers searching for exposed grain. Better. Still some rough edges.

Dust rose in the air and settled on his shoulders. He brushed it off his smock but only managed to rub it into the cloth. He sighed. So much left to do on the Cleveland man's order and only a week to finish.

The door slammed open, the lantern bobbing on its hook. He whirled at the interruption as young Emmett, pink-cheeked and black hair disheveled, sputtered, "Herr Bechtmann, there's a body in the river." He sank to his knees, his breath coming in spurts.

Fear clutched his throat as he grabbed the boy by his suspenders and pulled him to his feet. "Who? Who is it?"

Emmett's head jerked about as Benjamin shook him. "I don't know," he stammered. "Herr Guenther just told me to get you."

He shoved the frightened boy aside and fled out the door. If anything happened to her... He ignored several men who yelled to him as he sped down the hill, boots sliding on dew-covered grass. His heel caught on a tuft of grass and sent him stumbling, but he caught himself and continued to charge ahead, thoughts of Adelaide holding him upright.

Whyever hadn't he stopped her from going to the river? Alone. By herself. A *verboten* pleasure denied the Separatists. Admittedly difficult, redemption required constant vigilance, and self-denial was the bedrock of their beliefs. Why couldn't she understand? They had to follow the rules. Everyone did.

He crested the hill, fear numbing his limbs, and scanned the group gathered by the banks of the river. There she was. Water-drenched, shivering, her cap awry, but alive.

Seeing him, Adelaide ducked her head, shoulders hunched against the cold, her feet flying toward him. He crushed her to him, relief flowing out of him like the water from her clothes that pooled at their feet. He buried his head in her hair that smelled of river and fish and rotted wood, and he didn't care.

"I thought," he choked. "They said a body in the river—"

She stuttered, but he drew her closer. "It doesn't matter now," he murmured into her neck.

Footsteps crunched on the path behind them. Martin Guenther, the cow boss, stomped his staff into the ground and grasped it with burly hands as he caught his breath. His beefy, bullnecked body towered over them. "I need a coffin built."

"It was Johanna, Johanna Appelgate," she told him.

He felt the blood drain from his head. *Not Johanna.*

She stared at him, her face tilted in puzzlement. Auburn curls plastered against her face, green eyes confused. How could she understand his pain?

Raised in the Appelgates' household along with their many children, he had thought of Johanna as an almost sister, more beloved than any of the others because of her impish ways and adoring blue eyes.

"It couldn't be," he said, shaking his head. She's so alive, so forceful, so strong. "I'm sure you're wrong."

She laid a hand on his arm. "Benjamin, I pulled her out of the water. It's her. I'm so sorry."

He stared down at his wife, and her face told him she spoke the truth. "But how?" he asked them both. "And why?"

"Comes from giving the girls so much freedom," Martin said. Black hair flopped in his face, and he swiped it back with a practiced motion. "I try to tell them—"

"Tell them what?" Adelaide asked. "Not to be themselves, to catch a bit of fun whenever they can? They're innocent children. What are they supposed to do?"

"Humph. They're—we're—all sinners, even children." He spit on the ground. "And I need that coffin before nightfall," he told Benjamin.

"Today?" Adelaide slammed her hands on her hips. "What about her parents? No time to mourn her? Is that what they want?"

"They have no say." He yanked his staff out of the ground. "She's mine to decide."

"I thought Ilse Forster supervised the dairy maids," Adelaide argued. "Doesn't she have anything to say about it?"

"My decision," Martin said.

He gritted his teeth. Johanna, so laughing, so teasing, always able to cheer him whenever he thought of his own lost family. Just last night she'd tried to talk to him but he'd turned away. Her body ripe with womanhood had surprised him, and when she'd tried to tell him her secret, he couldn't bear it.

Now it was too late. But he wouldn't let Martin see his grief. "As soon as I can get some walnut," he said, his fingers clutched in Adelaide's hair.

"Don't wait for that. I want her buried by evening. And you," he said to Adelaide. "You best be readying the body."

"Nathan and Helga," Adelaide said, her voice shaking. "We have to tell them. I can't imagine…"

Martin flapped a hand toward her. "I'll handle it."

"We must go to Nellie," Adelaide said, heading toward their cabin. "No telling what this will do to her."

— Two —

Nellie thrust a squirming Olivia, overdue for feeding, toward Adelaide, her eyes widening at her sister's wet clothing.

"Hold her while I change," Adelaide said, her teeth chattering. Her hip banged the table and rattled plates, but she hurried past the upstairs ladder to grab her other weekday dress. She tried to rush before Olivia's squeals turned to screams, but her fingers, stiff with cold, struggled to undo the tiny buttons on her bodice.

If only I could keep this news from Nellie.

At last clad in dry undergarments and dress, navy apron, and a clean white cap tied over her damp curls, Adelaide settled into the rocker and took a wiggling Olivia from her sister's arms. She buried her nose in the crevices of Olivia's neck, inhaling her earthy, innocent scent.

"It's Johanna," Benjamin said in a tight voice.

"Wait."

"Adelaide, she'll learn soon enough. Best she hear it from us."

He was right, of course. "I'll tell her then." She reached out for Nellie, but her sister jerked away. She grabbed Adelaide's sodden clothing off the floor and clutched them to her body.

Nothing for it but to tell her. "I found her in the river and tried to get her out, but I was too late. I'm afraid she's dead."

Nellie stood as if frozen in place. Water dripped onto her skirts and puddled at her feet. She shivered, and that seemed to rouse her. "I'll hang your clothes outside," she said at last.

Adelaide watched out the window as Nellie spread her dress on a low-hanging branch. She'd shown so little emotion since leaving the girls' dormitory that Adelaide seldom could tell what her sister was thinking or, for that matter, feeling.

"You shouldn't have told her like that," Benjamin said as he reached up above the sink and pulled down a tin with a jerky motion.

"Just how should I have told her?" Her voice held an edge that she didn't try to control. He hadn't been the one to find Johanna, struggle to get her out and, most of all, fight off her own terror in the water.

He ran a finger around his collar and shoved at his disheveled hair. It curled a bit at his neck—she'd need to trim it soon, she thought absently. "I don't know. Warned her or something," he said as he added roasted rye grains to the coffeepot.

Olivia twisted away from the breast, and Adelaide realized she'd been clutching her too tightly. She repositioned her, and the baby grabbed on with renewed force. "See how my sister is? You want to send our baby to a place like that? Take away her smile, her laughter—"

"Adelaide, please, this isn't about us, our fight. Let's stop talking about it now." He wrapped a warmed coverlet around her and propped her feet on a stool in front of the stove's open door.

She sank back into the rocker with relief and irritation. Trust Benjamin to be reasonable. And to do a kindness for her just when she wanted to scream, lash out, hit him or someone.

Benjamin set the coffeepot on the stove and bent to stir the fire. How did he feel about Johanna's death? Grateful to Nathan and Helga for rescuing him from near starvation in Germany, he nonetheless had a special fondness for Johanna the way older brothers often feel protective toward a beloved younger sister.

He'd looked so stricken, though, when she told him who drowned. As if he'd lost his soul.

Coffee gurgled on the stove, its aroma filling the small cabin.

"I didn't see her at first," Adelaide said, keeping her voice level and her eyes on him. "She was caught under the tree, the one where I...it fell in the storm and she was trapped under it—"

"She was still alive?"

"No, no. She'd been dead a long time, since last night surely. Martin, he's the one who came along. Wanted to know what I was doing." She turned aside, keeping her fear to herself.

Her mind rushed back a few days. Johanna had come to her workroom wanting something for a woman's ailment. It was for another girl at the dairy, she insisted.

"To drown. I can't imagine a worse death," he said, his square jaw clenched tight the only sign of emotion.

Adelaide agreed, but she shoved the image aside. She'd come too near herself that morning to a watery death. Instead she rose to return Olivia to her cradle and wiped a dribble of milk off her face with the corner of the blanket before she turned to face her husband.

"She didn't drown."

"What?"

Nellie poked her head in the door. "Coffee's boiling," she reported and then asked if she could go to the Appelgates'.

"Ask them if they want you there," Adelaide said. "They just lost a daughter and may want to be alone right now."

Nellie toed the floor. "I could take the boys for them."

"I'm sure they'd appreciate that, but you ask to be sure, you hear?"

Her sister ran off. As if she were a normal fourteen-year-old. Had she really recovered that quickly?

Benjamin poured steaming liquid into a cup. His hand shook as he handed it to her. "What do you mean she didn't drown?"

She clutched her cup until her hands blanched white against the blue pottery. "There was no water in her lungs."

A shadow flicked across his face. "Then how'd she die? Was she sick?"

What did it mean? Pain?

"She wasn't ill."

"She drowned." A vein pulsed on his neck. "You must be mistaken."

"I have to tell Josef. He's our leader; he has to know."

"What can he do? It's too late."

"But we don't know why. She was dead when she went in the water, and that means someone put her there."

"Surely you don't think it's a crime of some sort. We're Separatists. We don't believe in killing, regardless the provocation. Or in spite of it."

"This isn't about our beliefs," she said irritably. "It's about Johanna and how she died." But what if her remedy killed Johanna? Was that a crime? Still, someone took her to the river. "Josef needs to know. I have to tell him. He can decide what to do."

"No. Don't talk about it. You'll only cause trouble."

"Trouble? You think I don't know if a person drowned or not?"

The clank of hammer on iron sounded in the distance. "Nathan's already back at work—and it's his daughter who died—and I have a coffin to build." He grabbed his jacket off the hook. "And Welby's order to finish before Saturday. You," he said, a square-tipped finger pointing at her, "keep your doubts to yourself."

The chair scraped as she jumped to her feet. "I don't care what her father is doing. Or you either, come to that. I will do what I need to. It's not yours to order me about."

"Do you know how she died? You don't, do you? You don't know anything for sure. Besides, you want them knowing about—"

"What? My time to myself?"

"No, but that, too. Think about what could happen. To you. To us. Think about that."

Adelaide slumped back in her seat after he left. Solitude helped her ready herself for her work and, goodness knows, she was uncertain enough of her skills. She rose from the table, her skirt dragging the floor. Outside she dipped a pail into the cistern and lugged it inside to the stove. She stood beside it, watching the water heat.

Had the herbs been for Johanna herself and not one of the other girls as she'd said? Had she made a mistake? Again?

The water boiled over and splattered the floor. She grabbed the handle with a towel and poured steaming water into two basins in the sink.

Was there a way to tell if someone died from the concoction she'd made? She'd recorded in her *Kasusbuch* that she'd given a herb mixture to JA on Wednesday last. It wouldn't take much for someone to realize that JA was Johanna Appelgate.

She scraped slivers of yellow soap into one of the basins and swished them around with a wooden spoon. The soap bubbled up into suds, and the scene at the river came rushing back, Johanna's waxy face rising as the sun hit it, turning it to clay. But she hadn't recorded the ingredients in the mixture she'd given the girl.

She shook off her thoughts. She must ready herself to face her friend. And find out if what she suspected about Johanna was true. Maybe her worry was for naught.

After the dishes were stacked on the shelf, she dried her hands and hurried out to her workroom, shivering from more than the cold of the unheated room. She reached up on the shelf above her workbench for the jar of rosemary and tapped some leaves into a tin cup, added lavender, and bent to sniff the delicate scent, calming herself if only for a moment.

Nellie returned and Adelaide called her out to the workroom to ask about Helga. Her sister stood in the doorway, twisting the corner of her apron. A sprinkling of freckles across her nose stood out in sharp relief on her pale skin and flushed cheeks. "*She's* there."

Gerda, Helga's sister and Johanna's aunt, who supervised the girls' dormitory where Nellie had spent too many miserable years. "She's not in charge of you now," Adelaide told her evenly.

Nellie rolled her apron into a spiral, her knuckles white against the navy fabric.

If only she could allay her sister's fear. "You don't have to go back today." She motioned to a cluster of herbs drying on a rack beside her. "Crush some thyme for me while I'm gone."

Nellie seemed to relax. She even wrinkled her nose in distaste. "That smells. I don't like it." She almost sounded like the girl she had been before she'd been forced into the dormitory.

"You need to start working with the herbs, Nellie."

Olivia whimpered, and Nellie rushed back into the cabin, sparing Adelaide from saying any more. If only she could change the rigid ways of the trustees. They had decreed that she should train Nellie to become a herbalist, and that was that.

After she had collected enough rosemary and lavender leaves

to suit her and snapped a lid on the tin cup, she made a note in her casebook and closed up the room. Nellie smiled up from the rocking chair where she had Olivia perched on her lap, giggling with her. At least Olivia brought Nellie out of herself, a blessing for certain. Adelaide slung the braided cord of her medicine bag across her body and prepared herself for what lay ahead.

Outside, the sun had paid no mind to death, its light glinting off the red-tile roofs of the log cabins that dotted the town. Nestled in a valley of gently sloping hills, the town, named Zoar for the place where Lot had found refuge much as the Separatists had in Ohio, reminded Adelaide of her long-ago home in Germany.

The village below pulsed with the rhythm of another workday. Along the main road, men with shovels, picks, or hoes propped on their shoulders led wagons to the fields, horses straining with their loads of seed. *Hausfraus* hurried on their errands, carrying baskets of just-spun flax to the weaving house or returning with finished coverlets or clothing from the sewing house. Yeast smells came from the bakery, its ovens already busy.

A sawmill shrieked in the distance.

Adelaide clutched her bag to her chest. What if her suspicions were true? Was she to blame for Johanna's death?

A light breeze stirred, rousing her. Johanna's body must be readied in time regardless of her own worry.

Determinedly, she propped her bag on her hip and headed down toward the town. At the main road she turned left and passed by the skeleton of their planned hotel, its massive posts thrust skyward. Two men centered a door frame along the front, studied it a moment, and then hammered it into place.

Smoke rose from the chimney of Nathan's blacksmith shop and hung over the cabinet shop next door where Benjamin studied a chair seat on his workbench. He'd ordered her not to report her suspicions. Why?

At the next corner her steps slowed. The Appelgates' cabin loomed ahead, its one room beginnings all but swallowed by the haphazard warren of connecting rooms that had been insufficient to contain their expanding family. Now just three little ones remained at home and, with Johanna's death, only two of their four grown daughters survived, though neither lived with Helga and Nathan. Maria was married to the innkeeper, Simon, and would soon birth her first child, and Brigit lived above the dairy.

After a few moments and no one had answered the door, Adelaide felt a brief sensation of relief. Maybe they took the body elsewhere, and she wouldn't be responsible for it.

Just then the door swung open and Helga, her eyes, red-rimmed and swollen, crushed Adelaide to her. "I'm so sorry," she mumbled into Helga's ample bosom.

A door opened at the back wing of the cabin, and footsteps clicked purposely toward them. Helga stifled her tears and patted her apron into place as her sister entered.

With her narrow eyes squeezed close together and a chin ending in a defined point, Gerda's face reminded Adelaide of a squashed pumpkin. She plopped a pail of water into the sink and turned a questioning frown on Adelaide.

"I brought herbs to wash Johanna," Adelaide said, her mind jumping back to Nellie's reports of the woman's cruelty toward the girls.

Gerda sniffed.

Ignoring her sister, Helga gathered herself and motioned for Adelaide to follow into the next room. Inside, Johanna lay on the bed, several blankets piled on top of her. "She was so cold," Helga said, straightening the covers warming her daughter.

"Do you have some heated water?" Adelaide asked Gerda.

"Cold water's good enough," Gerda answered. "Makes no difference now."

"I need some warmed for the washing," Adelaide said and turned to Helga. "I brought rosemary and lavender."

"What a waste," Gerda murmured under her breath as she left.

Adelaide bit her lip. Why didn't Helga admonish her sister? Was she afraid of her, too?

Gerda returned with a pan of water and dropped it on the bedside table with a clank. Water sloshed out. Heading back out of the room, she said to no one in particular, "That girl never had a switch to her hide." Her voice crackled with resentment. "How can you raise a child up right without that, I ask you?"

Adelaide cleaned up the spills beside the pan and lay the wet towel aside. "Why do you allow her to talk to you like that? At a time like this?"

"It's not Johanna that makes her angry. It's me." She stroked the clean linen sheet nestled in her arms. "After mother lost so many and I finally came along, well, they did spoil me, I have to admit. Maybe I enjoyed it too much."

"And you've been trying to atone ever since?"

Helga studied Adelaide, her head cocked to the side. "Maybe you're right. Did I ever tell you what she told Nathan after Johanna was born? She told him she hoped he wouldn't 'do that' again." Adelaide felt her face flush, but Helga paid no mind. "She never did take to Johanna, or any of my children."

"Why was she put in charge of the girls' dormitory?"

"No children of her own. I guess they thought she wouldn't show favoritism."

Not likely.

"Truth be told, I'm glad my girls were too old for the girls' house by the time we arrived here."

Adelaide crumbled a few rosemary leaves into the water and added crushed lavender. A sweet aroma filled the air. But she had to find out if what she suspected was true, and she needed Helga out of the room to do it. "I'll need more towels. Would you see what you can find?"

"More? All right," she said to Adelaide's nod.

As soon as the door closed behind Helga, Adelaide slid her hands under Johanna's tangled hair to feel for swellings, bruises, or abrasions. Nothing. She uncovered Johanna's torso, and her breath caught in her throat. There it was. What she hoped she wouldn't find. Darkened nipples and the telltale line down her abdomen.

"What are you doing?" Gerda said, the door slamming back against the wall.

"That's enough," Helga said, following. "You can say whatever you want to me, *Schwester*, but I've had enough of your rudeness to my friend. Go, get out of here."

Adelaide yanked the coverlet up over Johanna. "Helga, I—"

"Never you mind her, you know how she is."

If Helga asked what she'd been doing, what could she say? Reveal her daughter's sin? Never.

Helga clutched the towels to her. "She's always been my favorite," she said, staring down at her daughter's pale face. "You'll find out. When you have more, you'll see that, no matter how hard you try, one will be, well, special."

If I ever have another.

"I don't think I could love any other child like I do Olivia. Is it like that when you have the first?" The moment the words were out of her mouth, Adelaide wished she could retract them. Helga's oldest daughter, Ophelia, had killed herself the year before.

Helga slumped over the bed, and Adelaide rushed to her side. "I'm so sorry. I didn't think…" She hugged Helga, her own tears threatening. How could she have been so thoughtless?

"It's all right." Helga wiped her eyes on her apron. "Nothing for it but to get through this."

"You sit there," she said, waving Helga toward a chair. "I'll take care of Johanna." And keep her from seeing the revealing signs on her daughter's body.

"But I should—"

"I'll do it while you tell me about her." Adelaide dipped her cloth into the scented solution. "She had a beau, I heard."

Helga cleared her throat and a small smile crept onto her face. "They all liked her, they did. I think several wanted to marry her, but her, independent, she was."

"Anyone special?"

"Jakob Kirchner is sweet on her, that's for certain, but she led him a merry chase, she did. Liked all the boys. Even Benjamin."

Johanna's arm slipped out of her fingers and bounced on the bed.

Her Benjamin?

"Smitten with him, she was, back when they were younger."

Whatever had he been doing with Johanna last night? Returning home from a late visit, she'd caught sight of them beside his shop, out of view of the road. She started to approach, but something about the way they stood—Johanna's face tilted up to his—stopped her.

Helga's voice called her back. "Had her own ideas, she did."

"I thought," Adelaide said quickly, "that someone would have noticed she was gone. Especially with the storm."

Where was Benjamin last night?

"Always was a bit of a handful," Helga said wistfully.

Adelaide turned Johanna's hand over to wash it and stopped. Scratches criss-crossed the girl's fingers. She plucked a sliver of wood out of Johanna's hand. It looked old.

She hurried to the foot of the bed. Maybe it wasn't her herbs. Maybe something—or someone—else killed her. "Can you think of anyone who'd want to hurt her?"

"Hurt her? Why would anyone want to hurt her? Everyone loved her."

Not everyone.

"No one ever understood," Helga said, her hands clutched in her apron. "After they made her move away... However are you going to let Olivia go to the girls' house, her so young?"

Adelaide swallowed. She didn't have time to think about giving up Olivia right now. "You were saying that after she moved—"

"I just didn't see her much afterward. Martin, he made her work so hard."

Adelaide took the linen sheet that Helga handed her, tucked one long edge under the body, and turned her on her side. Lividity— bluish red where blood had pooled—stained Johanna's upper back. Her limbs had been flexible enough to move when Adelaide had first found her so she had been dead long enough for rigor to have come and gone, but she had lain on her back for some time before her body had gone into the water. Besides splinters in her fingers, Adelaide had found no other signs of trauma on her body. Whatever caused her death?

After she finished drying Johanna's back, she tugged the sheet through, and swaddled her in it. A few strands of fair hair escaped the shroud that framed her face. Pasty skin stretched tight over a sharp-edged chin, a dimple carved permanently into its cleft.

Helga joined Adelaide at her daughter's side.

"My baby," she murmured and sunk her face onto Johanna's neck.

Gerda came back into the room. "New linen. Humph. What do you think you're doing? Wasting that to rot away in the ground?"

Helga pulled herself up to her full height. "I wouldn't let her lie in something old."

"Waste nothing," Gerda said. "And burying in good cloth is a waste."

"I don't care. She's my daughter, and I'll bury her how I see fit."

Outdoors, Johanna's dress and underclothes hung motionless on a clothesline, as if waiting for her to fill them again. They would be given to another girl.

Now Adelaide knew. Johanna was to birth a child and both were dead. She flashed back to her mother's sweat-drenched face, her strength ebbing, her effort spent. *No, I can't think of that.* She brought her thoughts back to Johanna. The girl was a charmer, for sure, convincing Adelaide to relinquish the packet of herbs even as she still had doubts about who intended to take it.

Her casebook hung heavy in her apron pocket. A thought flashed across her mind, but she quickly dismissed it. She would not alter her record of treatment, no matter how damaging it might be to her own reputation. She might as well give up her practice if she bent to such deceit.

She turned at the corner next to an overgrown mulberry bush and nearly ran into Jakob, who was as startled as she. His loose jacket flapped behind him, and soot stained the shirt beneath it. He ducked his head, but Adelaide stopped him. "I'm so sorry about Johanna."

His head jerked up. A cut on his cheek seeped blood.

"You're hurt. I have something for it." She rummaged through her bag.

"My fault, my fault," he murmured as he scooted past her, his hunched back his only response.

His fault? Did he mean the injury to his face?

Adelaide watched him turn at the next corner and head toward the *Bauer Haus* where he lived with the hired hands who helped in the fields.

Could he be the father of Johanna's child? Or did he mean his fault Johanna died?

Three

Adelaide bypassed her own cabin, heard Nathan pounding on metal in the blacksmith shop, and spied Benjamin bent over his workbench in the cabinet shop on her way up the hill. Only one person could advise her. Emma. Her teacher, her friend, her surrogate parent.

Emma had taken her in after her own mother died and their father abandoned her and Nellie to return to Germany. Her sight fading, she struggled to serve as the village's healer. Nonetheless, she welcomed ten-year-old Adelaide into her home. Soon Adelaide was reading labels on herb jars to her and, standing knee-high at Emma's table, began her lessons in the herbal arts. And much more.

Adelaide knocked and identified herself as she entered, drinking in the comforting mixture of herbs, stewed apples, and soap that scented the tiny cabin.

Emma leaned forward on her rocking chair, her crinkled face breaking into a smile. "Ah, child. So good to see you." She patted the cap perched precariously on her topknot, but she only managed to shove it into a jaunty angle atop thinning white hair.

"You've heard about Johanna," Adelaide said, settling herself on a stool by Emma's side.

"People are saying she drowned, sometime during the storm." Emma fumbled on her lap for a strand of willow. Beside her on the table lay various lengths of willow strips. Several completed baskets of various sizes and shapes, with handles and without, sat beside her on the floor.

"I have to talk to you about that."

Emma fingered the base of her basket. Satisfied that it was the diameter she wanted, she shuffled through the willow strips on the table. Adelaide knew better than to try to help.

She found the piece she needed and returned to her work, weaving the strip in and out of the upright prongs, her fingers moving with an expertise that belied her arthritic joints. And her blindness.

"She didn't drown," Adelaide said, and explained how Johanna's lungs were empty of water.

Emma put her work aside and turned toward Adelaide. Sharp intelligence lay behind her clouded blue eyes. "Have you talked to Josef? Told him your suspicions?"

"I planned to, but then I thought about what would happen if I do. He'll have to investigate. Can you imagine how terrible that will be? Just by asking questions, he's saying that someone is lying. If only by omission. That's why I'm here. To ask you what you think I should do."

"You have to tell him, Adelaide. It's your duty to report anything untoward to him. It's just like if you didn't know what to do about an illness, you'd go to him."

"But this is different. And there is no way for him, or anyone else, to know that she did not expel river water when I lifted her. And I, uh, may have, uh—"

"May have what?" Emma's rocker jerked to a stop.

"She came to me, two of them did that day. The older woman said she wasn't about to have another child and then have to give it up in three years. She wanted to get rid of it now." Adelaide's voice quivered. "Not later when it would break her heart."

"Adelaide." Emma's scolding tone hurt more for being so rarely used. "What about Johanna?"

Adelaide swallowed. "She, too, wanted something for a woman's ailment. Not for her, she said, for another girl, and I gave her the usual remedy—blue cohosh, pennyroyal, and tansy—in the exact proportions you've taught me."

Emma nodded.

"I cautioned her that the girl should not take it if she was to bear a child. That it could cause her to lose it."

Another nod.

"When I told her how to prepare it, she balked. Didn't want the bother. Why couldn't she just mix it with water, she wanted to know. I told her it wouldn't work if she didn't cook it exactly as I told her. I explained that she had to boil the pieces of blue cohosh root first, then pour that over the pennyroyal leaves and dried tansy flowers, and let the mixture steep for a good while—long enough to milk two cows, I told her—to be certain she'd leave it long enough, and strain it before drinking the liquid."

"Did she agree?"

"Reluctantly, and I made her repeat my instructions."

"Go on."

"When I washed her body I knew for sure."

"Knew what?"

Although she knew that Emma couldn't see her, Adelaide blushed.

"What did you see? Tell me. Nothing is ever as bad when you share it."

"The color around her breasts," she couldn't say the word, "and the dark streak down the middle of her belly to her, her—"

"Nipples. Color of her nipples." Emma's voice held her impatience. "And a streak to her pubic area. My goodness, child, are you ever going to learn to say the correct words?" She slapped the table next to her, scattering willow strips about. "Whatever am I to do with you?" she murmured to herself.

"She was with child," Adelaide said.

"And your remedy had not worked."

Adelaide wrapped her arms around herself. "What if I killed her?"

Emma reached out for Adelaide's hand. "There, there, child, you didn't harm her. You wouldn't have given her enough."

"I gave her enough for two doses. What if she took it all at once? Maybe she wanted to be certain it worked."

"All that would have done is make her ill, cramping, too, but caused her death, no. That wouldn't have happened."

Adelaide whooshed out a breath. "It didn't work. She was still with child when she died."

"What about the other woman you treated that day? Did you give her the same mixture?"

"Yes, I saw her this morning."

"You see, she's fine. Your dose wasn't fatal. Did you tell Johanna she could come back for another remedy if her friend needed it?"

"Oh, I should have. Maybe that's what happened. She felt helpless and decided to do something to herself."

"It's still not your fault. Even if she ended her own life, she made the choice, not you."

"But her babe died, too." Adelaide shivered and drew her shawl closer.

"But you are not responsible."

Then why do I feel to blame?

"What about Helga?" Emma continued. "Did she know about Johanna's condition or suspected? Mothers sometimes know these things even if they weren't intended to."

"I couldn't ask her. If she didn't know, I wasn't going to add to her grief by telling her that she'd lost a grandchild, too."

"Then you must tell Josef. You cannot ignore what you saw."

"If someone put her in the river after she died, why didn't that person come forward right away? If it was an accident, then why cover it up?"

"Could be the father of her babe. Do you know who it is?"

"Helga said Jakob was sweet on her."

"Did he know about the child?"

"I don't know."

"And you don't want to ask him."

"I couldn't."

Emma sighed at Adelaide's embarrassment. "But they could marry. She wouldn't be the first to birth an early baby."

"But if she died of natural causes, why take her to the river? Her body could be anywhere by now if I hadn't found her."

"It may be that he's already married."

"No. Not here. Not a Separatist." *Not Benjamin.*

"Why are you so sure it's a Separatist? There's outsiders aplenty in and out of town."

"Yes." Adelaide allowed herself a moment to ponder the notion that an outsider killed Johanna. No worries about what discovering a murderer in their midst would do to the community. No suspicion of her neighbors. Or her husband.

Emma interrupted her thoughts. "Isn't that furniture buyer here?"

"Mister Welby, yes. He's staying at the inn until Benjamin finishes his order. But he's only been here a week. He couldn't have—"

"Ahem. Yes. I'm just saying that she may have met someone from the outside. A flirty little thing, from what I hear."

"However can I find out?"

"First, your duty is to report to Josef. Then it will be out of your hands." When Adelaide didn't say anything, Emma continued. "You can't turn away from this. It's as if you had a cinder in your shoe. You would want it out, wouldn't you? This information will chafe just the same. With every step, it will irritate and rub raw and eventually fester until you remove it. You know the right of it, don't you? Your heart is telling you or you wouldn't have come to me. So you'll tell him?"

Emma couldn't see her nod.

"Agreed?" Emma repeated.

"Yes, ma'am."

Interrupted by calls to attend a sick child who'd eaten too many berries, a woman who had countless complaints but one day might actually be ill, and several other minor health problems, Adelaide didn't have time to talk to Josef until late in the day. She found him in the corner of his cabin that he used for an office, the Bimeler family warranting no better housing than anyone else in Zoar.

Seated beside him while he finished entering figures in a ledger, Adelaide relaxed her jaw and spread her hands flat on her apron. He modeled self-control, so admired by the Separatists. If she intended for him to believe her and to act, she must not let her anxiousness show.

Josef wiped a quill pen on a scrap of graying cloth and set it aside, leaned against the high back of his chair, and nodded for her to speak. He listened as Adelaide told him her suspicions about Johanna's death. Rapid blinking betrayed his concern, but the lid on his left eye couldn't cover his bulging eyeball so it seemed as if he were peeking out even when his eyes closed. "If she had drowned," he began and held up his hand to stop Adelaide from interrupting, "could the water in her lungs have come out while you were pulling her out of the water?"

"No. Remember when the Hoffner boy drowned last year? The men pulled him out the same way I did Johanna and water poured out of his mouth even after they had him on the ground."

He chewed on his lower lip, staring into the middle distance. "How else could she have died? Had she been strangled or hurt in any way?"

"No, no signs of trauma." A flush spread up her neck, and she covered it with a cough into her handkerchief. That is an honest statement, she told herself. The other signs, well, she had no need to shame the family with that information now that Johanna was dead. Besides, how could she speak of such things to a man?

"Also, I treated her." As her advisors, Emma and Josef were the only two people privy to confidential information about her patients. She told him what she had given Johanna the day before her death, and he brushed off her concerns as Emma had.

"I know what happened." His eye seemed to pop out at her as he leaned forward. "She broke her neck. She slipped and fell in the storm, broke her neck, and then the water rose over the bank. That's how she died." He sat back and folded ink-stained hands over his paunch. "No one hurt her. It was an accident, an unfortunate accident."

"If her neck had been broken I would have noticed. Her head was still in alignment."

"Are you sure about her neck? Do you even know what someone looks like with a broken neck? And you weren't looking for that, were you? There might not be any visible sign. You'd just pulled her body out of the water, and you were chilled. You would have hurried, thinking you could save her."

"Josef, whatever killed Johanna we don't know, but I do know that she was dead when she went in the water and she didn't do that herself."

"What do you want me to do?" he said, raising his hand again when Adelaide opened her mouth. "I don't have to tell you what this could do to our community. Suspicion, distrust, animosity. All qualities we've worked so hard to eliminate even from our thoughts, much less our lives. Once begun, it can never be taken back."

"But there's something else you need to know. Jakob, he said something to me about it being his fault."

"I imagine he did. It happens when someone close to you dies. Blaming yourself is common even when we did nothing to cause the death."

Adelaide sucked in her breath. Either he did not see or he chose not to notice the reminder about her mother's death. "I think you should call the authorities," she said at last.

"Who?" he said, kicking the footstool aside. He plopped well-worn shoes on the floor. "I have authority here on our land."

With that, the subject was closed.

Adelaide stood outside for a moment in the fading light. Josef's reluctance to accept that Johanna's death had not been accidental wasn't surprising. Like the coverlets woven by Weaver Hamlin in his shop, the Separatists were inextricably connected one to the other. If he investigated, their community could unravel as surely as if they pulled a strand out of a coverlet.

Wind whipped around her, and she clutched her arms to herself. No matter. The fabric of her safe haven was torn, and she must try to mend it the only way she knew how.

Regardless of the outcome.

— Four —

Horses hitched to the open wagon stomped impatiently as Adelaide and Nellie joined others waiting in front of the Appelgates' home. Quiet talk accompanied the horses snuffling.

Burials required the presence of the entire community and, for once, Adelaide was glad for it. If her herbs hadn't caused Johanna's death, what had? And who had taken her body to the river?

"Crops in?" an elderly man asked another whose mud-caked pants bore witness to his work in the fields. Late spring storms had delayed planting and now, with May upon them, the men endured long days to ensure a plentiful harvest.

"Rye, barley, oats are, but the corn fields, potato fields," he coughed, "still too wet. But if we get more rain...wheat's sprouted, that's for the good."

One horse tossed his head, and talk turned to Johanna's death. A woman behind Adelaide spoke. "Sad," she said and then added in a whispered voice, "I always knew she'd come to no good."

Adelaide turned to see who had spoken, but the door to the house opened and the crowd silenced. Four men carried out the newly built coffin. At the head, Benjamin led the men down the steps—logs embedded in the slope of grass—stopping when one of them lost his footing. The men repositioned the coffin on their shoulders and continued down to the road. Fresh-cut wood smells blended with the faint scent of lavender as Benjamin slid the coffin into the back of the wagon and closed the tailgate, his face a frozen mask.

Josef followed the coffin out of the house along with Johanna's family. Lame since a runaway horse had crippled his left leg, he struggled to climb up onto the wagon seat and, after he was settled, Nathan gave his wife a hand up to sit beside him. Josef picked up the reins, jiggled them, and the wagon creaked forward.

The men fell in behind the wagon and the women, separate as usual, followed. Their dresses of muted reds and blues swished with their steps, toddlers tugged on their skirts, and infants swayed in slings like Olivia's. The soft rumble of guttural German sounds surrounded her. Whoever could she speak to about Johanna?

Ahead, Nellie looked up at Helga, who wrapped a shawl-draped arm around the girl and clasped her close. A pang of jealously jolted Adelaide, surprising her with its force. She held Olivia tighter and reminded herself that they were cautioned against such preemptory emotions. At least her sister was out of the dormitory.

Brigit Appelgate, Johanna's younger sister who had worked with her at the dairy, walked a few steps behind whispering with her friends. Adelaide waited for her to catch up.

Brigit smiled down at Olivia, who whimpered and then snuggled more deeply into the dangling cradle and went back to sleep.

"I'm so sorry about your sister," Adelaide said.

Brigit leaned toward the sleeping baby, the dimple in her chin a replica of her sister's. "She's so sweet."

"You're to become an aunt soon. Maria's about to birth her first baby."

"Oh, I know. I can't wait. But that Simon. So mean he is. Hardly lets me see her. Says she's working and such."

"He is her husband and they're responsible for tending the canal dock and the inn. There's much work to do, I imagine."

"He's just like Herr Guenther. Even when we've done everything, he comes in and wants the dairy scrubbed again. Work, work, work. That's all they think we should do."

"We all work."

She flipped the ties on her bonnet over her shoulder. "But not Johanna. She always found a way not to."

No minor transgression, shirking one's duty was akin to an attack on the community.

Brigit stole another glance at Olivia. "She smells good, too."

"That's milk smell. Baby's favorite food."

Brigit bumped into an outcropping beside the path. "She never wanted to get up to milk."

"Pardon?"

"Johanna. Said she was too tired."

"I can't imagine Martin Guenther allowed that."

"Oh, he didn't know. She always managed to be in the barn by the time he made his rounds. As if she'd been there all along."

Olivia cried out in her sleep, and Adelaide patted her quiet.

"What happened last night? Did she go somewhere?"

"Just like every night. Always sneaking out."

The dairy maids motioned for Brigit to catch up to them.

"She went out even in the storm?" Adelaide asked quickly.

Brigit waved off her friends and continued. "Did what she wanted to do, she did. Even Herr Guenther couldn't tell her what to do. Remember last summer? When he caught her and her friends swimming in the river? He wouldn't even let them put their caps on."

Nor much else, Adelaide recalled.

"She thought it was fun."

Adelaide blushed with remembering. Johanna had flounced along, the curves of her body outlined in the wet clothing.

"Nothing bothered her," Brigit said wistfully. "Sometimes I wish I were more like that, not so worried about what others would say."

"It's our way, Brigit, to keep each other—"

"From sin. I know. It's just that she seemed to have so much fun whatever she did. Surely you don't think God smites down someone just for having fun?"

"No, of course not."

Ilse Forster, the woman in charge of the dairy, fluttered bony fingers in Brigit's direction, and the girl hurried off to join her coworkers.

Adelaide pondered what she'd just learned. Johanna snuck out at night, even last night. To meet her lover?

Maria's husband loomed above the other men ahead, and Adelaide rushed up to him, Olivia bouncing on her chest. "Simon," she called out. "How's Maria?"

He turned his lanky body toward her. Light, slicked back hair topped a high forehead scrunched into a frown. "You. You're the cause of—"

Olivia squealed.

Adelaide lifted Olivia out of her sling and up to her shoulder to pat her quiet. Whatever did he mean?

"If she loses the baby…" Simon's jaw clenched.

"Is she sick? What's wrong?"

"Grieving, she is. Her sister dead. Just stay away from my wife."
He waved a long-limbed arm behind him.

"You don't have a say about that," Adelaide said to his back.

She stood aside to ponder his words. Whyever did Simon blame
her for Maria's grieving? And he had no right to order her away. Still,
she worried. Not that Maria wasn't healthy. She was. Or that Simon
could prevent her from attending Maria in her illness. He couldn't.
No, she worried that she might fail.

In the early years of her training with Emma she studied herbal
remedies, not birthing babies. Needing the women to help clear the
fields, construct buildings, and build the canal, the practical Separatists required everyone to be celibate, even the formerly married.
By the time women could be spared and marriage was allowed
again, Emma's sight was gone. Her hands, though, moved surely as
she coached Adelaide through the initial birthings.

But now Emma was too frail to help, and Adelaide was on her
own. Each time a birth neared, the same cloud of fear hung over
her. Would she make another mistake? She cradled her baby close
and fell into step with the others.

As the cortege cleared the woods and approached the final
incline that rose to the cemetery, rays of the setting sun fanned
out behind the rise to bathe them in warmth. Adelaide hoped it
warmed Johanna, wherever she might be.

Had she asked her fellow Separatists, they would have said that
Johanna had gone home to God. Adelaide wondered how anyone
knew that for sure but, having no better idea of what heaven might
be like and unable to even fathom the thought of an afterlife, she
usually let such thoughts drift away.

But not today.

She stopped. Did Johanna take her own life? Like her sister?

The wagon lurched to the side, and one wheel sank in mud. Some said then that Ophelia's self-murder kept her from heaven. Several men stepped forward and with a heave, the wagon came loose in a whoosh of freed suction.

They crested the hill to emerge into the clearing at the top of the bluff. The cemetery spread out before them. Mud lay piled to the side of a gaping hole aligned next to a softly mounded hillock covered with sparse vegetation, the most recent grave among all the others lined up in rows. Unmarked and unadorned, the gravesites were like the Separatists themselves: equal even in death.

Several inches of water stood in the bottom of the open grave. Beside it lay three wide leather straps. Josef positioned the wagon with the back to the grave, and the men slid the coffin out and laid it on the straps. Benjamin stepped forward and opened it for a moment of reflection. But he turned away without looking inside.

If Johanna killed herself, how did she get in the river?

Johanna lay wrapped in the cream-colored linen that Helga had so proudly selected. The outline of her body—a mere suggestion of her presence—was all that remained visible through the shroud. She seemed smaller now, encased in the plain wooden box, as if her spirit had departed and left only an empty shell. Her face, so lovely in life, had sunk onto her neck, her chin hidden in the folds of the cloth.

Murmurs rose in the crowd and someone yelled, "Take that off."

Helga stood mute, her sin apparent.

Benjamin's eyes swiveled to Adelaide. Don't say anything, he admonished silently.

She should have convinced Helga to forego the fine linen and exchange it for older cloth, but she couldn't deny her friend this one indulgence, however much her efforts came to naught.

People glanced from one to the other, quietly questioning. The wind picked up, and Adelaide drew her shawl across her body to warm Olivia.

Johanna's boss, Martin, shuffled up next to Josef and whispered in his ear.

Adelaide stepped forward. "Josef, please don't do this. Don't unwrap her here."

Martin stomped his staff in the ground. "We'll not waste good linen."

"But her parents. Don't do this to them."

"Adelaide," Josef said, with a glance at the darkening sky, "it's too late to return to town for another cloth. And Martin's right. I'm sorry." He nodded to Nathan, who knelt by the coffin, his knees squishing in the wet grass.

Helga cried out. "No. Don't, please, Nathan. Not you, not her father."

Adelaide moved to Helga's side. At least she could help Helga through this no matter how futile her efforts to keep her daughter's dignity had been.

Nathan continued to unwrap the body and, as he did, Johanna twisted to the side and her bare buttocks rolled into view.

A moan escaped from Helga's lips.

Adelaide's stomach clenched but she held tight to Helga's waist.

Josef studied a cloud that had moved above them, but Martin kept his face on the coffin's interior, a flop of hair obscuring his eyes.

Nathan tugged at the covering until it was free and then pushed himself back up. He wrapped the linen into itself and offered it to his wife who shook her head. Tears rolled down her creased face.

Josef nodded to Benjamin to close the coffin.

"Wait." Adelaide tugged the shawl out from under Olivia's sling and shoved it toward Nathan.

Nathan looked to Josef who nodded, and he laid her blue and gray shawl—one that had been her mother's—over his dead daughter's body. Benjamin slowly lowered the lid but it slipped out of his fingers and dropped down with a thump.

Howling came from the back, and Jakob pushed through the crowd. He flung himself onto the coffin, muddy boots pumping the air as he pounded the wood with his fists. Shuffling accompanied murmurs of disapproval for such an outward display of grief. Jakob's friend pulled him upright, and he stumbled backward, arms waving as if he could wipe the scene from his sight.

Josef nodded to the men who had carried the coffin. They gathered up the straps, lifted the coffin above the opening and lowered it, their labored breaths loud in the silence. The straps slipped and the coffin splashed into its watery home.

Jakob hiccupped and began to giggle. His friend tugged on his arm, but Jakob shoved him off. He jerked an arm over the grave, eyes darting from one to the other. "She loved the water," he said, giggles turning to frenetic laughter. "She loved swimming," he said as his friend dragged him away. Hysterical laughter could be heard well after they were out of sight.

Josef, who had remained quiet throughout the outburst, took a shovel from one of the mud-splattered men who had dug the grave. Propped awkwardly on his good leg, he scooped up a clump of mud and dropped it with a clunk onto the coffin.

Helga swayed, and Adelaide tightened her arm around her. "Do you want to leave?" she whispered, but Helga shook her head. One by one each man took his turn filling the grave until a mound of mud remained the only reminder that Johanna lay beneath.

As the community made its way back down to the village proper, Adelaide overheard someone say, "Drowning is such a sad death."

She kept her own counsel.

— Five —

Impatient with the chores that delayed her the next morning, Adelaide hurried through her work, left yesterday's dinner heating on the back of the stove, and put Nellie to work separating dried thyme leaves from their stems before she left. At the main road she turned right toward the block-square garden that anchored their town.

The gardener, August, waved her over to the fence. "You heard about Maria?" he asked, resting small, gloved hands on his spade.

He'd needed no prompting to address just what she'd come to ask him before heading to the inn. "What do you know?"

"Simon's worried, that's all. He said Maria's that upset about her sister's death, she is. Can't stop crying and Simon's worried, her with her, ah, illness coming. That's all I know."

"Surely not. You must know more." The man could keep little under his tongue.

"Humph." He turned toward a triangular plot behind him where a box of pansies awaited planting.

"I'm sorry, August, please tell me what you've heard."

"Nothing for sure."

"But?"

"I don't put much stock in it."

"Tell me."

He pushed his straw hat back on his head and wiped his forehead with the back of a gloved hand. "Someone told Simon that you gave Johanna something and that's why she died."

Adelaide studied the neat-edged paths behind him. The twelve paths of righteousness marched toward the center where a giant Norway spruce stood tall surrounded by twelve junipers. Christ and his disciples. Intersecting cross paths—temptations—awaited the Separatists if they strayed. Would they never let her forget her past? "Who said that?" she asked at last.

"Can't recall, I'm sure. Besides, she drowned."

"So how does he think I caused that?"

"I've been wondering about that myself. Maybe he thinks she fainted and fell in the river. That's all I could imagine."

"In the middle of the night? In a storm? She took something— some remedy I gave her—and fell in? Is that what he thinks?"

"I wouldn't pay it much mind."

Simon's anger with her at Johanna's burial now made sense, she thought, as she made her way toward the edge of town. He believed she was responsible for Johanna's death and thus Maria's grieving. Emotional upsets could cause the illness to come on. Was Maria's babe ready this soon?

"Adelaide," Nellie called from behind, Olivia bouncing on her hip. "You have to go. She's sick, Sophie is, and Matron won't help," she said as Olivia reached out her arms to her mother.

"Stop. Who's Sophie?"

Nellie's shoulders sagged, and she scrunched her head into her neck.

"Nellie, stand up and tell me what's wrong."

"Yes, ma'am," she said, straightening. "Sophie, she's only five, but Matron says she's a ma, ma—"

"Malingering?"

Nellie's head bobbed up and down. "Trude sneaked some hot water with lemon and honey—I told her to do that—but now Trude's locked up and Sophie, she's coughing and can't stop. Please, please, you have to help."

Olivia let out a cry.

"Take Olivia to Helga, and I'll see to your friend."

Adelaide swung open the door to the meeting house and caught the strong smell of lye soap in the darkened interior. She hurried through the empty building to the corner and up the steps to the second floor that housed the girls' dormitory. She hesitated, her hand on the doorknob. She'd have to face the room where her sister had spent too many wretched years sometime.

She stepped through the door.

Gerda, a small-handled broom tucked in the crook of her arm, stood over two girls scrubbing the floor. She lifted the broom and brought it down on the head of one of the girls who yelped in pain.

"Stop that," Adelaide ordered.

"You have no say here. I'm the matron, and I'll do as I please. Hard enough to beat sense into them." She waved the broom toward the second girl but stopped short of hitting her.

"I came to see about Sophie."

Gerda brushed invisible crumbs from her tight-laced bodice. "I told your sister the child's just putting on a show. She's not so sick. A few days without dinner should solve that problem. Usually does."

Adelaide pushed her aside. "I'll see for myself." Gerda stepped back, her mouth agape.

Sophie lay on a pallet in the corner and faced the wall. At Adelaide's approach, she scrunched up into a ball as if Adelaide intended to strike her.

Adelaide crouched down and whispered, "I came to see how you are."

The girl blinked at the sunlight streaming across her face. "I can't stop cough—" She raised up as spasms convulsed her tiny body. When she finished, Adelaide laid her back down, adjusted the pallet out of the sunlight, and wiped blood-streaked spittle from her mouth. When she reached for a frayed coverlet, Gerda jerked it out of her hands and tossed it over a cringing Sophie.

Adelaide stood and turned to Gerda, her jaw clenched. "I brought a remedy for her." She pulled a packet of dried horehound leaves out of her bag, thought a moment, then added a paper of hyssop. "Boil these leaves in a pint of water down to one and one-half cups," she told her. "Strain it and give it to her in one-half teacupful dose every two or three hours."

"You think I have time for that?" Sophie had turned back to the wall. "All these girls. All misbehaving. You'd understand if you—"

"Listen to me. If you don't treat this child, she will die." Adelaide narrowed her eyes at the taller woman. "And I will report you for it."

Gerda jerked back.

"I understand one of the older girls offered to take care of her. You best see to it." Adelaide stretched out her hand with the packet of herbs and, after a moment's hesitation, Gerda took it.

Back outside, she shoved her anger at Gerda aside and hurried through town and into the woods. She needed to see to Maria and calm Simon before he complained about her any more. As her feet sped along the pine-carpeted path, glimpses of sky peeked through the tangle of tree branches overhead, and she felt her temper subside.

Until her thoughts came whirling back.

If Josef investigated, he or someone else might come to wonder why she was at the river. If she had awakened so early, they'd ask, why wasn't she at work? Idle hands weren't to be tolerated. And alone? It was their duty to keep watch over each other. How else to keep them free from sin?

She should be ashamed. Here she was fretting about herself when her friend's daughter lay dead in her grave. Now Simon blamed her for the girl's death. She'd soon put a stop to that, she thought, hurrying along the path.

She steered clear of her favored spot. Still, when she neared the river, she couldn't help looking. The tree trunk and broken limbs had been hauled out of the water. Even the scattered branches had been gathered up and taken away to dry for kindling. Only the damaged stump remained.

The path rose up the hill and into the sunlight. At the top she paused, wiped her brow with the back of her hand, and adjusted her medicine bag across an opposite shoulder. Her remedy didn't harm Johanna, and she would insist that Simon stop saying that she did.

Ahead lay the bridge that spanned the river and the inn—little more than a tavern—that the Separatists had built after they had completed their portion of the Ohio Canal to house its crewmen and travelers. And where Simon reigned as innkeeper.

She crossed the bridge and spied a buggy parked next to the inn. *So Doctor Hertel has come from Bolivar to see someone at the inn.* Adelaide tried to quell her worry. *If he bled Maria...* She hastened her steps around a partially built platform and shoved open the door to the inn.

She stepped into the common room, empty this afternoon. Light from the open door spread across the polished wood floor, illuminating dust and dried mud collected in crevices along the edge. A breeze whipped up under Adelaide's skirts, and she smoothed them down hurriedly as Simon moved toward her, wiping his hands on a food-stained apron.

"We don't need you. Just turn around and get out." He shoved a chair under one of the crumb-littered tables along the wall and half-heartedly straightened others scattered about the room.

Adelaide squared her shoulders and looked up into the man's craggy face. "I need to talk to you about—"

"I have nothing to say to you, and I'm too busy to talk," he said as Doctor Hertel emerged from stairs at the back of the room, buttoning his vest over a corpulent belly. "Remember what I said, Huttmann, she needs to be careful. Try to keep her calm no matter her grieving. No agitating kind of exercise and. ..."

Simon nodded toward Adelaide.

The doctor coughed delicately. "Uh, she needs to keep her, uh, passions in control," he said aside to Simon, then turned to Adelaide. "What are you doing here?"

"I was just telling her we didn't need her," Simon said.

"How's Maria?"

Soft footsteps sounded on the stairs, and Maria staggered into the room, her hands gripping the heavy swell of her abdomen. The sleeve of her gown slipped away from her arm, revealing a telltale bandage.

"You bled her?" Adelaide demanded of the doctor. "How could you when she needs all her strength for, for her illness."

Doctor Hertel straightened his coat over his vest and snapped his medical bag closed. "You think your plants do any good?" He spoke to Simon. "Your wife needs real care, not some hocus-pocus dreamed up by that so-called medical man you call a leader."

"Don't worry, I'm running for trustee," Simon told him. "Wait till I'm elected." He wiped spittle away from his mouth with the apron. "Everything is going to change around here, yes it is."

"In addition," the doctor went on, "don't let her go outdoors in the night air. And keep the windows closed as well. The miasmas, you know. Not healthy for anyone, especially one in her, ah, delicate condition."

"What she needs," Adelaide said, "is rest." She started toward Maria, who leaned against the wall, her head propped on the molding.

"Don't let her give your wife anything," Doctor Hertel said. "Not if you want a healthy boy."

She shot the doctor a look. "I'll just help her back to bed."

Maria, her face pale and puffy, looked toward Adelaide with unseeing eyes.

So he had given her laudanum as well. The better to keep her quiet.

Adelaide held her temper. It would do Maria no good to give in to her anger right now.

"I need her help," Simon said. "Those girls do little enough as it is. Without her hand, they're next to worthless."

"I'm fine," Maria said. "I can work—" She slid down onto a step, and Adelaide rushed to her side.

"Put your head down," she ordered and shoved Maria's head below her knees. "Take a few deep breaths. That's it."

Maria raised her head and smiled at no one in particular.

"Look at this place," Simon complained with a wave around the room. "Sweeping, dusting, scrubbing all not done, so behind I am."

Doctor Hertel spoke. "Better let her rest, Huttmann. Today, at least."

Simon grunted agreement, and Adelaide helped Maria to her feet. She gripped her arm and they started up the stairs, but Simon called her back. "She can go up herself. Don't need you."

"Go on," Maria said as she hauled a foot up to the next step and made her way up the stairs.

Adelaide turned back to Simon. "I want to talk to you about something else. I can come back if that's better," she said with a pointed look at Doctor Hertel.

"No need. I'm not interested in anything you have to say. We don't need you here."

She jammed her fists onto her waist and stared at the man's stubborn chin. "I am not to blame for Maria's grief."

"Out! Get out before I do something I'll regret."

She backed up as he raised his hand that she thought to hit her. But he reached around her to shove the door open. She stumbled out, the door narrowly missing her as he slammed it shut.

"You best stop her," came Doctor Hertel's voice. "You know she'll be back to—" The solid wood prevented her from hearing the rest of their conversation.

Her hands shook, but she shoved them in her pockets and started down toward town. Maria will be fine, she told herself, as long as she isn't bled anymore. She could gain sufficient strength when her time came. But the thought failed to her calm her. Whatever could she do to stop Simon from saying she'd hurt Johanna?

— Six —

"As many of you know, I turned onto the broad road of destruction and remained there until God himself stopped me." Josef smoothed his wiry, gray hair back with a swift gesture. "I saw myself obliged to take another way, for I recognized that the road on which I had turned was the broad road, which would without a doubt lead me to ruin."

Squeezed between Nellie and Helga on the women's side of the cabin that served as their Sunday meeting house, Adelaide held a sleeping Olivia close to her. The austere room, its log walls covered with plain white plaster, was a stark reminder of the simplicity of their lives. No religious icons adorned the interior. Nor did they hold to any of the traditional sacraments, such as baptism or confirmation, seeing them as relics of the hated religion they'd escaped. The bare room allowed them to attend to their spiritual life without distractions.

But Adelaide never felt God's spirit here. She preferred her place by the river, water anointing the bank, air soaked with its presence, spirit everywhere and nowhere, not stifled nor stuffed into this box-like structure.

She glanced across the aisle at Benjamin, but his attention was on Josef, who leaned against the desk as he spoke.

"Sought God but he kept Himself aloof from me. He acted as if He did not want to hear my anxious sigh and my urgent cry. And no wonder, for I had very much offended Him." Josef swept his protruding eye across the assemblage. "Nevertheless He sent me his grace. Gladly I submitted to His guidance. Inestimable are the benefits, favors, and blessings that I enjoyed from that time on."

It was not a new story to Adelaide nor to anyone else in the community. What they called *Wiedergeburt*, or rebirth, the struggle and delivery, worked itself out over and over in their daily lives, lives of self-denial and redemption through living the life of the early Christians.

Or so they said.

She had never understood it. Life was difficult enough without needlessly denying oneself those few pleasures their world afforded. She studied Benjamin, his blunt-tipped fingers absently rubbing his thighs, and felt a shiver of longing. But she shouldn't. Even that pleasure should be denied. Especially that pleasure.

Now she'd added to her sin, determined as she was to prove herself right. That's the reason, the real reason, she thought ashamedly, that she wanted to show that Johanna's death wasn't an accident. Not for justice nor to punish a wrongdoer but, Simon's doubts notwithstanding, to be right.

She clutched Olivia to her and rocked the sleeping infant silently. She didn't have to be right. It would help no one to know what happened, in fact, as Josef pointed out, the investigation itself would damage their community. So why was she having so much difficulty letting go of her urge to know what happened to Johanna?

And Josef would soon speak of her. On the Sunday following

a death, he devoted a portion of his discourse to the deceased, speaking generally about dying, although not naming her, as was their way, and to lessons learned from the person's loss to the community. If the person had experienced a long and painful illness, he would laud the departed's patience, duty, and piety, which remained steadfast even at the hour of death. But Johanna had displayed none of these qualities in her brief life.

So what would he say?

"*Milch* is our basic sustenance," Josef said. A cloud momentarily obscured the light, throwing a shadow across his face. "It is the first food we have at our mother's breast and often the last food we are able to swallow at the end."

Adelaide reached for Helga's hand and patted it. Josef had referred, albeit obliquely, to Johanna's work. As he continued, however, he made no mention of her following the *Regeln und Ordnung* of their community. Regardless of however much she disagreed with him, she could trust his honesty.

She looked across the aisle at the rows of men. Nathan hung his head at the mention of his daughter. Martin looked straight ahead. Where was Jakob?

Josef cleared his throat, stared at something only he saw, and quoted from the Bible. *"The Lord is my shepherd. I shall not want. He maketh me to lie down in green pastures."*

Warm spring breezes drifted in through the open window, bringing the aroma of stew simmering in the cabin next door.

Josef allowed himself a glance outside. *"He leadeth me beside still waters. He restoreth my soul."*

She hadn't told him all that she knew. Was that a sin? To withhold information? But to tell a man, even her leader, that an unmarried girl was to birth a babe?

Nor had she told him that Simon blamed her for Maria's ill health. Nor how he'd let Doctor Hertel bleed his wife when they all were expected to seek care for their ills only from other Separatists, namely her and Josef. Besides, how would Simon pay the doctor? Their money was held in common in Josef's safe. Only he and the trustees could decide its allotment.

Maybe she should give testimony about Simon's behavior here in Meeting. She had always considered their practice of shaming wrong-doers at Sunday Meeting barbaric. The culprit was forced to sit in the front—so there'd be no mistaking the sinner—then face the congregation and admit the error of his ways. She smiled as she thought about that.

No, she would not let her anger affect her judgment. Simon was too much under the influence of Doctor Hertel, who often disparaged Josef's and her treatments. Maybe Simon was simply anxious about his wife's health. He wouldn't be the first father that Adelaide had had to calm.

Josef spoke again. *"He leadeth me in the path of righteousness for His name's sake."* He stopped, removed a graying handkerchief, and coughed into it before replacing it into the pocket of his vest. *"Yea, though I walk through the valley of the shadow of death, I will fear no evil for Thou art with me. Thy rod and Thy staff they comfort me."*

Adelaide drew herself close to his words during the silent meditation that followed. Johanna's funeral discourse had ended, her official mourning complete. They would return to their duties, some more sad than others, but no one would ignore their tasks to mourn, not even her parents. She need only return to her work. She needn't say any more, ask any more questions, nor ponder her death.

Josef motioned for them to stand to sing the final hymn. Helga gave her a quick smile and she and Nathan left. As the music ended, Adelaide arranged a wiggling Olivia in her carrying sling, and positioned it around her neck.

The door slammed open and banged against the opposite wall as Simon strode toward the front. Unlike the other men dressed in their formal Sunday wear, Simon's head was bare, and he wore his workday shirt and trousers topped by a loose smock. Simon straightened himself up to his full six-foot height and settled his arms to his side.

He pointed to Adelaide. "You think you know her," he said, his quiet tone all the more threatening.

Nellie clutched at her sleeve.

Simon poked a thumb to his chest. "I've had all I can take. My wife," he choked, "my wife, I'm that worried."

"Take Nellie and Olivia home," she whispered across the aisle to Benjamin as she struggled to free herself from Olivia's sling.

He shook his head and mouthed, "I'm not leaving you here alone."

"Go. I'll be fine," she whispered.

"No, I'm staying," he murmured as Olivia squirmed and twisted her face into a scowl.

"Please. I can handle it."

Olivia arched her back and let out a scream.

Olivia's screams continued, and Adelaide shoved her into Benjamin's arms. He gave her another glance, then scooted to the end of the bench and rose. The door blew back against the inside wall, and a gust of wind caught Nellie's dress and raised it behind her. She clutched at it with embarrassment, and Adelaide's heart ached for her.

Simon directed his gaze around the room. "Do you want to know what she did?"

No one moved.

Ice blue eyes stared down at her. "She killed Johanna."

She jumped to her feet as chattering broke out. She wobbled for a moment as words swelled and crashed around her. Momentarily dizzy, she lowered her head.

"I've seen her," Simon said, his words measured, his stillness unnerving. The pace of his words picked up. "She sits there by the river in the moonlight communing with whoever knows. And it's not the first time she's made a mistake. You all recollect, don't you?"

Adelaide shuddered with remembering. The young mother. The wrong medicine. Both dead.

"She gave Johanna something."

Adelaide raised her head and swallowed her shivering. She would not defend herself over the past. She had done enough penance then.

"Maybe it was an accident, maybe she didn't do it on purpose, but the result is the same and my wife's grieving, her with her illness upon us…" His voice stumbled.

She opened her mouth, then closed it. What could she say? Tell them about Johanna? Violate her own strictures against revealing her patients' problems? Especially Johanna's condition. No, she must keep silent about that.

Simon's eyes swept the assembly. "Maybe it was something that hurt her, caused her to fall."

"I did not harm Johanna." Her voice quavered however much she tried to settle it. She dug her fingers into her palms, then deliberately unclenched her fists. "I did not give her anything that would hurt her."

"Is that your complaint, *Bruder*?" Josef steadied himself against the desk. "And what makes you accuse our *Schwester* of such an action? If you have proof of wrongdoing, man, it's your duty to speak it."

Simon snorted. "I have it from a reputable source. She's not the only one 'treating' people here. Is this the person you want deciding if you live or die?" he asked with a nod toward their leader. "Instead of a trained medical man?"

Only a bulging throb on his temple showed that Josef recognized the snub. "This is not how we settle our disputes. We have a mechanism in place to deal with them."

"The so-called board of arbitration. A bunch of your toadies, bobbing their heads to whatever you say. I won't let her treat my Maria. That's all I have to say." He turned on his heel and left.

Josef settled the murmuring. "We all know that poor Johanna drowned on Thursday night last. An accident, for certain." He gazed pointedly around the room. "Let no more be said about it."

The crowd filed out silently, and only a few directed sidewise glances toward Adelaide; some even smiled at her. She waited until everyone else left and then dragged her feet toward the entrance.

Clouds hung overhead, leaching color out of the town. Adelaide stared upward toward her home, but a three-story house, recently clad in white-washed boards, obscured her view. A wagon rumbled by, the men returning to the fields. But today they seemed to move slower, as if time itself had slowed.

Whatever was she to do? If she defended herself against Simon's accusation, she would have to say how and why she treated Johanna. No, she had already decided that she would not breach Johanna's privacy. Would people believe him? Or would they remember the past?

The wind caught one end of her shawl, twined around itself, and tugged it out of her hands. She scrambled after it as it fluttered along the ground, but it seemed to leap out just beyond her grasp. August stepped in front of her and scooped up the errant fabric.

"You're not letting him bother you, are you?" The gardener handed her the shawl.

She clutched it in front of her. "How dare he accuse me. I did nothing to Johanna, and now he's, he's…"

August wrapped an arm around her shoulders.

She should shrug him off. Touching a woman not his wife would set tongues wagging if they were seen. Instead, she leaned into his strength. "Why would Simon think I would hurt Johanna?"

"It's not about you. It's Bimeler he detests."

"Why? I've never known."

"Simon's never forgiven Josef for deceiving him. You were just a child when we decided to become communal." A gust of wind caught his high-crowned hat and sent it scurrying into the tall grass beside the road. August dashed to retrieve it. He brushed bits of leaves and grass off the crown and went on. "Simon argued that it wasn't fair to those who worked harder than others."

"Some people still complain about that."

"Even Josef was against it at first, didn't think it would work. But eventually he voted with the rest of us, Simon the only dissenter. He thought he'd been betrayed."

"But that was years ago," she said as they stopped to view the progress on the hotel. The posts Adelaide had seen Friday morning now sported crossbeams, and a double door centered the front.

"Some people hold onto hurts, never forget."

She swiped a hand over her face. Her past would never go away. Someone would always be sure to remind them the way Simon had today. "Then why is he the innkeeper? I heard several men wanted that position."

"I think Josef wanted him out of the way or maybe just to appease him."

"And now he wants to replace Nathan as trustee. If he wants to be elected, he can't go against our rules."

"Unless he plans to change them."

"He'd still only be one among three, and any change such as that would require everyone to agree, or at least a majority."

"It's just that he might have a better chance at being elected now."

"Why? People don't know him well."

"They don't but with folks thinking that Nathan's had two girls die. Suspicious, it is."

"Lots of people die. It has no bearing on reelecting Nathan trustee."

"Think about it. One girl hangs herself. Another drowns, presumably self-imposed. Doesn't that make you think something's the matter with the parents?"

"Not at all. Both girls were old enough to decide for themselves. Besides, Johanna didn't mean to die." She had said enough. More than enough.

"I wouldn't pay Simon's accusing you any mind, though. He said he's talked to folks, people from the outside he meets at the inn, especially now that we get more and more traffic on the canal. He says Josef's homeopathic treatments are old-fashioned. And now he's met that doctor from Bolivar who doesn't think Josef's medicines are any more than plain water. All the real medical men go to universities and use scientific treatments like Doctor Hertel."

"I've seen what the doctor's treatments do." She told him about her encounter with him at the inn the day before. "Maria's so weak from his bleeding her that I'm worried about her when her illness comes."

"Don't worry, Adelaide. Everyone knows you, they trust you."

"Do they?"

"Of course." He sounded almost certain.

— Seven —

It took all of Benjamin's resolve not to return to the meeting house after he'd delivered Olivia and Nellie to their cabin, but Nellie's demeanor held him back. Expressionless, as she'd often been since she returned from the dormitory, she lurched around the cabin with stilted movements. Finally, he suggested that she finish preparing their dinner. She stopped, looked around as if she didn't know where she was, and then took dishes down from the cabinet and arranged them on the table.

Whatever was happening at the meeting house? What was Simon saying about Adelaide? Did he know what she did?

Johanna. She'd tried to tell him what was wrong. He wanted to understand, but when she began to talk about Jakob and what they'd done, he couldn't abide it, and he stopped her. He could have helped her. He should have helped her. But no, he had to send her away with nothing, not even a by-your-leave.

Benjamin stopped pacing when he saw Adelaide approaching their cabin. He bent to stoke the fire in the stove, hiding his impatience as she came through the door.

Adelaide headed straight for Olivia, restless in her cradle, but the baby was too distressed to feed and squealed and tossed her head from side to side until finally she wearied, and Adelaide was able to coax her to the breast.

"So what happened?" he asked her at last. "Did you do something to make someone mad? I knew you wouldn't stop. I heard you were up at Josef's asking him to investigate her death and that he refused, but no, that didn't stop you. Tried to get to Maria to tell you something, I suppose."

"How do you know what I've been doing? You have someone who follows me around and reports on me?"

"You know how they talk. You can't do anything here that someone doesn't notice and mention."

Nellie stood watching them, a fistful of silverware clutched in her hands.

"Will you go to the cellar and get some apple butter?" Adelaide asked her, and the girl disappeared down the stairs. "He thinks I treated Johanna and somehow caused her death."

"Did you?"

"You know I can't say." She lifted Olivia from one breast and the infant, momentarily sated, let out a sigh. "Emma's told me. Josef's told me. Why can't you understand?"

"Be reasonable. There are no secrets here in spite of your keeping quiet about your treatments. People usually know anyway." He did know, and that's what worried him. Before he sent her away, Johanna told him that Adelaide gave her a remedy for what ailed her.

At least she'd tried to help Johanna. That was more than he'd done.

Following dinner, Nellie left for afternoon Sunday school, and Adelaide finished scrubbing the table. She hung her rag to dry, poured tea into cups for them, and joined him at the table.

Benjamin warmed rough hands on the cup, staring silently into its contents.

"I can see the worry on your face," she told him. "Nothing will come of this, I'm sure. Everyone has much more to think about than an accusation from a man who's seldom about."

"I'm not so sure. Once a rumor starts—"

"Until another comes along."

Arguing with her wouldn't change her mind so he moved on to the question he needed to ask her. "Nathan asked me to be a candidate for the standing committee, the one we'll have when the Articles of Incorporation are approved. To mediate disputes, that sort of thing."

"Sounds like the board we already have for settling problems, although Simon thinks they just do Josef's bidding."

"Maybe that's why the trustees thought it should be expanded. In any case, the standing committee will replace the board but instead of three members, now there will be five."

"What did you tell him?"

"That I'd talk to you."

She smiled, and he knew he'd pleased her. Few Separatist men would have asked their wives for their opinion about such "men's business," and fewer still would have shared with another man that they were doing so.

"Is this important to you?" she asked.

"If I'm an elected official, then we're safe." Whyever couldn't she understand? Their place in the community would be secure.

No longer alone. Hungry. Wandering the streets in search of food or help or someone to care. No, nothing would get in the way of his making sure they were safe. Nothing.

A spasm of alarm passed over her face. So she feared their being banished, too.

"Josef's delivered the funeral discourse," she said, as if reassuring herself. "Johanna's death won't be at the forefront of most people's minds. Within a few days everyone will be so busy that they won't have time to think about it."

"You said yourself that she didn't drown. But isn't it possible you're wrong? That you made a mistake?" He didn't say "again." He wouldn't hurt her that way.

Adelaide bristled. "I told you about the water. If she had drowned, water would have poured out of her mouth."

"That's just what you think. No one saw her. Maybe there's some other reason why there wasn't water in her mouth. Maybe she was caught on something that pushed against her, I don't know, Adelaide, I don't know how it happened. I just know you need to keep quiet about something you can't be sure about. Don't make people any more suspicious than they are. You weren't there. You didn't see it happen. Admit it, you could be wrong."

Adelaide stared over his shoulder to the sleeping baby in the cradle behind him.

"That's what I thought," he said in response to Adelaide's silence.

After Benjamin left to return to work on Mister Welby's order, Adelaide busied herself in her workroom, but her mind wasn't on her tasks. It wasn't worry about Simon's accusation or even that the elders might investigate Johanna's death that worried her. Her fear was that talk about the past would gather momentum, as such talk often did in their confined community, until her very practice was threatened. Without her work, who would she be?

Nellie returned and reported on Sophie. "Her cough's no better," she said, her face pinched with worry.

Adelaide hurried out to see to her young charge. She must help Sophie, not just for the girl, but to reassure her sister. And herself.

"I told her," Gerda said from the top of the stairs. "Whatever you gave her is no good. It's just as Simon says."

Adelaide stomped up to the second floor, and Gerda stepped back just in time to keep a determined Adelaide from running into her. "Let's try something else." She pulled a packet of dried mullein out of her bag. "Sometimes it takes a few different medicines to find one that works. This, too, must be boiled, reduced, and strained. Add some honey, too."

"Humph. Waste, that is. She want it, she take it without honey. Coddling them, that's what it is." A bun of gray hair under a too-tight cap added to Gerda's sour expression.

Adelaide quelled her temper with effort. She needed Gerda's willingness to care for Sophie, and making her angrier wouldn't help. The child smiled as she neared, and when Adelaide bent to her ear, Sophie whispered, "Thank you," before a coughing spasm took her.

Adelaide grabbed a blanket off the pallet next to Sophie and spoke before Gerda could. "She needs to be kept warm. And have someone bring a pan of hot water up to her, steaming." To Sophie she said, "Put this in the water," she said, handing her a packet of bergamot. "Then you bend over it and breathe in the steam."

Sophie nodded and lay back down.

"Next thing you know I'll be cuddling her like a baby," Gerda said with a huff.

"That would be an excellent idea." Adelaide smiled as she let herself down the steps. The image of Gerda with her mouth hanging open cheered her.

On the path ahead, a woman emerged from Emma's cabin, folded her shawl around her scrawny shoulders and shuffled unsteadily toward Adelaide, who greeted her with a nod though the woman did not return the pleasantry. What her illness was neither she nor Josef had been able to determine, but the rising on her breast grew larger. She had even let Doctor Hertel lance it, but even he could not release the pus. More and more the woman disappeared into her clothing, bones protruding as weakness overtook her.

This was not the first time that a villager had turned to Adelaide's teacher, rather than her for advice, especially if the illness worsened. And Emma seemed unable to turn people away no matter how often she insisted that she was no longer in practice and that they should let Adelaide attend them. She shook off the slight. She had too much need for Emma's comfort to let it bother her.

"I brought you some more willow bark." Her hands shook as she placed the packet of grayish pieces in Emma's swelled hand, recalling the loss of the tree where she'd found refuge as well as healing bark. What else could she use to ease Emma's stiff joints? "Have you thought you should give up making baskets? There are others making them now, you know."

"No more than you could give up your work."

Adelaide clutched her medicine bag to her and sank onto a stool at Emma's knee.

Emma leaned forward, gnarled fingers splayed on the rocker's arms. "You're bothered, child. Tell me."

"He shamed me, Simon did. In front of everyone. Telling them I killed Johanna. And bringing up the past. You know I didn't mean to harm that woman nor her babe. I only wanted to help. And now everyone's talking, and I don't know what they'll do." She wrapped her arms around herself and rocked back and forth.

"Hush, child. The past, well, it's over. We only have today."

"No, Emma, the past remains."

"You made a mistake one time. Need I remind you that you're not perfect. None of us are. For all we try to make it so. Besides, we don't know for sure what you did caused Frau Mendelsohn's death."

"I do. And her babe. I know that if I'd had my casebook with me instead of hurrying—as you often remind me—I would have given her the correct remedy."

"Adelaide, she might have died anyway. You're not in charge."

"I know that. It's just…" She knew Emma would try once again to reassure her that nothing she could have done would have saved the woman. Nevertheless, she was unable to let go of the lingering sense of failure that dogged her work.

"What bothered me the most was when Simon said that he'd seen me meditating by the river or, as he said, 'communing in the moonlight.' That sounds like he thinks there's something, oh, I don't know, supernatural, about me."

"People have always been suspicious of women *Heilerin*. Ever since ancient times the official healers—who are, of course, always men—have been the most harsh opponents of women." She stroked her fingers. "Doctor Hertel wants to discredit those of us who use natural substances, those less toxic to the body. Even among Separatists, some grumble that only a man can treat their ills."

"But they know me," Adelaide complained. "They know I come to you or Josef if I need help."

"Ah, Adelaide, it goes back to the beginning of civilization when men took all the power. They couldn't believe a woman had any abilities, especially not healing ones." She sat back in her rocker and rested knobby fingers on the chair arms. "Black magic. If a woman healed someone, they accused her of using magic."

"And if they didn't recover?"

"They blamed her then, too. Even today, much as we've learned about science, we don't know what causes illness or injuries or why the crops fail. So people have always tried to find a cause, something they might control."

"A woman."

"Of course. Then some started saying the woman entered their mind and made them do something, usually bad."

"The better to put the blame on another."

"Indeed. The cause, they thought, was the devil. The devil had entered into the errant woman and must be destroyed. You should be glad you live in modern times. A woman accused of using such tricks, as they called them, was, uh, tested."

"What do you mean, tested?"

"They'd throw her in the river...bound."

"*Ach.*"

"If she had magical powers, they reasoned, she would survive."

"And if she did?"

"She was burned at the stake."

"You're frightening me."

Emma laughed. "We're more enlightened these days, thank goodness."

"Good, because I can't swim with or without bindings."

"But you jumped in the water for Johanna."

"Yes, I did. I didn't have time to think about what happened before." Emma reached for Adelaide's hand, but she pulled away. "But what if he brings charges against me? Accuses me of practicing something like you said, unnatural."

"Settle yourself, child. No one believes that anymore."

"They could force me to stop, though. Have me watched. I couldn't work. Not like that."

"Josef would never allow it. He's too busy to attend to illnesses. He needs you."

"I've never known anyone else to meditate like I do."

"We're each challenged to find God in our own way. You know that. It's why we came here, where neither the Church nor the State can say how you worship." She folded her hands in her lap. "Or don't."

Adelaide took a moment to still her breath. What did happen during that time? Did God come to her? Or some other spirit? It seemed as if it came from inside her but she couldn't admit that. It would be saying she was equal to God. She kept her thoughts to herself. Even Emma might not understand how differently she had come to believe.

"You more than most need that period for reflection to be able to do your healing work," Emma continued. "You need to be somewhere away from the community, and you need not let anyone tell you otherwise."

She felt Emma's stillness and it calmed her. "Thank you. Yes, I do. And I'm not letting Simon or anyone else tell me how to prepare myself for my work."

"That's much better."

"I am worried about Maria." She told Emma about Doctor

Hertel bleeding Maria and how Simon had ordered her out. "And after Ophelia's death last year... I don't know how Helga can take it."

"She's suffered as we all have, but maybe her more than most."

"What did happen to Ophelia? Do you know?"

Emma righted her rocker.

"You do know, don't you? Why did she do it?"

"Do you really want to hear any more tales about death? Don't you have enough to think about now?"

"Please tell me. Maybe it will help me understand more about Johanna's death."

"I doubt there's any connection."

"You know I can keep a confidence."

Emma settled back in her rocker. "It was shortly before we gave up on celibacy. She came to me with her problem."

"What problem?"

Emma cocked her head to the side.

"Oh," Adelaide said. "I heard the rumors about her, but I didn't know they were true."

"I tried everything I could think of. First I used the concoction that you did. When that didn't work I tried peruvian bark, snake-root, rue, angelica, even bryony," she said with a grimace.

Adelaide watched outside the window where a hummingbird fluttered around a bud on the apple tree. "Did you ever think it was wrong?"

"Child, what's right and what's wrong aren't always that easy to know. Would you have the girl punished? Flogged? Shunned? Would that have been right? And I doubt I could have prevailed over our more sanctimonious members, regardless. They'd want her sin to be punished. Even if it killed her." Emma shoved thin white hair up into her cap. "But nothing worked. Either that or she had waited too long."

"Did Josef suggest anything?"

"She wouldn't let me ask him."

"Who was it? Her baby's father? Did she tell you?"

"No, but I had my suspicions."

"Not Josef?"

"No, forget that old rumor."

"Rumor?"

"That it would be an honor to have his child."

"Oh?"

"Sure. That such a child would be the Separatists' one child. That we'd grow him up to replace his father eventually."

"But Josef already has a son. Peter."

"Yes, the farmer. But this supposed child born during the celibate years would be the son that belonged to all of us. Trained by us. We'd be his community of parents and, because no one else was having children, we could concentrate all our efforts on perfecting him."

"What happened? I never heard any of this."

"Only a few of the more radical adults talked about it." She chuckled. "The usual result. They couldn't agree on what woman would bear his child. Then what if she had a girl? Others, including me, thought the whole idea was barbaric."

"And what did Josef think about all this?"

She laughed. "I doubt he knew. They tried to keep it from me, but you know eventually I hear everything. This came from a man on his deathbed. He didn't think we should do it, and he wanted to be sure someone knew. That's when I became involved. The idea died out after that."

"So who fathered Ophelia's child?"

"I suspected it was Simon Huttmann."

"He found her hanging in the horse barn."

"And later married her sister."

"Now he's trying to keep me away from Maria. So you're saying you think he suspected that you had something to do with Ophelia's death? That doesn't make sense. She killed herself."

"Or she killed herself because I had no way to help."

"And that being the reason he wants Maria cared for by a real doctor?" Adelaide finished. "August thinks it's about Josef."

"Simon has always been ambitious," Emma said, wincing as she resettled herself. "Josef, too, but he's ambitious for all of us. Simon only wants it for himself. Have you talked to Josef?"

"He didn't believe me. He thinks she broke her neck and fell into the river in the storm. He said if he started asking questions it would disrupt our community, which it seems to have done."

"People won't believe that you harmed Johanna, not knowing you, they won't."

"Maybe not deliberately, but if they think I made a mistake… don't you see, Emma, with Simon accusing me I have to find out what happened to her?" Never mind her chastising herself that she was only trying to prove herself right. Not anymore. Now she had a legitimate reason to investigate Johanna's death, and she relished the thought.

"What if you find out someone killed her? Or dumped her body after she died? Then what? Think this through, Adelaide, before you do anything."

"Causing more trouble, you mean?"

"She's already buried, and everyone thinks she drowned. You could forget about it."

"That's what Benjamin wants me to do."

A niggle of worry teased the back of her mind. Why did Benjamin want her to stop investigating? Did he know something about Johanna's death that he hadn't told her? If so, why wouldn't he have reported it in the beginning? Or told her about it?

"Maybe you should listen to your husband."

"I can't. Simon accused me, in Meeting, no less. Emma, let me ask you this. What if I don't find out who did it and it happens again? Someone else dies under suspicious circumstances? You've told me I have responsibility for the greater good. It's just like a sickness. I must investigate, find the cause before I can prescribe the treatment. There's only one reason the cause of her death needs to be kept secret and that's if someone caused it or covered it up. I cannot let that happen."

Emma nodded her agreement, however reluctant.

Josef stopped his carriage outside of Emma's cabin. He looped the reins around one hand to steady his mare who shied at a wagon rumbling by. "If you're letting Simon's accusations bother you, I wouldn't. He won't be saying any more about it."

"He'll have to confess at Sunday Meeting, won't he?"

"No. I advised him to not speak of it again."

"After he accused me, made everyone think I did something wrong? You're going to let him get by with that?"

"I'll tell you what I told him: Let it be."

"Josef, it's my reputation at stake. I want him to pay for his crime."

"Crime? He only said what he thinks he knew. There was no malice in him, just worry about his wife. You can't let words bother you. Goodness knows, I have plenty of complaints against me.

That's what being a leader—or a healer—entails, and you must let it be. There's no substance to his words, and that's all they are, just words."

"Still." She shuffled her feet and stared at Josef's mare, who turned a bleary eye toward her. Nothing she said now would change his mind, that she knew about her leader.

"I told him to keep Hertel away from my people," Josef said. "Said his wife wasn't 'my people' as if any of us aren't. Just how did he think he would pay him? I doubt Hertel—have you seen his fancy carriage?—would treat anyone for free."

"Did he agree?"

"Of course not. Said that was his business, his wife, and he'd do as he pleased."

Should she ask him the one question that might help her find out what happened to Johanna? His mare swished flies with her tail, and he reached toward the reins he'd hooked around the carriage post. "Do you remember who was on watch last week?" she blurted out.

"Didn't I just say to forget that nonsense? Nobody killed her. No one here would do such a vile act, nor violate their beliefs. They'd be damned for eternity if they did."

"Josef," she said, shading her eyes from the sun, "if the night watchman saw Johanna, or anyone else, out at night, maybe he could help us figure out what happened to her."

"I know what happened." He gathered the reins in one hand and pointed to Adelaide with the other. "You're as bad as Simon. Stop all this talk about it."

Adelaide studied a stone on the ground. She lifted it with her toe to reveal the other side. A spider scurried away.

"Well, will you?" he demanded.

"I'll ponder it," she said in a small voice. It was the best she could do. She wanted to scream that she would never let it go no matter how much he insisted, but few in her community dared go against his wishes. And she never had.

Back home, Adelaide headed straight for the sanctuary of her workroom. She grabbed her apron off the hook by the door, wrapped it around herself, and brought the ties in front to secure them in a knot. Nothing for it but to keep busy.

Long clusters of drying herbs hung suspended from ceiling rafters, and a breeze through the open window released their musty scents. She sneezed, comforted by its ordinariness. Her eyes roamed around the room, her seedlings at the window, buckets and baskets at the ready, cups and spoons scrubbed and stacked on shelves, her jars and bottles of medicines safely stored up high. Four jars on her top shelf held her poisons.

She settled onto the high stool positioned in front of her elevated worktable and reached up for the jar of slippery elm.

Was something out of place? The stoppered jars had been Emma's and already labeled with their Latin names in paint on the outside, poisons labeled with the characteristic X. No, they were in alphabetical order as always, arranged so that she could grab whichever one she needed without having to hunt through them. They weren't lined up at the same distance from the edge as she usually kept them, but occasionally when she hurried she knocked them a bit out of line, like now.

She tapped a few leaves of elm into her mortar and set to work with the pestle, grinding the leaves and flowers to a powder. She tapped the pulverized herb onto a paper square, folded the four corners to the center, and labeled it for Herr Holz. It was all she had until last year's bark was dry enough to be crushed into powder. If his indigestion had not improved, she'd leave it with his *Frau* to make into a paste to dilute with boiling water. If he'd take the distasteful fluid. She'd have to remember to suggest that Frau Holz add honey to the mixture, too.

She chewed on her pencil. Was the mullein she left for Sophie too strong for such a young child? She stared at the top shelf. *Bryonia alba* could alleviate an intractable cough, but she had never used it for a child. No, too powerful. She couldn't take the chance with the girl's life. Or to her reputation. Not now, she thought, with a tinge of guilt that she even considered the consequence to herself when a child was ill. *Why can't I remember everything Emma's taught me?* If it weren't for the records in her casebook, she might never know what to do.

Now Simon was trying to stop her work. Or probably Doctor Hertel. He was the one who had put these crazy notions into Simon's head about her treatments. Simon had jumped to the conclusion that she had given Johanna a lethal medicine.

Tears welled in her eyes. *No, I won't cry. Not now, not ever. Not even when Mother died.* Everyone had said what a brave little girl she was, but she knew better. If she gave in to her grief, her body, her whole self, would crumble into dust.

Only ten years old, Adelaide had clutched her mother's hand during the agonizingly slow labor while the doctor stood by, offering little help. Confined in the cramped upper room they shared at the house where they worked as domestics, she covered her ears, but she couldn't shut out the screams echoing off the rafters above them nor the cloying smell of her mother's sweat.

Her mother's words lingered still. "Take care of the baby." But she couldn't do even that. All she saw was the top of a downy head swaddled in a blood-stained blanket before the scrawny infant, whom her mother named Nellie, was turned over to Helga, whose latest infant had died at birth a few days before.

While the baby prospered at the breast of her surrogate mother, her mother lingered for several days. One night, as she slept next to her, her mother's soft breath simply stopped. She lay awake until morning, hoping she'd only dreamt her mother's death. Nor was she able to save Nellie from being sent to the dormitory later.

Doctor Hertel. She flung the jar across the room. It clattered against a shelf and fell in broken shards to the floor. *Now look what he made me do!*

Her hand shook as she gathered fragments, and she cried out as she jabbed her finger. She wiped her hand on her apron and kicked the remnants into a pile. Back at the table, she flipped through to the back of her book, creased the page with her bloody finger, and printed "Cause of Death" at the top. Only one explanation made sense: Johanna had been poisoned. Under that she wrote "Plant? Food?" And finally, "Who?" Had someone deliberately given Johanna poison? Who would have done that? And why?

Tomorrow she'd begin her quest. She couldn't, she wouldn't, let Josef stop her. Her leader. However could she defy him? But how could she not? She was the only one determined to find how and why Johanna died, her baby barely conceived inside of her.

But she could lose all this. Her life's work.

I am not going to let another mother die in vain.

— Eight —

Word of a revivalist's return to town spread rapidly. Brigit rushed into their cabin, breathless, Nellie trailing.

"Can she go with us?" Brigit asked Adelaide. "They've set him up outside the inn for when it gets dark. Lots of people coming from all around, they said. Isn't this exciting?"

Nellie ducked her head.

"Please, she's never seen a real preacher, only Josef, and he just talks." Brigit's words tumbled out on top of each other.

"What's he like? The preacher?" Nellie asked, her face flushed. "Maria says he calls everyone sinners."

"But not like Josef. He makes it so awful," Brigit said with a delighted shiver.

"No." Adelaide's knife sliced through the roll of summer sausage and banged the cutting board beneath it. She had heard more than enough from a traveling preacher when she was twelve. After he had described the bowels of hell, she'd suffered nightmares for weeks. But she hesitated, reluctant to quash her sister's new-found interest, even for a revivalist preacher. "He's not of our faith," she said finally.

Benjamin glanced at Adelaide with raised eyebrows, then turned to the girls. "He's not speaking the truth, not the truth we believe in, any case. At the end of the day, you're still Separatists. Or you will be when you're of age."

Seeing Nellie bob in agreement, Adelaide softened. "All right." Before she could say any more, Brigit tugged Nellie out the door, letting it bang against the cabinet inside.

"Why did you object?" Benjamin asked her. "Aren't you glad to see her making friends? That's good, isn't it?"

"Yes," she admitted. "But I won't let her go without me." She dumped the sausage slices onto a plate and grabbed a fresh loaf of rye bread. "She goes, I go," she said, sawing into the bread.

"He's not so bad. I heard him last time he was here. And that Johanna, my, she marched right in front, flipped those bonnet ties around to get his attention."

"Did she?"

"Did she what?"

"Get his attention?"

"Oh, I suppose so. Every time he railed about hell, she giggled. Started the other girls giggling, too, until Martin marched them away. Know what she did then?"

"Johanna?"

"She turned around and stuck out her tongue at him."

He's proud of her, Adelaide thought. *Why does that bother me so?*

"I thought he'd have a stroke, his face turned so red. And that broke up the meeting. I guess he's back to try again to convert us sinful Separatists to his way of thinking."

"That's not likely. Doesn't he know we escaped from such a harsh religion? Whyever are people going to hear him?"

"Some excitement in their lives, Adelaide. God knows we work hard enough. You wouldn't deny them such a harmless distraction, would you?"

In the end, though, Nellie took to her bed with a stomach ache, and Adelaide left her with a cup of ginger root tea. She decided to go, nonetheless. It would give her a chance to see to Maria.

Adelaide heard the man before she saw him. His voice carried through the woods, but she couldn't make out the words until she came into the clearing in front of the inn. Reverend Truesdale— she'd learned the preacher's name on the walk—glared down on the crowd from a makeshift wooden platform a foot off the ground. Lanterns dangled on poles at the four corners of the dais and illuminated his elongated face. A draft sent smoke wafting over the assemblage.

He paced back and forth, his gait uneven as if his frame was too heavy for his legs, and his head arched forward above a slightly rounded back. Frayed suspenders held up flapping black trousers.

"Sinners! Sinners! You're all sinners!" He punctuated his words with the tattered Bible he held in one hand. Bony fingers of the other hand shot out from the worn cuff of a shirt turned gray. "Fire—scorching, roasting, boiling, blazing, burning, searing, blistering, seething, suffocating, stewing, bubbling—fire," he blared at the silent listeners.

"You've tamed the land." He spread his arms wide to encompass them all. "Now it's time to root out sin, tame your bodies, clear away the underbrush of sin, decay, wanton desires. The enemy is always lurking nearby, ready to crush you, so you have to be vigilant, on the alert for temptations that sneak into the house of the Lord, pretending to be pious, believing, worshipful but, oh no, they're the devil in disguise. Kill those demons in your hearts. Cleanse your souls, brothers and sisters!"

"Amen. Amen," came a few shouts from the outsiders in the audience. Most of the Separatists had gone to their Sunday evening meeting, something Adelaide had shirked. Maria stood at the front, her hands cradling her swollen belly, her face pale in the lantern light.

As Adelaide made her way up the side, glances shot her way. One woman grabbed her skirts and swished aside, an audible sniff making the snub obvious.

"Now, you Separatists," the preacher continued. "Think you're so perfect. Don't believe in fighting or war or such. Hah! As if that could save you from damnation." His eyes roamed over the audience. "And your leader, so-called. You've all been fooled into thinking he's a saint, haven't you? But I heard about him from the Quakers. Yes, sir, they know about how he has you all bewitched, how he rules over all of you. How he's fooled you into thinking you are your own savior." He huffed. "Whoever heard of that? Only Jesus Christ can save you from sin."

Her attention captured by the man's words, Adelaide failed to notice a tree trunk that sprouted on the path, and she stumbled. A strong arm reached for her and, righted, she turned to thank the man. Martin held her in a too-tight grip, his bulky arm throbbing against her, his face in shadow. For a moment they both stood still. Sound seemed to disappear into the smoke from the lanterns, its heat soaking her dress. He dropped her arm, mumbled a few words she couldn't hear, and backed against the tree as if he could shrink into it. Beneath a fringe of dark hair, his eyes glittered in the lamplight like two black pits.

Adelaide tugged her kerchief across her chest, surprised to find it still tucked into place.

"Oh no, woe is he who sins for he shall be denied the kingdom of heaven forever and ever." The preacher stretched his arms high over his head and appealed to the sky. "Forgive them, Father, for they know not what they do."

Martin jostled people aside as he turned away.

August trailed behind him. "Where you headed?"

"On watch tonight." Martin shoved black hair off his face and nodded toward the preacher. "But he has the right of it."

Reverend Truesdale laid the Bible aside, gathered his coat from a nearby branch, and moved forward to the edge of the platform. "Death comes when we least expect it," he said, conversationally, dangling his coat by one finger. "So, what to do?" He lowered his voice "Beware, you Separatists. Your religion…you are not saved. Woe to you," he wailed, rocking back and forth, the coat flapping to and fro with his movements.

Maria looked as if she could swallow his words.

"No one among us born is not a sinner. Let this be a lesson unto you." He pointed one finger across the crowd. "I say to you if you are not saved, you are condemned to eternal damnation in the fires of hell. Come now to Jesus. Be saved. Will you be saved?" he asked, his eyes on Maria. "Will you confess your sins?"

Maria shoved outstretched arms in the air. "Yes! Yes!" she screamed, her face twisted in pain. "Save me before I die! Before I go to hell!"

Adelaide slapped her.

Maria started, her screams muted to mewing cries as her husband slammed out the door and headed toward them. Adelaide leaned forward to hear her friend's next words. "I'm not going to live through this. I don't want to go to hell."

"You're not going to hell, Maria," she said, "and you're not going to die. I'll see to that."

Someone grabbed Adelaide by the neck of her dress and shoved her aside. Before she could say a word, Simon had scooped up Maria in his arms. "You," he said over his shoulder to the preacher, "clear out by morning."

The door banged behind him.

— Nine —

Mister Welby stood back from examining the chest of drawers, its finish glistening in the morning light. "The boat returns Saturday, Bechtmann, and it seems like you've too much to do yet to finish. My customers are wealthy men, and they expect the best their money can buy. I don't want a rushed job."

Benjamin bit back a response. If he came back to the shop every evening as he had been doing for the past week and if Nathan could supply the locks, hinges, and pulls in time then, yes, he could meet the man's deadline. They needed the money too badly for him to fail.

The man fingered the dovetail joinery that connected the sides of the top drawer, then pointed to the walnut trim inlaid along the front. "You do good work, Bechtmann. Better than I've seen from any Yankees, no doubting that."

Benjamin dipped his head and struggled against his pride. "Thank you."

"What about the locks?"

"The blacksmith will have those today." He smoothed the top with his rag. "We'll still make it by Saturday, I'm that sure."

He consulted a list in his hand. "Two more chairs—"

"They only need final finishing." Benjamin grabbed a chair and held it up for his customer's inspection.

Welby stroked its smoothly turned legs, shrugged, and returned to his list. "Another cabinet, three shelves, several traveling trunks that I don't see."

"They're all cut, ready for joining."

"Drawers, too?"

"All ready." Benjamin turned away as he spoke. It was almost the truth. Admittedly, the drawers existed only in his imagination, but that's how they all begin. And he'd soon put truth to the lie.

"Although I've enjoyed this time in your pleasant little village," he said as he brushed nonexistent sawdust from his sleeve, "it's time I make some money."

"And you will, sir. Do not trouble yourself." A pleading tone colored his voice, however much he rued it.

The man pushed pudgy fingers into dove-gray gloves. "I'm depending on you, Bechtmann." He tipped his hat to Nathan coming in the door as he left.

Nathan dropped a handful of hinges on Benjamin's workbench. "Are we to finish on time?"

Benjamin grabbed a hinge, fit the eye onto a cabinet door, and positioned the flag and rat-tail accordingly. "I told Welby we could," he said, marking the hinge's position. "I need the escutcheons and locks and keys for these drawers and the desk over there."

Nathan slapped a hand against his leather apron, and sawdust scattered in the air. "That Jakob. I need his help, but he's barely been around. And when he is, his mind's not on the work. He nearly dropped hot tongs on my foot yesterday and then ran off."

Benjamin adjusted the hinge on the matching cabinet door, marked its location, and stuck the pencil behind his ear.

"He's still on probation," Nathan continued. "He better come back to work if he wants to stay here."

The door snapped open.

"Humph." Martin stomped into the shop. "That outsider's still here, I see."

"If you mean our buyer," Benjamin began, but Martin interrupted.

"Polluting our young people, that's what he's done. We need to get him out of here before anyone else gets hurt."

"What do you mean anyone else?" Josef asked, stepping inside.

"Why are we doing business with outsiders, anyway?" Martin said in response. "We can make everything we need. We did just fine before."

"Before?" Josef asked. "Let me remind you. Not enough cabins, food even. We've been blessed with plentiful bounty. God's bounty. And the industriousness of our people." He tipped his head toward Benjamin.

Benjamin bent to his work, rubbing linseed oil along the cabinet's top. It sounded as if his leader was about to begin a sermon, and he had no time for it. His fingers felt the grain, slightly raised, just enough to show differing shades of color. Exactly what he wanted.

"Their work," Josef said with another nod to Benjamin, "makes possible much we would not have. And do you know how close to starving some people are?"

Benjamin's mind jumped back to the time when he'd wandered the countryside and through the villages in *Deutschland*. Only eight years old, he didn't know why his parents and brother had been taken, just that his mother had shoved him into a cabinet under the sink and told him to be quiet. The last words he'd heard was his father telling the officer that there was no one else in the house.

When Nathan came upon him in an alley many weeks later, he was scraping maggots off a piece of chicken. He shoved the decaying meat into his pocket, but it fell through the worn fabric. He scrambled on the ground to retrieve the first meat he'd found in many a day. He wasn't going to let some stranger steal it now. Nathan picked him up and told him he need never be hungry again.

Josef brought him back to the present. "Starving right here in America. Not faraways, no, right nearby, right today."

"Don't lecture me," Martin said. "You heard that preacher." Josef's face flushed at the mention of the revivalist, but Martin went on. "You think you're not sinning." He poked a finger at one and then the other of the men. "Lying with your women." He spat. "It's against God's will, it is."

"Martin," Josef said, "let me remind you that you did not want such restrictions just a month ago. In fact you wanted to—"

"That was then. I've seen the light and you should, too."

"We are not going to outlaw marriage, no matter how much you want that. Even when we practiced, ahem, lived apart, it wasn't in our rules."

"You want to outlaw marriage?" Benjamin asked.

"Besides," Josef said, "it's not necessary now. We have dormitories for the children so the women can work as they did before." He hooked his cane over the edge of Benjamin's workbench and grabbed his left leg to prop it on a lower brace. "Martin, you're free to be celibate. But it's your way. It's not everyone's."

"Just because you wanted to marry—"

"Leave Josef out of it," Benjamin ordered.

"Let it be, Benjamin." Josef turned to Martin. "*Bruder*, don't let what's happened in your life affect other people."

Martin opened his mouth, then raised his arms in a shrug and left.

"Try to understand," Josef said. "He's, well, he's suffered for his faith."

As have we all. A wave of sadness washed over him. Tales of prisoners beaten haunted his nightmares. Had his own parents been among them? "What did you mean, 'What happened to Martin'?"

"You heard some died in prison? Martin's wife was one."

Benjamin swallowed. "I didn't know."

"He accepted it, though, as God's will. Said she was better off dead than forced to practice a faith she didn't believe."

"He had a wife and yet he wants us to go back to living apart?"

"He convinced his wife to become a Separatist. Then when she died for it, he blamed himself. If he had his way, we'd outlaw carnal relations for everyone." Whiskers bobbed on his chin. "Many think—and you know this—that being celibate brings one closer to God. We came here to be free from the Church's oppression. We can't allow Martin to enforce his beliefs on us, say that everyone has to believe exactly the same."

"We would be hypocrites."

"Yes, Benjamin, we would."

Adelaide sniffed at her dress. She could swear she still smelled river water.

Before daylight she had trudged down to the river's edge, but her attempt to settle herself had failed. Standing next to the ragged stump, she felt naked, her strength sapped as surely as her beloved tree's.

Smoke billowed from the chimneys of the washhouse even as she returned in the early dawn light. Wash day. No matter how impatient she might be to find out about Johanna, she must nonetheless do what was expected of her. She didn't want to give Benjamin or any of the others reason to think she wasn't following their rules.

She dropped the dress into the pile of laundry and took up Nellie's apron, crumpled from her sister's repeated twistings. If only she could undo the damage living in the dormitory had done to her. And keep her own sweet baby away from there.

Laughter sounded outdoors as two women greeted each other, then moved along, bulging laundry bags propped on their shoulders. Adelaide stuffed Nellie's apron into the bag with the family's dirty clothes and let herself out the door.

The women were close enough that Adelaide could have joined them. Instead, she took her time and allowed the distance between them to grow. Would anyone shun her the way one woman had scooted away from her the night before? Would people be afraid to allow her to treat their ills now that Simon's accusation had tainted her reputation?

Outside the washhouse, clotheslines waved with dresses, pants, shirts, towels, and bedclothes of residents, each item embroidered with the person's initials or their house number. A gust of wind puffed up a bed sheet to reveal a woman's drawers hung underneath it, and a woman in front of Adelaide turned aside. Having seen most everyone's underclothes and more, Adelaide nonetheless felt herself blush as if she had just peeked unbidden under a woman's skirt.

That morning as she dressed, she'd found a puzzling bruise on her arm. Then she remembered. Martin grabbing her, the rough fabric of his jacket against her cheek as she turned to thank him, and the moment when time stopped and the world disappeared around them. Whatever was the matter with her? Surely she imagined that rush of feeling, she thought, as she stepped inside the washhouse.

Frau Sander grabbed Adelaide's bag, dumped their laundry onto a sorting table, tossed the bag back to her, and waved her aside for the next woman in line. Another washwoman stood in front of the brick-encased double stove, steam rising above two washtubs on top of it. Sweat stained the woman's back as she stretched over the soapy water to churn a wooden paddle through the clothing inside. White linens bubbled up in the blue-tinted rinse water next to it.

Before Adelaide was out the door, her laundry had been separated according to color: whites in one pile, blues, grays, and blacks in another, and the next family's clothes were being sorted. She slung the empty bag over her shoulder and stepped outside.

"You don't think she did anything, do you?" one woman asked another next to her. "I've always thought she was as good as Emma."

"No, of course she didn't. That's just Simon causing trouble, that's all it is. I'd trust Adelaide over that Doctor—" The woman stopped in mid-sentence when she saw Adelaide, then gave her a small smile.

"Good day to you, *Schwester*," Adelaide said with dip of her head. If they had to gossip, at least it was in her favor.

Her relief didn't last. At her next stop, Frau Holz barred the door and asked what she wanted.

"How's Herr Holz's indigestion?" She kept her tone neutral, however much she wanted to scream at the woman's scowl.

"He's poorly. Thanks to you."

"I have some slippery elm—"

"We don't want your so-called medicines."

Adelaide groaned in frustration. If she could just figure out how Johanna died, people would know she hadn't harmed her.

"Pay him no mind," Helga said, leading Adelaide toward the kitchen. "Simon's complaints are baseless. Don't trouble yourself over him."

"I couldn't bear it if you thought I'd harmed your daughter."

"Hush now. You should know we wouldn't believe anything so ridiculous," she said, motioning Adelaide toward a stool at the table. She pushed up her sleeves and plunged both hands into the bowl of dough. Stalks of tangy rhubarb with stubs of rippled leaves lay ready beside the bowl.

"Helga, I know this is distressing, but I have to find out what happened to Johanna."

"No." She scooped a ball of pie dough out and slapped it down on the table. "Nathan doesn't want any more talk about her."

"I have to, Helga. I'm sorry. If I don't, people will think I'm to blame." No matter how much she cared for her friend, she could not let her feelings for Helga stop her.

Helga attacked the dough with wide sweeps of a floured rolling pin. "He says it will only cause trouble."

"Trouble? Doesn't he want to know what happened?"

Helga picked up the flattened dough, folded it in half, and dropped it onto a pie tin with floured fingers.

"Don't you?"

Helga perched the pan on the palm of one hand, raised it to eye level and, with quick cuts of a long-handled knife, chopped the overhanging dough off the edge. "He says it will just stir up everything about Ophelia." She turned aside and the pan dropped to the table with a clunk.

Adelaide reached across the table and took Helga's hand in hers, automatically brushing off a bit of pastry.

"But Johanna did not do this herself, in case that's what you think," Helga said, her voice thick.

"I know she didn't."

"She would not have hurt herself, not my Johanna, no. That girl loved life, she did. From the day she was born." Helga blew a wisp of graying brown hair aside and allowed herself a slight smile. "It was always something, something she was into, doing, asking. My, that girl could ask questions. It wasn't until she moved away that I realized how much I missed her."

Adelaide patted her hand.

"I'm just so angry." Helga wiped at threatening tears, leaving a dusting of flour on her cheek. "I know I shouldn't be. God knows my sister keeps reminding me—not my will, God's will." She slumped onto a stool. Her dress hung loose on an ample frame that seemed to have shrunk since her daughter's death. "You don't think it was God's will that Johanna died, do you?"

"Of course not. If I believed that, why would I try to help people? Or try to find out—"

"No, you must stop, stop asking questions." Helga tossed the knife on the table. It clattered across the surface, narrowly missing Adelaide's outspread hands. She jumped up and knocked her stool to the floor.

"Oh, Adelaide, I'm so sorry." Helga reached for her and clutched her hands in her own. "I don't know what to do. Nathan says the talk must stop but I, I— "

"You want to know what happened."

Head down, Helga nodded.

"One more question. Do you know if Johanna ever went to Doctor Hertel for anything?"

"She was never sick. Not a day in her life."

Raised voices came from the blacksmith shop, and Adelaide hurried ahead to the door. She needed to find Jakob regardless of whatever argument was going on in the shop where he worked.

"I want to know where you stand," grunted a guttural voice. "That will decide my vote." Martin leaned against the wall, thickset arms folded across his chest, his face flushed from the heat of the forge. Or his anger. He turned when he noticed Adelaide and frowned at her, heavy brow ridges shadowing dark, deep-set eyes. "What are you doing here? Don't you have woman's work to do?"

Adelaide pulled herself up to her nearly five-foot height. "I vote too, you know."

Martin studied her with an intensity she found unnerving.

Absently she rubbed her bruised arm. Had she imagined last night? "What is it you want to know?"

Nathan answered. "He wants to know how I'll vote on the Articles on Incorporation—for or against." He shoved a piece of iron into the coals and flames shot up to lick the metal. Adelaide's face warmed, but she ignored it. "I thought everyone's agreed to accept them. You haven't?"

Martin snorted. "Women. Never should have allowed them an equal say."

"We wouldn't have stood for that."

Nathan's hammer struck the iron.

"Besides, we outnumber you men two to one," she added over

the clanging. She had been about to say "and we could vote you men out," but her better judgment prevailed.

"See," Martin said to Nathan, "what happens when a man can't control his wife?" He waved toward the door where they could see Benjamin working in his shop.

If he decided to complain to Benjamin, life could get much worse with her husband. So far she'd ignored his demands to keep silent about Johanna's death. She knew that it was only his fear speaking, fear that they'd be banished from Zoar.

"You need all the votes you can," Martin said to Nathan.

"He has everyone's vote," she shot back.

"Let me know," Martin said and left.

Adelaide sucked in the earthy soap-drenched scent that lingered in his wake.

"You need something, Adelaide? Speak up, I'm busy," Nathan said.

"What did he mean that you needed votes? You're not worried about Simon winning, are you?"

"It's more complicated than that." He clamped his tongs around a newly selected piece. "Now, if there's nothing else, I have work to do."

"I'm looking for Jakob," she said to his back.

"You find him, send him to me. I can't go much longer without help, not with Welby waiting on his order. Plus, three horses can't be used until I repair their shoes, and one of the wagons has a wheel off." He looked up, his face flushed by the heat, a streak of coal dust slashed across his forehead. "What do you need him for?"

She hesitated. Even though she knew Nathan wanted Johanna's death to be a closed subject, she had to say it. "He might know something about Johanna."

Nathan pumped the bellows to fan the fire until the coals glowed hot. "I don't want you asking him about her."

"Don't you want to know what happened?"

He looked up. Whiskers framed a down-turned mouth. "She's dead; that's all I need to know."

— Ten —

No one answered her knock at the *Bauer Haus*. Adelaide started to leave until she heard voices through an open upstairs window. She pushed through the door and called out. *"Guten tag. Das ist Adelaide,"* she said in case any of the hired men were present.

"She was evil," pronounced a deep voice that resounded through the building. "You couldn't stop the devil from claiming her as his own any more than you can stop the rain."

Adelaide hurried up the stairs toward the sound.

"She had to die," Reverend Truesdale intoned as Adelaide shoved open the door to the room Jakob shared with the other men. He lay facing the window, his body curled into a ball beneath the preacher who loomed over him. "But you, you can be saved. Confess your sins, my brother. God forgives."

"Get out!" Adelaide screamed at him.

"You!" Reverend Truesdale raised a fist at her.

"It's all right, Adelaide," Jakob said, righting himself.

"A woman," the preacher said. "Man's downfall, that's what you are. You and all your ilk."

She faced the preacher, who stood with a satisfied smirk on his face. "I'll get some men to throw you out if you don't move now."

He stared at her for a moment. "The devil will come for you, too, woman." With that, he disappeared down the stairs, threadbare coat flapping behind him.

She turned to Jakob. "Why do you let him talk to you like that?"

"You think I'm not man enough, don't you?" He scrunched fingers into light-colored hair grown shaggy and rocked absently. "I should have thrown him out, not you."

She had to agree.

"He's right. I am a sinner, but how can I confess it? No one, not even the preacher, can forgive me."

Blood drained out of her head. Had he killed Johanna? Was he about to admit it? "What did you do?"

"I only wanted to help her, make her feel better. So sick, she was."

She stomped her foot, the sound echoing off the walls. "Tell me what you did!"

He shrank back as if she'd struck him. "I made the drink that killed her. I didn't know, honestly I didn't. Fixed it just as she told me to."

What was he telling her? That she killed herself by making him prepare the poison? That didn't make sense.

"She didn't want anyone to know about it, especially the other girls. She said Martin would find out and he'd be angry."

"What was it? What did you give her?"

"Those herbs, or whatever they are." He turned narrowed eyes on her. "Your remedy."

Her confidence wavered for a moment, but she quickly righted herself. Emma told her, Josef told her. Her remedy was safe.

"What I gave her wouldn't have harmed her."

"Are you sure? It made her frightful sick."

"I'm certain. Did it help?"

"Not so's you could tell. She was that doubled over with pain, she was."

"I sent two doses. You only gave her one, didn't you?"

"Just as she said, yes, I did. If only I'd been there—"

"What? I thought you were."

"Not the night she died. The night before."

"The night before? That's when you gave her the drink?"

He nodded, his head in his hands.

"Listen to me," she said, and quelled the desire to grab his hair and pull him upright. Instead she bent to his face. "Whatever you gave her the night before wouldn't have killed her. My remedy or anything else. Not more than a day later, it wouldn't."

He stared up at her. "I loved her. I wanted to marry her. I should have been with her but no, I had to go—"

"Jakob, there's nothing you could have done."

"If only I'd—"

A shout came from downstairs. "Jakob!"

"That's Nathan. I have to go. But your remedy, if you want it back, it's downstairs."

"You didn't throw it away?"

"I didn't know what to do with what was left. But don't worry. I hid it so no one will find it," he called as he bounded down the steps.

She hadn't convinced him he wasn't to blame for Johanna's death, she thought, as she descended to the first floor, and she wasn't all that certain that he had told her the truth, however much she wanted to believe him.

The building was empty at this time of day with all the men out in the fields so she detoured into the kitchen, the only room with hiding places. The women who came in to cook and clean for the men had left it spotless. Where would Jakob have left the packet? She'd best remove it before someone finds it and rumors about her involvement in Johanna's death escalate.

In the cabinet along the wall stacks of plates nestled next to serving crocks and platters, and cups hung from hooks above. The drawer below held metal forks, knives, and spoons lined up between dividers with serving spoons along the back. She tugged on the drawer, but it wouldn't budge. Kneeling to eye level, she spied a scrap of paper jammed in back. She wiggled the drawer back and forth. It still wouldn't move. Finally, she slid her fingers along the edge until she felt the paper, then she gently tugged on it and, at the same time, jiggled the drawer. The packet fluttered to the floor, and loose herbs scattered across the boards.

The front door banged open.

She scrambled along the floor, sweeping dried flowers, leaves, and bits of roots into her apron. Footsteps headed toward the kitchen. She swiped up the paper, rolled her apron to her waist, and held her breath. However was she to explain this?

The footsteps clanked up the stairs, and Adelaide let out a breath. She shoved the herbs in her pocket and hurried out the back door. Josef's carriage rumbled by, and she hung back until he disappeared around the corner.

Ahead lay the dairy and beyond it, Martin's cabin. Adelaide shivered, with apprehension or longing, she didn't know. The thought of the man who had touched her arm the night before brought a wave of feeling that she tried, and failed, to ignore. She might be pressed to talk to him about Johanna, but first she'd try others. With fortune, she'd discover what happened and have no need to ask him about her.

Adelaide pushed open the door to the dairy and all chattering stopped. The pungent smell of cheese and soap-scrubbed wood filled the room.

"If you're wanting Frau Forster," Brigit said, grunting as she and another girl lifted a round of cheese out of a brine vat, and solution drained from the pressed curd. The two girls swung their load onto a shelf to join other rounds of cheese in various stages of maturing. Several had aged long enough to sport the characteristic holes of Swiss cheese. Brigit laid a clean cloth on top of the cheese round. "She's not here. Cleaning the master's cabin," she said to snickers from the others.

"Do you know anyone who might have hurt Johanna?" she asked them all.

A girl at the table scraped butter from her bowl into a one-pound mold. She patted it down flat with her hands and stamped it with the Zoar insignia while the others glanced at each other.

"She drowned, didn't she?" asked a blond-haired girl from a corner, her hand resting momentarily on the dasher of a butter churn bigger than she was. "At least that's what everyone says."

"Brigit, could I speak with you?"

"You already are, aren't you?" she said to giggles all around.

"Outside."

Brigit shrugged, wiped her hands on her apron, and followed Adelaide out. They stopped beside a dogwood tree whose branches, heavy with white blossoms, dipped low, partially shielding the view of the dairy as well as the path.

"The night she died. Do you know why she went out?" Adelaide asked.

"Thought I was a bother, that she did." She pulled a branch down, snapped off a shoot, and fanned herself with it, scattering petals in the air. "Little sister, humph."

"Why would she go out in a storm?"

Brigit bit off a leaf and chewed it. "Phew." She spit it out on the ground. "To meet him, of course."

"Jakob?"

She wriggled her nose. "She didn't care one whit about him. Not like I do, no indeed."

"But Jakob wanted to marry her."

"She wouldn't, would she? Just a tease. Like with all the men. Thought Mister Welby liked her, she did." She patted her cap, tawny hair tucked inside. "He gave Johanna that bonnet—did you see it? The 'Bonnet of Many Colors,' she called it. Silk, too, it was, made for royalty, she said, called Johanna a 'princess.' Made of ribbons— all colors I don't even know their names—dark and rich, woven together like a basket. It sparkled even."

"What does that have to do with the night she, uh, died?"

"And the tassels." Brigit continued without answering. "Tassels on the ends of the bonnet ties. Have you ever heard of such a thing? And gold they were. We all wanted it. But she," Brigit stamped her foot and a strand of hair escaped from her cap. "Wouldn't let us even try it on. Slept with it under her pillow and even when Herr Guenther told her to return it, she refused."

"About Johanna—"

"Wore it whenever she spied him about. She flipped the strings on it around like this." She demonstrated with the white ties of her cap. "But she didn't know him. He says I'm the only interesting woman here."

"Brigit, you don't want to have anything to do with him. He'd only be trouble, believe me."

"You want to know about trouble?" She tossed the branch aside.

"What trouble? Johanna?"

Brigit nodded and turned to leave. "What do you think? What trouble does a girl get into?" she added, skipping away.

Adelaide sank onto a boulder by the side of the path. So Brigit knew. Presumably all of the dairy maids did as well. Her face flushed with more than the heat of the day. Whoever else had discovered Johanna's secret? She untied her bonnet and fanned herself with it. Even if someone did, would that be reason to kill her?

Across the road Ilse Forster lugged a bucket toward the door to Martin's cabin. Charged with supervising the dairy maids, Ilse surely knew more about Johanna than anyone else.

Adelaide side-stepped around Ilse to hold the door for her and followed her into the cabin. Two unmatched chairs sat beside a battered table, a cupboard held a few chipped dishes, and a narrow bed hugged the wall. The room was cold, its cast iron stove unlit.

Ilse fluttered slight fingers about her face as if to ward off Adelaide's intrusion. "If it's more milk you want, or sweet cream, you're too late; I gave the remainder to the girl for the dormitory."

"It's not that. I wanted to ask you about Johanna."

Ilse fingered her apron, damp at the hem. "I don't think—"

"Please, may I talk to you?"

Ilse shook her head, loosening a cap that topped straggly, straw-colored hair. "He wouldn't like it." She pushed the cap back into place and retied it.

"Wouldn't like it if I'm here?"

"Not you. Anyone. So much to do. He wouldn't want me stopping to talk."

"Go ahead with your scrubbing."

"If he comes back—"

"We can talk while you work." Adelaide pulled out a chair and sat.

With a glance toward the door, Ilse gathered her skirts behind her and lowered herself to the floor, her knees cracking audibly. "If he thought as much about people as he does about those cows…"

She swished her hand in the water, stirring chips of leather-colored soap into scrawny suds. She dipped a brush into the mixture and leaned into her work, scrubbing a floor that looked to Adelaide clean already.

Ilse had shown up in town one day looking for work, and Josef had sent her to help Martin in the dairy. Some in the community wondered if Martin would marry her like Josef had married his housekeeper after marriage had once again been allowed. Although Ilse proved herself a diligent worker, she had yet to apply for membership so the question of marriage was moot.

Adelaide fingered the bruise on her arm. "He sounds like a tyrant," she said, her eyes darting to his bed, its tattered coverlet drawn tight across the straw-filled mattress.

"It's nothing like that. It's just that he works so hard, and he expects everyone else to do the same. Do you know the girls have to scrub the cows down every day, and he comes along behind them to check? I have work here, and I'm to see what the girls are doing at the same time."

The swishing sound of the brush reverberated in the sparsely furnished room.

"I shouldn't be complaining. I deserve what I get."

"Deserve what?"

Ilse mumbled a reply and bent to her task, the wood planks squeaking under her knees.

Maybe a different approach would work. "You take good care of your girls, don't you, Ilse?"

The woman dropped the brush into the bucket with a splash and sat back on her heels. "'Course. Best I can."

"Cook, too, for them."

"Always wanting more. Or something special. Particular they are, but they get the same as me. No more, no less."

"What did they have to eat that day? The day Johanna died."

"Why ask that? She drowned, didn't she?"

"But she went outside that night, in a storm. Was she sick?"

"Those girls, always some complaint or other. But I'd know if she was sick."

"So you were awake?"

"No, I gotta sleep sometime, don't I?"

"Was Johanna someone you had to watch?"

"I don't want to speak ill of the dead."

"Was anyone angry with Johanna that you knew?"

"Angry? Not so'd you'd notice."

"Really? I don't understand."

"You know young girls, always fussing about something, the slightest word can touch them off, and then some of them will decide they don't like another, and by that time I've got one in tears. He doesn't like that, I can tell you."

"He doesn't mistreat them, does he?"

"Do you know how much work I have? Keep the girls milking, scrubbing, churning butter, making cheese—we can barely keep up. And this house. He wants it as clean as his cattle. Too old I am," she added as if she'd talked too much, and went back to her scrubbing.

Adelaide left her to it.

Emma leaned crooked hands on the arm of her rocker and felt her way to her seat. "I hope you're being careful. If someone murdered Johanna," she winced as she settled herself, "he won't want you finding out."

"I've only talked to her sister and Ilse. No one knows what I'm doing."

"You think not? Even I heard you were at the blacksmith shop looking for Jakob. People are talking. Some think you're just trying to find someone else to blame."

"Emma, I've been accused and until I find out how Johanna died, people will continue to blame me. And I need your help. I can't figure this out alone. I need you to talk it through with me, just like we do with an illness. Please, Emma, please help me."

Emma stared at something only she could see until finally she spoke. "If I don't, I suppose you'll go right on anyway, won't you? Never mind, I know the answer. I haven't spent sixteen years rearing you in this work to not know what you'll do. So, all right. What do we need to do?"

We? Adelaide smiled to herself and pulled her casebook out of her pocket. "It had to be poison. It's the only way that makes sense. I've thought about how easy it would be. We have so many plants in the woods, in the garden, growing by the side of the road even. It would have been so simple to find something and use it."

"I doubt it would be that easy. First, it had to be a potent substance. Most anything could be lethal in large enough quantities, but I suspect the killer preferred to use something that could guarantee quick results."

"Foxglove, it's in the woods. Oleander's growing in the green-house. Or lily of the valley blooming now. Anyone could soak a few leaves and they'd have poison. Oh, Emma, however are we to discover what happened?"

"Slow down, Adelaide. I don't think they'd be so open about collecting them. Someone would be too likely to remember even if the person was only gathering flowers for the table. Could mean one of your remedies. They're dried so they're more potent than freshly-gathered ones. And they're labeled so there'd be no mistake. Any sign that someone's been in your stores?"

"Maybe. I thought they might have been disturbed."

"It had to be a concentrated, fast-acting poison," Emma continued in her no-nonsense voice. "Otherwise someone would have noticed, or she would have been obviously ill. It had to sedate her soon after she'd taken it. Deadly nightshade, or something similar, would work the fastest."

She steeled herself to keep her mind on the conversation as if they were discussing a medical case. "How much would it take?"

"Very little. So someone steals some from your stores, intending to mix it in her food or drink."

"How? Ilse said they all ate the same. For sure the headstrong girl would have resisted anything forced on her."

"What if he, or she, told her it was something for what ailed her?"

"She might take it, especially after my remedy didn't work. But what about the taste? Nightshade would be bitter."

"Maybe he covered it up with something. And she might expect something stronger to be bitter."

"What would it do to her?"

"Numb, first, then excited, delirious, until it paralyzed her lungs."

Adelaide couldn't seem to catch her breath. "How long?" she whispered.

"It depends on the dose. With enough, I'd say quickly. Less than an hour."

Poor child. Alone. Terrified.

"Adelaide, I'm speaking to you."

"Sorry. What did you say?"

"When was she last seen?"

"Brigit said she sneaked out, like most nights. To be with Jakob, from what she said."

"Did he know about the babe?"

"I, uh, didn't ask him." She ignored Emma's snort. "But he wanted to marry her."

"So he says."

"I just can't see him hurting her, no matter what."

"When you've seen as much as I have, you'll know that people often are not what they seem."

Adelaide bristled. "I know that, but you've taught me to pay attention to my instincts, and they tell me he didn't do it. Besides, he wasn't with her that night."

"You sure?"

"You think he did it, don't you?" Jakob had that cut on his face. Could he have fought with Johanna? She fingered the herbs in her pocket. Could he have made another drink with an added something?

"Did you see anything else on her body?" Emma asked. "Any clue to what happened to her?"

"No, no injuries. Nothing except the, uh, signs I told you about." She sucked in her breath as a memory surfaced. "Her fingers. There were splinters in her fingers."

"Splinters?"

"Dear God, could she have been locked in somewhere? Struggling to get out?" Her voice rose. "Like a coffin." Adelaide bent double, her arms clutching her body. "Who? Who could have done something so horrible?"

"Hush now. It's all over for her."

"But what she went through, she—"

"You must stop that kind of thinking. We'll never be able to solve her death if you don't calm yourself. It's up to us to find out who did it. Isn't that right?"

Adelaide stared out the window as the wind plucked a blossom off the apple tree and flung it to the ground. She brought herself upright. Arguing with Emma had calmed her, helped her let go of imagining Johanna's suffering.

"Who else might harm her?" Emma asked.

"What about her sister? Brigit seems smitten with Jakob, but Johanna was the elder. She had first right to marry."

"The trustees do seem to favor the oldest girl with so few men available."

"If Johanna died, Brigit would have Jakob to herself."

"If he wanted her. Besides, I doubt she would kill her own sister. Not after Ophelia's death a year ago. She wouldn't do that to her parents, if for no other reason."

Adelaide had to agree. She studied her casebook open on lap. "Gerda didn't approve of her niece, nor like her from what I've seen. Johanna would have trusted her and probably would drink something she gave her."

"What reason would she have to kill her niece?"

"Family disgrace. When everyone found out about Johanna's situation, she'd be shamed."

"Adelaide, no one is responsible for what another person does, no matter their relation."

"She might not see it that way."

"Self-righteous, stern, I'll grant you, but that alone would prevent her from doing harm. Goodness knows, she keeps track of everyone's misdeeds." Emma winced as she repositioned herself, then leaned back in her rocker with a sigh. "What about Martin?"

Adelaide swiped her hand in front of her face as if she could wipe away the thought of him.

"He was her boss, wasn't he?"

"Uh, yes, well, strictly speaking, he's Ilse's boss. He wanted—no, demanded—that she be buried that same day."

"Why?"

"He wouldn't say. But mad, he was."

"Same day burial is not unheard of, and some people react to grief with anger. Again, what motive would he have? I doubt he had much to do with her or any of the other girls. Besides, now he needs another dairy maid."

"Then there's that preacher. Benjamin said she'd taunted him when he was here last. He certainly wouldn't have approved if he knew about her, uh, sin."

"And what? Killed her to save her soul? No, Adelaide, no matter how he might condemn, or even chastise her, he wouldn't harm her. Even to further his cause."

"Doctor Hertel. She could have gone to him when she first noticed her illness, and he could have given her some medicine. Then when she died, he tried to cover it up by dumping her body in the river."

"His treatments might be useless, if not downright dangerous," Emma mused, "but I don't see him purposely covering up a death. He'd be the one asked to ascertain the cause, come to that."

"He would expect everyone to think she drowned. He didn't count on my finding her and knowing that she couldn't have drowned. Then he told Simon that I had given her something to cover up what he had actually done." She sat back, a satisfied smile on her face until Emma shook her head.

"That doesn't make sense. Why would he even suspect that you or anyone else would discover his deception?"

"Maybe he told Simon just to make sure he wasn't accused. Maybe he thought she'd told someone he had treated her. One of the dairy maids or her parents or her sister. Or Jakob."

"So he turned the suspicion on you? I suppose that's possible."

"I have to keep trying to find out what happened, who wished her harm."

"If you think you should."

It isn't Benjamin.

"I can't let her death go, I just can't. It's the only way I can be certain."

Be certain Benjamin had nothing to do with her death.

"But stop and think. It's all well for you and I to discuss this, but if we have a murderer out there, you could be putting yourself, maybe your family, in danger."

"Wouldn't you do the same?"

"I'm not the one who could be ostracized nor harmed. I just want you to think this through before you do something that you wish you hadn't."

She kept any more misgivings to herself.

— Eleven —

Alone again, Benjamin grabbed a smoothing plane by its horn, steadied himself against the piece, and slid the plane along the grain, the wood squawking as he dug into its uneven surface. The scent of linseed oil lingered in the air. Finally, he felt the wood give way under his fingers, and he continued scraping until the grooved edges had smoothed out to barely rounded ridges. He brushed the cuttings to the ground and stood back to review his work.

He often imagined that he was just one in a long line of German cabinet makers that stretched across the ocean and back through the generations of wood workers who felled the trees in the forest, lugged them home, and fashioned even the most recalcitrant logs into furnishings. Though he had never said it aloud, Benjamin felt a oneness with the wood as if he and it had once grown strong together.

Adelaide stepped inside the door. "Beef and noodles." She looked around for a place to leave his dinner bucket.

He scraped wood shavings aside to clear a corner of his workbench and took the bucket from her. He pried the lid up with a
knife, and the hearty scent of beef broth filled the tiny shop.

"Looks like you'll finish in time."

"Much more to do before Saturday," he mumbled between bites.
"We can't afford to lose him as a customer. He says he has much
more business for us if his customers are satisfied with the initial
shipment."

Had she heard about Martin's campaign to outlaw marriage?
Should he tell her? Maybe if she thought they'd have to live apart,
she might listen to him and stop asking questions about Johanna.
If she keeps this up, the only person who will be implicated is
her. And why won't she admit she gave a remedy to Johanna? He
stopped, his fork in mid-air. Johanna. *Whyever didn't I listen to her?
Why did I turn her away?*

"Did you hear me?" Adelaide asked.

"What?"

"I said, who was on watch last Thursday night?"

"Not again!" He stuck his fork upright into the bucket. "You
must stop this. No one knows anything."

"Maybe he didn't think about it at the time."

"And he wouldn't have stopped her? Or told someone?" His
appetite gone, he picked up the plane to resume his work.

"Maybe it didn't seem suspicious at the time."

"Isn't it enough with Martin threatening—"

She flinched as if he'd struck her.

"But no one's listening to him. He's the only one wants it."

"Wants what?" she asked in a strangled voice.

"To outlaw marriage again."

"Marriage?"

"He's campaigning to write it in our Articles. But don't worry, it won't happen."

"That's what you meant?"

"He's not going to win."

Brigit burst through the door. "Come quick. Maria, she's ill."

Outside, Adelaide grabbed Brigit's arm. "He won't let me treat her. You heard him at Meeting. He thinks I hurt Johanna. He's ordered me away." But it wasn't Simon she feared. It was her own doubts clouding her mind.

Brigit pulled her along. "If you don't help, she said she'll die, that's what she said. You have to. And he's not there. There was some trouble with one of the locks on the canal upstream, and he went to see to it."

She had never turned away a birthing mother, and she wouldn't now, despite her worry. "All right, Brigit, I can try. It's all I can do. If he comes back, well, we'll deal with that then."

At the inn Adelaide examined Maria. "You were premature to call me. Sometimes mothers have these pains," she explained, relieved that she needn't face a birthing today. "It's a way for your body to prepare for the birth."

"I'm probably imagining it." Maria drew herself up to a sitting position and shoved damp tendrils of pale hair under her cap. "I'm sorry I bothered you."

"It's no bother. It tells us it's almost time. But you look a little peaked. Have you eaten today?"

"I thought I might be sick, but I am hungry."

Adelaide sent Brigit for a tray for her sister.

"Best you rest today just to be sure."

"He won't like it," Maria said, dull eyes darting toward the door.

"If he knew you were here... I can't lie. That's a sin. Reverend Truesdale says we have to confess our sins."

What about my sin? I'm a fool as well, imagining desire from a man who wants to outlaw carnal relations.

Maria shoved at her bedclothes and winced. "I can't get comfortable, no matter how I sit or lie."

"No help for that until your time. Have you been working on your breathing? To relax your stomach?"

"I've tried, but with this lump on my tummy—"

"It will help when your time comes." She moved around the bed, neatening Maria's bedclothes. "I need to ask you about that. Do you want me to come when your illness starts?"

"Of course I do, but Simon insists I need the doctor."

"You had the doctor here before."

Maria scrunched down in the covers.

"What is it? What did he do?"

"Oh, Adelaide, I couldn't bear it if I have to have him here." Her face flushed. "It's, it's not proper."

"He didn't—"

"No, no, nothing, but if he comes then... I don't know how I could tolerate a man... seeing me." She tugged the coverlet to her chin.

"So why did you let him bleed you?"

"He told Simon he needed to so my blood wouldn't be too much for the baby. I thought it made sense."

"That isn't how your body works, Maria. Your body knows how much blood the baby needs and makes enough for both of you." She did know this. And much more about birthing babies. Why did she doubt herself so often?

"That's another reason I don't like him," Maria went on. "He talks to Simon about me as if I'm a child."

"You are not a child, Maria. You're a grown woman. You can make your own decisions. How did you feel afterward?"

"I've been feeling poorly. Tired all the time. I don't have any strength. That's normal, isn't it?"

"The bleeding didn't help."

"I'm so lonely. He won't let me go outside. The girls, they have to work even if I can't. If men are downstairs, Simon says I have to remain up here. Like he's ashamed of me."

"That's not unusual, Maria. Most women don't want to be seen."

"You did. You never stopped working, going to people who needed you. You even went to Bolivar for a woman one time when you looked like you would burst."

She had no response to Maria's criticism. It hadn't occurred to her or Emma, or even Benjamin, for her to stop working. She was well and healthy, if a bit awkward near the end.

"Just stay in bed today. Then if you feel better, go ahead with your work. No lifting anything heavy, though, and take plenty of rests. Lying down is best." She patted the coverlet over Maria's bulging abdomen. "You don't have long now."

"Even if I sent for you, he'd tell the girls who work here and they'd keep you out."

"Maria, you have control over your own body. Even your husband does not have a say about that. We are all free here."

"But men are more free, aren't they?"

She sat back on her heels. Maria was right. Little by little power had slipped away from the women. Once they'd finished the canal and paid their mortgage, the women fell back into their old roles as cooks, bakers, sewers, and caretakers. Men did the important work—building homes, plowing fields, raising animals. And made the decisions.

"I want to be a good wife. Like my mother. But my parents seem like they're of the same mind, partners. And Simon, well, he's different. Old-fashioned."

"You are his partner. And your own person."

"I know you're right. It's just that he wants our baby so badly. He wants him to be well."

"Then it's up to you to convince him. Or insist. It's your decision." When Maria remained silent, she said, "It's about Johanna, isn't it?"

"Oh, Adelaide, I'm so sorry." She sat up in bed, the covers tossed to the side. "I'm the one who told him," she said, her words coming in a rush. "After she died, I couldn't stop crying. Johanna and I, close, we were. I knew she went to you and he pestered me. Wanted to know why I was so distressed. Finally I told Simon what she'd said. That you gave her a remedy, and he said that's what caused her to fall in the river. Now God's going to punish me, I'm going to die."

Adelaide grabbed her hands. "You are not going to die and you're not being punished for whatever sins you're imagining."

Maria swallowed.

"Listen to me," she demanded, sinking onto a chair. "You are giving birth like millions of women before you. As much as I knew, I was still afraid. And now Olivia's three months old and, as you can see, I'm fine."

Maria shifted her body toward Adelaide and gave her a wan smile. "So it wasn't so bad?" she asked in whispered words. "Your sickness?"

She wasn't about to share the pains she'd had with Olivia's birth nor her worry that she would have no other children. "I have to talk to Simon. That's what I'll do. I'll ask him right out why he thinks my remedy harmed Johanna."

Maria let out a harsh cry. "Oh, no. Don't do that. He'd only get angrier. He'd blame me." Her fingers dug into Adelaide's arm. "He's a good person, really he is. He just wants the best for me and his son," she murmured, lying back down.

"Then you need to help me."

"Me? How?"

"You knew why Johanna needed a remedy."

She nodded.

"Why did she go to the river that night, do you have any idea?"

Maria burst into tears.

Adelaide jumped up to hug her.

"All the time I'm here and she's dying," she said between sobs, "drowning, no one to help."

"You couldn't have done anything."

"My own salvation, that's all I thought about."

"Your salvation?"

She sank back on the bed, her face as pale as the pillowcase. "Sunday night outside when Reverend was speaking, I saw the light. I mean a real light. Some power shot right through me. For a moment I thought my baby was coming, it felt so strong. Hasn't anything like that ever happened to you?"

Adelaide had to admit she'd often sensed a power greater than herself but nothing so visual, or visceral, as Maria described. "Yes," she said, finally.

"The preacher prayed with me, let me confess my sins."

"I thought Simon ordered him away."

"This was before. Besides, he was busy with the ruckus downstairs and that went on most of the night. Josef, he told me my faith was between me and God. But it's not enough, not for me, not now. There's nothing wrong with confessing your sins to a preacher, is there? Nothing that says we can't do that?" She didn't wait for Adelaide's answer. "Worrying about myself and all the while... I should have been with her, but, no, I had to save myself. Don't you understand? I was right here, more worried about my salvation than my sister's life."

"You mean the night she died? The preacher was here with you that night?"

She clutched the coverlet, her fingers white against its woven pattern. "We heard the tree crack and fall on her." She hugged her knees and rocked back and forth. "Oh, dear God, I heard her killed!"

"No, you didn't. The tree didn't kill her."

Her rocking stopped suddenly. "It didn't? Then what did?"

"I wish I knew. But I'm surprised Simon let the preacher up here with you."

"I told him I had to see him if he wanted a healthy boy. Besides, I think he's done something wrong."

"Who? The preacher?"

"No. Simon."

"Something wrong? What?"

"I know," Brigit said, entering with a tray. "He's been talking to Herr Guenther."

"You know what about?" Adelaide asked.

"Herr Guenther says Simon should get the authorities," Brigit said.

"Authorities? Whatever for?" Maria asked.

"Our sister, how she died," Brigit answered.

"He's not going to the authorities," Maria said as Adelaide helped prop her up in bed.

Brigit arranged the tray on her sister's lap and topped buttered dark bread with a slice of Swiss cheese. "He said maybe he would."

"I know my husband," Maria said, and took a sip of heavily sugared tea. "He will not go to the authorities."

They left Maria to her meal and as they descended the stairs, Brigit asked, "She'll be all right, though, won't she? In the end? I've already lost two sisters. I couldn't bear it if I lost another."

"I'm sure she'll do fine." She added a smile for confirmation, and Brigit seemed satisfied. But Adelaide worried about how much pain Maria's fear would engender. Sometimes when people say they're going to die, they do.

A man's voice sounded outside.

"Go out the back," Brigit said. "Hurry."

Adelaide turned, intending to follow Brigit's advice but then stopped herself. "This is as good a time as any," she told Brigit, facing the door, her hands on her hips.

— Twelve —

"Your wife is well," Adelaide said to Simon as he came into the common room. The high pitch of her voice belied the calm demeanor she intended. "She's all right, but she needs to rest today and be careful from now on."

"How can you show your face here?" He wiped the stubble on his chin with the hem of his apron. "After what you did."

"I did nothing. I know you think I harmed—"

"You did. Your remedy. Killed her, it did." He waved the apron about as if he could shoo her away.

"I did not kill Johanna," she said, enunciating each word.

"Admit it, you gave her something, something that killed her."

She could not, she would not, betray her patient's confidence, never mind that the girl was dead. Still, she could tell the truth without revealing that Johanna had come to her and why. "I never gave her anything that would have harmed her," she said at last.

"Ah hah! So you admit you gave her something?"

"I didn't say that."

"So did you?"

"I can't say."

He flapped his apron toward her. "And you wonder why everyone worries about you treating them. You can't even tell the truth."

"Simon, listen to me. I did nothing to hurt Johanna. Why are you so certain I did?"

He studied her face for a moment, then collapsed into a chair. "It's Maria." He shot a glance toward the stairs. "The grieving. It's been so hard on her."

"She'll be fine. She's a healthy young woman. I shouldn't worry about her. She'll come through her illness, and your babe will be well." She knew, and he probably did, too, that no one can predict what will happen when birthing starts.

His shoulders slumped, and the lines in his face deepened. "She's not like her sister."

"Brigit?"

"No, Ophelia. She was strong, knew her own mind. Maria, well, she needs more direction."

Adelaide bit her lip. His words to his wife seemed more like commands than direction. But having his favor would help her attend Maria so she kept quiet. "I'll be back later. See that Maria rests today." She let herself out the door.

On her way home Adelaide saw her husband in conversation with Nathan in the blacksmith shop so she used the opportunity to pick up Benjamin's empty dinner bucket from his shop next door. She wanted no more talk about what she should or should not do. Back home, she shared a quiet dinner with Nellie, then nursed Olivia and put her down for her nap. She longed to join her, but she'd neglected her responsibilities in the community garden for too long.

Mister Welby was taking his daily constitutional along the garden path, she saw, nearing. The man, with little to do except wait for Benjamin to finish his order, often strolled about their village, greeting people as they went about their business. And Brigit had said he'd given Johanna that bonnet.

She hurried through the garden, grabbed her rake from the greenhouse, and headed back out.

"Missus Bechtmann." He tipped his hat. "A handsome garden you have here."

"Thank you, sir," she said with a dip of her head. The garden had sprouted in the last few days. Splashes of pansies filled triangular beds, a row of geraniums edged a bed overflowing with clusters of purple phlox, and a dogwood tree guarded crimson bleeding hearts that bobbed along the fence.

"Though much work, I warrant."

Words seemed stuck in her throat, but he looked as if he was about to move on. "I think you knew our Johanna," she blurted out.

"I heard, yes. My condolences to you all."

"You gave her a bonnet, they tell me."

He threw back his head and laughed a deep-throated guffaw. Finally, he pulled a fine linen handkerchief out of his pocket and wiped his face. "I do apologize, Missus Bechtmann, for my inappropriate hilarity. Of course I did not gift any of your lovely young girls with anything. I fear it would have been misconstrued, and it seems as if I was correct."

"Apparently a false rumor."

"Little place like this, stranger in town. Yes, I've had a few curious stares and whispered conversations."

"So you didn't agree to take her with you back to the city?"

"Hardly. Why back in the city…let's just say I don't need young country girls to fill my social calendar." He fanned himself with his hat, then twirled it around on his finger, the diamond on his ring catching the light. "So many pretty girls around here, well, they would be if they dressed up a bit. Why do all your clothes look alike? It's as if you're trying to disguise your attractiveness. I hear some talking about the 'old ways,' and when I asked them, they said you all forsook matrimony. Espoused celibacy."

She dropped her rake. Martin. How could he want to outlaw marriage? *I saw desire in his face, his body. I know I did.*

"That true, Missus Bechtmann? You didn't marry?"

Adelaide bit back her answer; it would be rude to answer his inquisitiveness with an ill-mannered response. "It's not that we didn't believe in…living together."

Did I imagine his yearning?

"I thought that was why you're always scrubbing, cleaning, trying to purify yourselves."

She upended her rake and yanked off dead leaves that clogged the prongs. A breeze stirred and tulip petals, their red color leached pale since they had dropped, skittered into a bed of columbine.

Her face reddened with shame. How could she have been so foolish to think that a man committed to celibacy desired her?

"I heard tell that you consider yourselves all brothers and sisters." He adjusted his hat at a jaunty angle.

She wiped her face with the back of her glove. "We are all one family." *Not that I believe it.*

"So that's why you call each other by your first names. Though few people would agree to work without pay."

"Look what we have," she said with an encompassing wave. "Food a'plenty, clothing, homes—"

"You won't starve, I'll give you that— "

"Do you know why we came to America? We didn't believe as our neighbors did. Not that anyone had a choice." She chopped into a clump of dirt. The clod burst apart. "You believed as the state decreed or…" Memories of childhood friends being carted off came rushing back, their parents distraught. And helpless. She bent over the raised perennial bed. Choked with dead leaves, its stench of decay mixed with the scent of newly turned earth.

"So that's why you call yourselves Separatists. Because you're different, not like everyone else. Do you believe in all that 'burn in hell' the preacher was spewing last night?"

"He's not a Separatist, and I personally don't believe in the hell he described, but don't take my word as the beliefs of everyone else. We may dress alike, live in similar homes, but each of us believes in our own way."

What do I believe? It seemed a sacrilege—this thinking about God in the abstract as an amorphous universe. When she meditated, she didn't have any thoughts—religious or otherwise. Each works out salvation in his own way—way to heaven, according to Josef. Truth be told, she seldom thought about anything as esoteric as salvation.

"No offense, Missus Bechtmann. Religious freedom. That's what America was founded on, but I must caution you, as the years have passed, there's been more and more effort to make everyone conform. The Catholics, for example, haven't had an easy time settling here, but you're close enough to the Puritans—my, you put their rigidity to shame—that I doubt anyone will try to get you to abandon your ways, strange though they might seem to me." He waved a gloved hand. "You people don't know what's going on outside your little village, do you? Tucked away in the middle of the Ohio countryside."

"That countryside, sir, is our land."

"All this belongs to the Separatists?"

"Five thousand acres." She pointed uphill toward the east where in the distance they could see the tiny figure of a man criss-crossing a field, a bag of seed slung on his back. To the left of the fields, cows grazed in the high meadows. "And that's not all." She swung about before he could speak. "Those woods down there, the river, it's all ours, more than sufficient for our needs."

She spun around, her world whirling by in a kaleidoscope of sights and colors—pink flowering trees and tall dark junipers gave way to the glass-fronted greenhouse, the sewing house, the Bimeler cabin, the bakery, and the tin shop before her steps slowed. It was as if she was seeing her world for the first time. This was her home, her people, caring for each other, no matter their differences. She allowed herself a moment of pleasure. "This town? Built it ourselves, yes we did."

"Whew!" he said. "I didn't mean to get you so riled. You deserve much credit for all you've done, but I meant the world outside of yours, this country."

"I know everything about America. We learned it in school."

He tipped his hat back on his head. "I'll bet you don't know anything about our president. Jackson's his name. Though I know few men who voted for him."

"That's of no interest to me."

"Of course. You can't vote."

"I do vote, sir. Every year like everyone else."

"But not outside your town."

"As I said, it's of no interest to me."

"You think this country's laws don't apply to you?" He chuckled. "Probably not here in your idyllic world. Although for one of the utopias, it's equal to any I've seen."

"Utopias?"

"You're not the only ones. The Amish, Mennonites. They're not communal, but they have their own ways and they do marry."

"As if anyone's like the Separatists. We have our own beliefs, sir."

"You just don't know, do you? Lots of folks believe like you people. The Harmonists for one. I think they came from *Württemberg*, like you did, but earlier. They don't believe in war, either, though we wouldn't have an America today without one. And the Shakers. All of them are celibate. I don't know where they think the next generation is coming from," he said with a wink. "All you folks work hard, I'll give you that. None are as clean as you Zoarites. I'll swear, you women would scrub the leaves on the trees if you had any more time. What do you do for fun?"

"Fun?" She blew an errant curl out of her eyes. "We're not here for fun."

"So what are you here for? Prepare for heaven? If there is a heaven."

"Of course there's a heaven," Adelaide sputtered, her words automatic, her doubts held at bay.

"Me, I believe in money. And what it can buy." When she kept on working, he said, "Quaint though it might be, your little village isn't the modern world. You should see what's happening in the city."

"I'm perfectly happy here, thank you, sir," she said as she tugged on a weed embedded in the ground. It came free with a jerk, sending her and a spray of earth backward.

Mister Welby reached forward to brush dirt off her apron, and she jumped away.

"*Was ist das?*" Gerda said to Adelaide. She snapped her apron at Mister Welby. "*Was machst Du?*"

Mister Welby doffed his hat in a bow and left.

"You're a married woman," Gerda said, lips clamped together. "Stay away from him or you'll end up like Johanna."

"What do you mean 'end up like Johanna'?"

"You should be glad I came along when I did. He almost—"

"Mister Welby is buying cabinets from Benjamin," Adelaide said, though she didn't wish to defend the man who had, a few moments before, belittled her world, even unintentionally. However much she criticized it herself, she didn't want anyone else to do so. And she wasn't about to explain why Mister Welby had reached toward her. Not to Gerda Schlechter, she wasn't.

"That doesn't give him the right to go after our girls."

"You saw him do that?"

"Oh yes, he did. And her," she spit out. "No better than she should be."

"Who? Johanna?"

"Swishing her skirts about. Maybe if I'd had her in the dormitory for a while, I would have straightened her out."

At least Johanna had been spared that.

"She loved the men, she did." Gerda clicked her tongue. "She'd flip those ribbons around—you see that bonnet?—tassels flying about. Coy, she was. Any man looked at her she'd flutter around them like a bee after nectar."

Adelaide gritted her teeth. The woman was too perfect by half. Before she turned away she saw Gerda's face flush red.

"I can help with that," she said, reaching for a packet of sage. It wasn't the first time she had noticed that Gerda suffered the signs of a woman's change of life.

"I told you stay away. Besides, I've got all the help I need from a real doctor." She shoved up her sleeve to reveal the tell-tale bandage.

Doctor Hertel had bled her.

"That's his cure?"

"It makes sense. Too much blood makes one hot. I thought even you knew that."

"That's nonsense." Why couldn't anyone understand? Emma had told her that the body regulates its blood and never needed to be reduced.

"Nonsense? He went to medical school. And blood-letting is commonly taught and accepted as a treatment for many ills."

"Well, they're wrong."

"And just how would you know that? Went to medical school, did you?"

"You need some help, Adelaide?" August asked, coming up behind Gerda. He rested his arms on his hoe and watched the woman stomp away. "What's her complaint this time? More about the man from Cleveland?"

"How did you know?"

"Some are saying he knew Johanna more than he should."

"I just asked him. He barely remembered her." But she wondered. Could his talk about not knowing Johanna been a lie?

"He's from the outside, so different from our ways. But I heard you're spreading some rumors of your own." He squatted down beside a flat wooden box of Sweet William plants.

"What rumors?"

He lifted the first plant out of the box, slipped it into a harrowed row, and tamped soil around it. "That you're saying someone killed her, that she didn't drown."

"Who told you that?" The moment she asked she knew it was hopeless to expect that August would tell her even if he remembered.

"Word just gets around, that's all. Is it true? Is that what you think?"

"I don't know how she died." Her words were not all that far from the truth although, strictly speaking, she did know Johanna hadn't drowned. There was no mistaking that.

Who knew about her suspicions? Benjamin, of course. Emma and Josef. Could someone have overheard their conversations? Maybe someone walking by? The Bimeler cabin sat close to an oft-traveled road. They'd made no effort to keep their voices low so used as they were to windows closed through the winter. She couldn't remember if any windows had been open. She did know Dorothea Bimeler had been close enough to hear them, although she was so timid that Adelaide had dismissed Josef's wife from her mind once they had begun to talk. She doubted that Dorothea would spread gossip. Few others, though, would be above passing along a juicy story like this, a rare *Schadenfreude*.

"I'm still worried about Simon's accusations." She piled her collected debris to the side and examined the new shoots sprouting in the bed.

"Only people listen to him are just those don't want to work so hard. Always grumbling about this or that. The others, they don't know the innkeeper that well and they do know you, so they're not inclined to give him much mind. But there is one thing."

"Tell me."

"Simon's saying he's going to call the authorities. Apparently, he talked to Josef but he wouldn't budge, said Johanna died, was buried, and that was that."

"Maybe he meant Lewis Birk. He is our official here."

"And just what crime has he investigated?" Zoar had never had a crime in its sixteen years of existence. "No, I'm worried about them sending someone from Tuscarawas County."

"I don't think Simon will go to outsiders." Maybe it would be best if the authorities investigated. Not that she wanted Simon to circumvent Josef's authority but sometimes, like with Johanna's death, his usual wisdom eluded him. That Josef put the good of the community first, Adelaide had no doubt, but he had never dealt with murder before, and he seemed to believe that murder was so unlikely as to have been impossible. If Simon informed the authorities, then at least someone would investigate Johanna's murder.

"Just mind yourself."

"You going to the town meeting tonight?"

"I wouldn't miss it for anything." He turned his hoe upside down and pulled a wedge-shaped piece of wood out of his apron pocket. "Simon and Nathan." He waved the wedge in the air. "Each telling how they'd be best for the town." He scraped dirt off his hoe blade with the wedge. "I can't wait to see them go after each other."

But Adelaide worried. Would Simon say anything more about her?

It had taken only a few words from Matron to convince Benjamin that Adelaide should stay away from *her* girls. Still, when she criticized his wife, he wanted to defend her, but the woman had the right of it.

Adelaide couldn't have disagreed more. "Who is she to tell me what I can or cannot do?"

He should have said request, then maybe she might have agreed. "What do you want me to do? Matron is in charge. She has the say of it."

"You think I'm not good enough? I don't know what I'm doing? Is that it?"

That's exactly what he feared.

She squared a potato in the center of the cutting board and

balanced it with one hand. "I am the herbalist for this community. I will treat whoever needs me and neither you nor Gerda nor anyone else has a right to tell me not to." She raised the knife and slammed it down, sending potato halves flying.

He gathered the potato pieces and placed them back on the table. "Adelaide, please, just for me. Let someone else care for her."

"Is that the woman you want to give your daughter to? Haven't you seen how Nellie still cringes at a raised word? Can you imagine how she was treated for all those years? You want Olivia beaten or worse?" She scooped up potato peelings and tossed them into a pan.

"It is three years away."

"Two years and nine months," she shot back, her voice choking.

"Two years and nine months. So why are we arguing about this now?"

He knew she felt that Nellie's being sent to the dormitory had been her fault. Whyever he couldn't imagine. She'd been too young to care for her sister at the time. The blame fell on her father, who had deserted the girls to return to *Deutschland* and left them to be raised in America. That, he supposed, she also imagined she caused.

"It's not for us to question the rules," he said.

She cleared her throat. "Well, I won't allow it."

"No," he said. He had to stop her. For their safety. "You can't defy the trustees. We'll be banished, sent away with nothing."

"That's not going to—"

"You remember the Holstein family had to leave? Disobedient, the trustees decreed. Put out with nothing but the clothes on their back."

"And the trustees offered to loan them some money, which Herr Holstein in his pride refused."

"You know what happened to the family—"

"I don't want to hear."

But he wasn't to be stopped even as she covered her ears. "The children indentured to wealthy families in Canton, the mother dead shortly after they left, and the father, he hasn't been heard from since."

"If I get the other women with children—"

"I said no." Benjamin, his patience gone, gritted his teeth as he said each word distinctly. "You've caused enough trouble, all that talk about Johanna and how she died."

"I have a vote—unlike the rest of America, I might add."

"Some of the men are already vowing to take away the women's vote. Don't do anything to upset them or you may find that—"

"Twice as many women as men here. Just how do you think they can prevail? Tell me that." She grabbed another potato and chopped at its skin as if flaying the man himself.

Olivia squealed from her cradle.

Adelaide gave him a look and then hurried to her infant.

Now he knew. No matter what he said, what he did, she'd never agree. Not to stop treating the girl. Not to stop questioning Johanna's death. Not to stop fighting to keep Olivia out of the dormitory.

He said no more.

— Thirteen —

The bell announcing the meeting rang while Adelaide settled Olivia for the night, and then Nellie needed help untangling her embroidery thread. Still she delayed, reluctant to return to the meeting house where just the day before Simon had accused her of killing Johanna. By the time she left, the streets were deserted.

Benjamin had returned to work right after their evening meal, but his angry words echoed in her head. Was it only three months ago she first saw her infant, her red face squished and screaming against the world she'd been so abruptly thrust into? In that instant she knew love. Not like the love she felt for Benjamin. No, one's husband didn't inspire such rapture no matter how much one enjoyed his face or his arms or his body. A husband is a helpmate, a companion and, yes, Adelaide admitted to herself, a lover. But a baby is so much more. The issue of one's loins, literally tied for so many months to one's own body, now forever bound by an invisible cord linking child to mother.

Her stomach tightened every time she thought of the date when she would be forced to relinquish her beloved Olivia to the girls' dormitory, never to return home again. She couldn't abide the thought, no matter that Benjamin insisted the time was far off. To her it felt as if the day would dawn tomorrow, her pain that great.

The meeting house was filled with the low murmuring of people visiting with each other as they waited for the meeting to start. The press of bodies, smoky lanterns, and muggy air made the room oppressive. Several heads turned as Adelaide entered, and a wake of whispering followed her as she went to join the women. She raised her chin and kept her eyes straight ahead.

Nathan sat with Josef and the two other trustees behind a table at the front of the room. In spite of the heat, all four dressed in their formal Sunday wear: black woolen trousers topped by rounded cutaway coats and white linen shirts buttoned to the neck. Simon sat in the front row, his head held high.

As Adelaide settled herself, Josef stood and held onto the desk for balance. The room quieted. "I hereby declare this meeting of the Society of Separatists convened," he announced. "We need your consent for the Articles of Incorporation to be approved," he reminded them. "To make the Society a fully incorporated entity for business purposes. A two-thirds majority is required, and I'm expecting everyone to vote. Voting will take place as it does every year on the second Tuesday in May, Tuesday next. I'm sure you've all seen the notice posted outside."

Josef gave the names of the five men proposed for election to the new standing committee to mediate disputes. At Benjamin's name, a couple of heads turned her way, but their expressions were more curious than disapproving.

Adelaide stole a look at the casebook in her lap tucked under her apron. She slid her pencil out of her pocket and, keeping her apron tented over the book, opened the book to the page near the back where she'd written, "Who?"

"This week's meeting," Josef said, "is to afford the two candidates for trustee an opportunity to speak and to answer any questions you may have about their ability to lead. Our first candidate is Nathan Appelgate, who has been a trustee in charge of our industries for the past six years. Herr Appelgate, we thank you for being with us in this your hour of woe." Josef settled himself as Nathan came from behind the table to address the audience.

Nathan cleared his throat, nodded to Josef, and turned to the assemblage. "I am called to serve," he said, "regardless of my personal concerns. And I am honored to be called."

Adelaide wiggled her pencil onto the page and wrote DH. Doctor Hertel. Regardless of Emma's belief that the doctor had nothing to do with Johanna's death, Adelaide couldn't help hoping the man had treated Johanna and caused her death but, she had to admit, maybe she simply wanted him gone from the town.

"We have made significant strides since we arrived from Germany in 1817, sixteen years ago," Nathan said. "Some of you remember." Beads of sweat stood out on his face. "God gave man this world to tame, and He led us to this place, and we found that He had blessed us much."

She added JK to her list. Jakob, who loved Johanna and wanted to marry her. So he said. He'd given her the herbal tea. If he knew about the babe and didn't want the child…

"Today we have paid our mortgage in full," Nathan said with a nod to Josef, "built a canal that enables us to conduct trade with cities to the north and south to replenish our stores of items we can't produce ourselves. We're building homes—more than log cabins—two- and three-story structures to house several families so that no one is overburdened with chores and all are fed, clothed, and housed."

The woman next to her shot her a glance. Adelaide turned to the side, shielding her book from the woman's view, and returned to her list.

Martin Guenther. His voice, deep, resonant. And his arms, sleeves rolled up to the elbows, powerful muscles bulging on his forearms. She shoved the image away. But could he have lain with Johanna? Had her flirtatious behavior tempted him regardless of his claim of celibacy?

She added Simon's name. He had accused her of killing Johanna, but that was Doctor Hertel's doing. Simon had no motive she could imagine, but maybe she enticed him. She didn't seem particular, flitting about any man that caught her fancy. Even her sister's husband?

Or could either Martin or Simon have forced himself on her? Catching her unawares? Certainly she would have fought him and, from what she knew about Johanna, she would have told someone. At the least her behavior would have changed in some noticeable way. The girl was nothing if not obvious.

Nathan continued. "Our industries are expanding and thriving. And we're still buying and clearing land. You can see the hotel near completion; it will bring us more income. I accept your vote if you so want." He wiped his brow with a handkerchief and sat down to murmured approval.

One name she'd omitted. She would not commit her husband's name to the list.

Next was Simon's turn. Adelaide resisted an urge to shrink into her seat. Instead, she slipped her casebook into her pocket and directed her gaze to him as he stepped to the front.

"You have heard about all we've done in the past." Simon waved dismissively toward Nathan. "Now I ask you: Isn't it time to look to the future? Josef Bimeler's not the only one here with business acumen. I handle financial transactions regularly with outsiders. I have some ideas for production, suggest we purchase more canal boats, and invest in industries outside of Zoar."

A man in the back spoke up. "You think you can do better?"

"What are we doing with all the money Josef says we have?" Simon said by way of an answer. "Nothing. It sits there in his safe. We collect much custom—overmuch, I suggest—and where is it?

"Why did Bimeler insist that our mortgage be only in his name? And when the Quakers in Pennsylvania urged him to sign a title allowing us to share the land jointly, what did he do? He refused. Bimeler owns us, that's what I mean to tell you. Every part of Zoar, he owns it free and clear thanks to our work. If we want to live here, we work for him." He shook his fist toward Josef. "Right now, if he died, only his direct heirs would own our land." Simon pointed one long finger at Josef's wife and family.

Rustling murmurs spread through the room. Nathan started to get up, but Josef motioned him back down.

Simon continued. "I suggest it's time for a new order. We should be investing in bank stocks, bonds, and issuing loans—farm loans, personal ones, too, with our money that's just sitting there. I tell you one lesson I've learned," he leaned forward, "that money can make money. All by itself. But not confined in his so-called safe." He directed his gaze around the room. "One more matter. Why can't we decide for ourselves if we want to see Doctor Hertel?"

People looked at each other, some nodding, others clearly puzzled.

Josef jumped up. "No. His remedies, they will hurt you, not help."

"He's warning us about Hertel," Simon said in an aside, "as if he'd know."

Josef opened his mouth, then closed it. He balanced himself on his cane and said, "Just how would you pay him?"

"Ah, yes. I'm glad you asked that, *Bruder*," Simon said, looking over Josef's head to the assembly. "Bimeler's ideas might have been all right in the past, but this is the nineteenth century in America. Commerce is America's way. And freedom where each person's work is his, not owned in common."

"Are you saying we should end our communal life?" Josef asked. "Leave each one to fend for himself?"

Gerda spoke up. "With our own resources, we could have whoever we wanted to care for us in our need."

How had Simon paid Doctor Hertel? For certain, the man didn't come to Zoar for free.

Simon's words drew her back. "I'm just saying that we should consider the times and the place. What's served us in the past may not do in the future." He dipped his head to the few who nodded agreement and left.

After a brief intermission during which the Bimeler family left, Josef addressed Simon's complaint. "About the man from Bolivar."

Interesting that he didn't mention Doctor Hertel by name nor that he was a physician. For some time Adelaide had wondered about Josef's animosity toward the doctor, at first believing it simply a difference of opinion about treatments. She had come to suspect that Doctor Hertel was the one person who could intimidate her leader.

"As your physician, I am advising you that Hertel's treatments cause more harm than help."

"Isn't that why we came here?" a woman asked. "For the freedom to decide for ourselves?"

"No," Josef said. "We came to be free of the tyranny of religion and—"

"Isn't illness God's way of testing us?" a woman asked.

"Or punishing us," Gerda offered.

Josef held his hand up until the room quieted, but Gerda went on. "You can't tell us who we can see for our ailments. Maybe if Doctor Hertel had treated her, my niece would be alive today."

Josef's face paled.

Gerda cleared her throat and stared straight ahead, tears pooling in her eyes. *Tears?*

"I will say no more on the subject." He thumped his cane on the floor in front of him.

The trustees behind him stood, signaling the end of the meeting.

"You'd think Bimeler was another Moses," Adelaide heard someone say going out. "Ordering us about like we were children."

"Not everyone's voting for *his* man," another woman said. "Some of us want a change."

— Fourteen —

Benjamin stepped inside the blacksmith shop, its heat suffocating. Although the morning had barely dawned, the day promised to be hotter than usual for early May. He fanned himself with his apron as he watched Nathan pounding on a strip of metal. Steady flames flickered in a bed of coals in the forge.

Nathan had yet to notice his arrival, and it gave him time to consider the words that he'd delayed saying for several days. He wanted to tell Nathan that he was sorry about Johanna, but talk about death did not come easily to him, nor to many in Zoar.

His reluctance to speak of her death, though, was tainted with remorse. He'd ignored her plea for help. However could he speak of his failure to her father? His friend. The man who'd saved his life so many years ago. The man whose daughter he might have saved.

Nathan jarred him out of his thoughts. "You heard about last night? Simon attacked Josef and—"

"Attacked him?"

"Not physically, no, but he accused Josef of, of, I don't know." Nathan stood up, arching his back. "Lord, I need some help around here—" He pulled worn leather gloves off and wiped his face with a neckerchief.

"What happened?"

Nathan stuffed the neckerchief under his leather apron and picked up his tongs. "It's about Josef holding title to our land. Some—I guess Simon's one—can't accept that we have to follow the laws of the state." He raised the piece to the light and sighted along its length. "I guess it's no wonder. We all knew what the 'state' meant back home.

"A group of people cannot hold land if they're not an organized body, not easily, anyway. For many reasons—tax purposes, legalities, and for business dealings—it is better to name an individual as the official owner for state purposes. Josef did, after all, sign the mortgage. Fifteen thousand American dollars that he would have been responsible for even if we'd all up and left. Simon seems to have forgotten that."

"And if we approve the Articles of Incorporation next Tuesday? Then we could own the land collectively, correct?"

"Umm. I imagine so."

"Is that what Josef's planning to do? Sign over the title to the corporation?"

"He hasn't said."

"Maybe if he agreed to do that, Martin and Simon would be satisfied."

"Simon wants us to rescind our communal agreement, as if we can't see his motive in that. He'd be the only one to benefit, what with the traffic on the canal bringing him more and more transit."

He selected another metal piece and shoved it into the coals. "But that's not what Martin wants. You heard him yesterday. He wants to outlaw marriage. And put it in the Articles."

"Why? Even when we lived apart, it hadn't been written anywhere. We all knew to follow the rule," Benjamin said, moving to the doorway where a light breeze stirred. "Few would agree to outlaw marriage. Martin's the only one I've heard say it. It sounds as if all of this is to undermine Josef."

"If Simon becomes a trustee," Nathan said. "He'll try to get others to come around to his way of thinking, maybe even get them elected trustees. You know in three years we could have all new trustees." He pulled the reddened metal out of the fire and plunged it into the barrel of water beside him. "And new rules." Sizzling steam rose from the cask.

"That won't happen. You'll be reelected, of that I'm certain."

"Not with Martin saying I'm not fit for the job."

"Not fit? You've been a trustee for three years. Whatever could he say?"

"It's a question of my morality." His face contorted into a spasm of pain.

"Your what? You are the most moral person I know. In all your dealings you are rigorously honest." He laid a hand on Nathan's soot-stained arm. "You're responsible with your wife, your children, your work. However could he accuse you of anything immoral?"

"Hints, only hints."

"Pray tell."

"That I've had two daughters die in suspicious circumstances."

"That's not your fault."

"No, but he's making it sound as if somehow I caused their distress, and that's why they killed themselves."

"Martin's saying that Johanna killed herself?"

"Lots of people are."

Not Adelaide.

"I don't know how Johanna died. I just want everyone," he gave Benjamin a knowing glance, "to stop talking about her."

"Maybe we should find out what happened. For certain. That would stop Martin's talk."

"No. Please, can't you make her stop? Tell her," he swiped at his eyes with the back of his glove and left a charcoal smear on his cheek, "tell her she's only making it worse for us."

"I'll do what I can, but you know her."

Nathan's voice was thick. "Please try."

"If only I could," he mumbled on the way back to his shop. Does he know something about his daughter's death? Is that why he's so adamant about stopping Adelaide? *Maybe he's trying to spare me by asking me to stop her investigating.* Does he believe Simon and suspect Adelaide of harming Johanna? *Do I?*

Adelaide finished her morning chores without delay. She resolved to renew her hunt for Johanna's killer. One person might have answers to all her questions, no matter how reluctant she might be to add to his store of information.

Down the road men clambered over the hotel roof joists, balancing themselves on rafters as they jostled roof boards into place on the sloping frame. While she often chafed at the restrictions placed on the work allowed to women, she didn't begrudge men the danger their work entailed.

She joined August outside the greenhouse. Rose bushes, their flowers still locked into buds, hung over the walk.

"Tell me," she began, and August's eyes brightened. "About Johanna and Jakob."

"He wanted to marry her, but he couldn't, you know. That's why he's grieving so poorly."

"Why not?" She lifted a rose stalk off the path and a thorn pricked her finger.

"Jakob's not a Society member yet and both of them have to be. Or born of members, which Johanna was." He squatted to clear leaves cluttering a bed of strawberries still in first leaf. "He has six months more to complete his two years' probation."

By that time... Adelaide imagined the horror Johanna would have experienced when her expanding belly announced the awful truth.

Maybe Jakob was afraid he'd be blamed. That made sense. To be admitted to the Society of Separatists required untainted morality. Johanna's condition might have destroyed his chance for membership.

"You heard about Martin, though, didn't you?" August asked.

"Martin Guenther?" She sucked on her finger, drawing blood into her mouth.

"He planned to ask the trustees for permission to marry her."

"No!" A wave of jealousy shot through her. Martin, who tempted her, then vowed celibacy, desired Johanna? She spit into the grass.

"All I know is what I heard. You don't want to believe me, don't."

Maybe he offered to marry her because she was with child. He knew Jakob couldn't, and he wanted to save her from humiliation—or worse.

She squeezed her finger, and watched her blood drip onto the ground.

Trude, two tin pails balanced on a yoke across her shoulders, walked ahead, and Adelaide called out to her. "How's Sophie?"

The girl jerked and her buckets bounced about, splattering milk.

Adelaide helped her lower the buckets to the ground and apologized for startling her.

"She's much improved, Frau Bechtmann, that she is." Trude glanced up the road toward the dormitory.

"Her cough?"

"It's, uh, I don't know how to say it."

"Loose?" Adelaide demonstrated as best she could, and Trude laughed at her effort. "That's like it, yes. She ate some porridge this morning. And milk. I went back for more, you can see. But I best be hurrying."

"Just one question."

Trude flicked a look up ahead.

"It will only take a second. You remember the night of the storm?"

"Yes, ma'am. Terrible it was upstairs. Shutters banging. We thought they'd crack right in two—"

"Do you remember where Matron was?"

"'A course. Right there with us. Like she is every night."

"You're sure she stayed with you all night."

"Between Sophie's coughing and the thunder and the lightning, we was all awake. Is that all, begging your pardon, *Frau*?"

"On with you. Tell Sophie I'll check on her later."

Trude rearranged her yoke on her shoulders and bobbed a nod at her.

Adelaide contemplated what to do next. Her workroom. Her sanctuary. She had some serious thinking to do and, with fortune, she'd be undisturbed until dinner time.

At home she stoked the fire in the stove where it had been damped during her absence and when the pot on top began to gurgle, she lifted the lid and stirred the broth, the aroma of stewing chicken filling the room. A bowl of dough sat ready for scoops to be dropped into the potage for dumplings.

The door to her workroom stood ajar. Had she left it open earlier? No, she always made certain it was shut. She shoved the door wide and for a moment she couldn't move. She blinked once but nothing changed.

The cabin door opened behind her.

"Benjamin, don't!" She flung both arms across the doorway as if she could obscure the sight within.

"What is it?" He grabbed her arms and pulled her aside. "Now, look what you've done."

"What I've done?" She stole a glance inside the room.

Scattered remnants of her work littered the floor. Dried herbs and powders, shards of glass bottles, tin funnels, scoops, corks, measuring tins, an overturned drying rack, clusters of herbs, seedlings, and soil spilled over the floorboards as if they'd been flung about in haste. Honey dribbled from a crock and puddled in the cracks.

She dropped down, her skirts dragging through the honey. She jerked them away and leaned forward to pick up the stopper to her bottle of lemon balm, clutching it to her chest as if she could taste its comfort.

A shaft of sunshine spilled across the room, dust dancing in its light.

"Adelaide," he said, his jaw clamped around the words. "You have to stop this! You have to stop talking about Johanna. You have to."

The savory aroma of her herbs, usually so reassuring, smelled sour, a bitterness lingering in the air.

"And that." Benjamin pointed to a knife impaled in the middle of her worktable. "Doesn't that tell you—"

"What? That I'm getting too close, that I've discovered something they don't want me to know?"

"That you could get hurt."

"Don't you see, this means someone did kill Johanna. Once I find out who and report it, this will end."

"I don't care if you never find out. Don't you understand? I care about you, about Olivia, that's all. If they want you to stop, then stop." He pulled the knife out of the table and smoothed the roughened edges of the wood with his finger.

"I can't. I just can't." She turned away, but he caught her arm. "Please, Adelaide, for me, for us."

She jerked out of his grasp.

Benjamin threw his hands in the air and slammed them back onto the bench, the knife skittering to the floor. "What if everyone believes you did do something to her? What then? Haven't you worked too hard to learn everything, to have a trade that others need?"

"You shouldn't worry about that," she said. "We have skills. Both of us do. We could make our own way in the world."

"You want to leave? Throw away your life here?"

"Of course not." His worry was for naught. But did someone destroy her medicines to stop her work? What if she couldn't find more herbs before someone needed them?

"And do you think Simon will keep his accusation to himself? What if he goes outside to the government? Americans hang people for less."

"Benjamin, stop it. Stop imagining trouble when there's no reason." But had Simon gone to the authorities despite Josef's orders? If they decided to investigate Johanna's death, what would they do? Dig up the body? Confiscate her casebook? From her entries they might conclude that she had treated Johanna, but that was a long way from suggesting, much less proving, that she caused her death.

"You think you're so powerful, so strong, you can fight anyone. But you're not. You're just one small person in this community. And a woman at that."

"A woman? You've been listening to some of the men going on about keeping your wife in her place." She spit out a bit of leaf. "My place is where I say it is. Not you or anyone else is going to tell me where."

"You're my wife, and I say don't talk about this," he said, leaving. Dust scattered in his wake, the taste of it sharp on her tongue.

How dare he order her about!

Adelaide grabbed a broom from the corner and tackled the floor. The culprit was mistaken if he thought this would stop her. She'd find out who it was and bring him to account. After dirt, dust, and herbs were piled in the corner, she dug honey out of the cracks and dumped it on top of the debris.

She stepped over to the window and shoved it open, breathing in the scent of fresh cut grass from an early morning mowing. A sewing maid passed by, a dress draped over her arm. She glanced around quickly, then started to skip. Adelaide smiled at the girl's antics, supposedly unobserved. She set a tray upright, scooped soil into it, and tucked spilled seedlings in dirt before sliding the tray into its place on the window shelf.

Back in the cabin she grabbed a bucket and filled it with water warming on the stove, the smell of cooking chicken gamy now. If she continued to investigate Johanna's murder in spite of Benjamin's orders, what would he do? She chopped chunks of soap into the wash water, gathered a scrub brush and rags, and returned to her workroom.

He might order her to stop working as a healer, a midwife even, or the trustees might order it if he requested their help with his disobedient wife. She plopped the brush into soapy water and started scrubbing in the far corner. None of the Separatists had been divorced, although some couples lived apart even after celibacy ended. The trustees allowed people to move if they quarreled with their housemates. If Benjamin requested it, he could move to another house.

If the trustees agreed that she had disobeyed her husband—and given the recent complaints about her and the gradual shift diminishing women's rights—they might order her to move to one of the larger homes where she'd be the lowliest woman in the household.

She bent over and hugged the floor, her head whirling with fear. No! They weren't going to take this from her. Not her work, her life.

She righted herself. Her place was here, in Zoar with her fellow Separatists, however much she resented its limitations.

Finally, the floorboards gleamed like fresh cut wood. She dumped the dirty water outdoors and returned to her workroom to right bottles and tins on their shelves and fasten lids.

Benjamin had no right to tell her what she could do or not do. She fully intended to make up her own mind. In earlier days, she had worked alongside the men, learned her trade from Emma and Josef, and believed she was equivalent in every way to her husband.

She wasn't about to take any place but beside her husband as an equal.

Why couldn't Adelaide understand his fear, Benjamin mumbled to himself, even as he realized her reasoning about their valuable skills made sense. He trudged through the underbrush toward the sawmill, its blades screeching up ahead. *I hope that's not my maple they're sawing. I told them I'd come as soon as I could.*

Although it was a longer way, he'd chosen to this route to avoid the main road and possibly encountering anyone who might complain about Adelaide's meddling. Of course she didn't see it as meddling. Oh, no, she was just doing what was right. Doesn't she realize that some people blamed her, believed that her remedy caused Johanna's death? And he wasn't altogether certain that they were wrong.

He kicked at a clump of dirt and sent fragments flying. She had never been cold, hungry, wandering the streets, searching for a family that never returned.

At first he couldn't believe the Appelgates would keep him. Helga had spread her arms, and he'd walked into them and into his new home, a frightened eight-year-old struggling to be strong. But that didn't last. The moment he felt he felt her warmth, the flood of tears came. He tried to stop, fearing they'd send him away for being such a baby, but Helga and Nathan only looked at each other, smiled, and welcomed him into their family.

Now he and Adelaide had built a life together in this new land, safe among their countrymen, with a warm home, plenty of food, and work that was good and satisfying. And she risked their losing it.

Water tumbled over paddles at the mill, but the scream of a blade on wood drowned out the sound. Benjamin nodded to the men loading planks onto a wagon as he hurried inside. Wind whipped in through the open door and stirred up dust and a burnt-wood smell.

The sawman lifted a board off the conveyor and the blade ground to a halt.

"My curly maple, Kurt?" Benjamin asked and then spotted the log to the side.

"Waited, as you said, *Bruder*," Kurt answered. He banged the sawed board on the floor several times to loosen sawdust, wiped its edges with a gloved hand, and stacked it on top of others along the wall.

"But I should be working on that for the hotel." He wiped a sprinkle of dust off his face. "So far behind they are now."

"The exterior's up, I see."

"Siding boards, they be needing and right away."

"Only this log. It's all I need."

Kurt nodded and they lifted the maple log onto the belt. Benjamin pointed out the curly pattern at the end.

"Never seen one of them," Kurt said. "Not very big is it? No more than nine inches, I'd say."

Benjamin had found the rare tree in the woods and directed its removal. The narrow diameter was perfect for a tapered set of shelves—it was his last piece—for Welby's order. Now it was ready for splitting into boards.

"Curly maple's so hard to find," he explained. "So I wanted to be sure it was fed into the saw at the correct speed. Too fast and the blade will tear the wood, too slow and the blade could burn it." Still, he winced as Kurt brought the blade down for its first cut. He studied the split log, nodded his satisfaction, and Kurt continued.

This work with his countrymen, it was his lifeblood. Whatever would he do without it? And his community. His mind jumped back to the time when they had built the canal. When he'd first noticed Adelaide. She stood out from the other girls, who mostly giggled whenever he walked by. Not Adelaide. When he made some teasing remark to a gaggle of girls nearby, she skidded to a stop, flung herself around, and yelled at him. He couldn't recall why. All he saw were her eyes—green, sparkling with flecks of gold where the light caught them.

Although he couldn't court her—marriage was still disallowed then and he doubted she'd agree to his advances—he began to time his treks to and from the canal to hers and finally, they fell into an easy comradeship, no matter how much the others frowned at them.

"Looks good." Kurt waved to the stacked boards to the side. "I'll have them brought up on the next load."

Benjamin stood outside the sawmill and looked back toward the town. He couldn't explain why Zoar meant so much to him. Not specifically. He only knew that if they had to go, he'd leave part of himself behind.

— Fifteen —

August beckoned her over to the fence. He glanced about, then leaned over the picket spikes to whisper, "I told you, I told you. I told you your complaints would bring them here, Adelaide, didn't I?"

"Whatever are you talking about?" She'd spent the morning with an infant too hungry to nurse and a young mother too anxious to allow her milk to let down. Finally, she put the hungry baby to her own breast, letting the mother watch until the baby was sated enough to transfer to his mother. She left them contented and herself exhausted. Now August was agitated about something.

"They sent a constable. A constable from New Philly. From the coroner," he added with studied patience. "He's here to investigate Johanna's death just as I told you they would. You should get away—"

"I'm not going anywhere. I'm going to find that constable and tell him what I think happened to her."

"Don't. Please, Adelaide, I'm begging you." He clutched gloved hands together as if in prayer.

The attack on her workroom told her that the killer was one of them, a Separatist, not an outsider as she'd hoped. What would happen to him? To them?

"It's you he'll suspect. Do you know what the jails are like? It's no place for a woman, that I know."

She made up her mind. "I can't stand around, or hide for that matter, while I'm accused." And she'd promised herself she wouldn't let anyone keep her from her work. "What would my life be worth if people believe I killed Johanna?"

August squared his shoulders, but his face showed the strain. "Have it your way," he said and turned his back on her.

Josef stood in front of his cabin in animated conversation with a stranger, a crowd congregating around the pair. A dappled mare stood tethered to a nearby oak tree.

The man stood apart from Josef, hands on his hips, waistcoat unbuttoned in the warm air. Stocky with the build that would turn to fat with age, he faced their leader with his chin in the air. "You're the only landowner, they tell me." He nodded toward the group. "They all related to you? I hear you Zoarites don't believe in marriage."

"We're not Zoarites," Josef shot back. "Separatists. The Society of Separatists. That's who we are. And we're legally married. Besides, you have no jurisdiction here," Josef told the man, his voice tight. "Lewis Birk is our law."

"He another of your brothers?"

"He's our justice of the peace, duly authorized by the state of Ohio."

"It's a suspicious death and that makes the coroner of Tuscarawas County in charge."

"Johanna Appelgate died Thursday night last. She fell in the river and drowned. It was an accident. Tragic, yes, but not suspicious."

"According to you, but, sadly," he said, though his voice made it apparent he felt anything but sorrowful, "the coroner will decide that."

"Sir," Adelaide said.

The constable turned to her and shielded his eyes from the sun. "And who might you be, young lady?"

Josef flapped a hand toward her. "Adelaide, I'm handling this."

"I can tell you about her."

"Constable Helling," he said to introduce himself, then led her toward the shade near his horse. "Now, tell me what you know." His eyes lingered on her bodice where her swelled breasts had begun to leak.

She crossed her arms in front of her. "I found her in the river."

Josef shooed bystanders away and limped over to where they stood. "Adelaide, you don't know—"

"Let her tell it," the constable said. His hand, steadied on his horse's head, caressed her mane.

"That's why everyone thinks she drowned, but there wasn't any water in her lungs and—"

"She died accidentally," Josef said.

"You couldn't know that for certain, could you?" he asked and turned to Adelaide. "Your cooperation is appreciated, miss."

"Missus. Missus Bechtmann."

Josef shoved himself in front of the constable, forcing the man to take a step back. "If you're through here, you best be on your way."

The constable studied Josef for a moment, then stuck one boot into a stirrup and swung himself into the saddle.

"What will happen now?" Adelaide asked.

"I report to the coroner and he'll decide if he wants to hold an inquest."

"We've already buried her," Josef said.

"Oh, don't worry about that. We dig up bodies all the time." With that, he flicked the reins, and he and his horse cantered up the road that led out of town.

"Why did you do that?" Josef asked as they watched the man ride away. "The authorities are involved now. And whom do you think they're going to suspect? I can't protect you, you know, nor our community."

"I don't need protecting. I spoke the truth. Isn't that what everyone here is supposed to do?"

Josef said no more.

Somehow, that made her feel worse.

Nellie dumped the cloth-wrapped package of bread on the table and flung her bonnet off beside it, spilling disheveled auburn curls out of her braid. She charged up the steps to her sleeping loft.

Adelaide called up after her, and when Nellie didn't answer, she bunched up her skirts and clamored up the ladder. "I know you're up here," she said, standing upright. Nellie scrunched down in the corner, head sunk onto her knees, arms clutching her legs.

Adelaide stooped to kneel beside her sister. Heat that had collected under the eaves pressed down on her, but she ignored it. "What happened? Why are you hiding?"

Nellie rocked back and forth wordlessly.

"Whatever it is, we'll help. You know that. Benjamin and I love you."

"They said, they said, you're going to hang," she said, her words smothered in her folded arms.

"Who said?"

"The women at the bakery." She raised tear-stained eyes to Adelaide. "I handed over my cloth and one of them went over to pick up our loaves and I heard them talking. That the constable's come and, and—"

"The constable wants to find out what happened to Johanna as we all do. Whatever he finds, it won't be about me."

"What about Benjamin?"

"Benjamin? He doesn't believe them either."

"That's not what I mean. Brigit, she said it was Benjamin with Johanna the night she died."

Her mouth went dry. Did everyone know they'd been together? "Benjamin was working that night trying to finish the work for the man from Cleveland."

Nellie worried her lower lip. "I've seen them together other times."

"Of course you have. Benjamin grew up with Johanna and her sisters. He's like their big brother. Don't pay any attention to that Brigit. She's all full of romantic notions. I doubt anyone is."

"If you hang—"

Adelaide shook her. "Stop that talk right now."

Nellie blinked hard. "They'll take me away, I know they will."

"That's not going to happen. No one's taking you anywhere. I'll see to that."

"You won't be able to stop them. Not if they say so."

"I'll never let you away from me again. Not ever." Adelaide clasped her sister to her bosom and patted her back until she felt Nellie's still-small body relax. "Come on, now, it's too hot to stay up here. Come downstairs. You have to go to Olivia. She'll be waiting for you."

She watched Nellie out the door, but her sister lingered on the path, her head down, her feet kicking at cinders. She wanted to scream, "Go. Go. Stop letting the gossipmongers upset you." But she only dug her fingernails into her palms and tightened her jaw. She could wait no longer. She must do what she had delayed until now.

Despite her determination, Adelaide hesitated as she approached the cow barn. Stepping under the forebay, she stopped to mop the sweat from her face and gripped her casebook in her pocket, soothed by its worn leather covering.

The two wide center doors swung open. Martin stabbed a pole in the ground, jammed it under the door's brace and turned to the second door. He squinted into the setting sun that sent long shafts of light across the front of the barn. "What are you doing here?" With slow, careful movements, he rolled up one sleeve and then the other. Tiny hairs glinted on the skin below the blue fabric.

She drew herself up. "I came to ask you about Johanna." When he started to interrupt, she spoke quickly. "What you know about her going out that night."

He studied her for a moment, a frown on his sun-weathered face. "She was one stubborn girl, that Johanna. No matter what I tried with her, she wasn't one to be told what to do. Shame, that's what it is."

"Her death?"

"If she'd just listened to me—"

"You think she'd still be alive?"

He shook his head and turned into the barn.

Adelaide followed him, her eyes taking a moment to adjust to the darkened interior. The smell of cow dung lingered no matter how much lye soap tried to cover it. "How well did you know Johanna?" she asked to his back as he started up the steps to the second floor.

She squared her shoulders and began the steep climb, gripping the sides of the ladder. As her head emerged at floor level, Martin picked up a pitchfork. She grabbed the rim of the opening to keep her balance.

Martin dug his pitchfork into a pile of hay and pulled it out in one smooth movement. He swung his load over to the wall where he stuffed it down into the opening that led to a trough below.

She pulled herself up over the edge of the hatchway and scrambled to her feet. Bundles of hay and barrels of feed stood stacked along the wall. "Why did she go out that night?"

He stuck his pitchfork into the floor and leaned an elbow on it. "I can't watch them every moment. That's what the dairy mother's for. Ask her."

"I did and she didn't know."

"Well, then, that answers all your questions, doesn't it?"

"Why did you insist, uh, want Johanna buried the same day she died?" she asked, thankful that her voice didn't betray the quivering in her chest.

"No business of yours." He dug into the hay and turned, the loaded pitchfork seemingly light in his hands. "What I do know is I need to find another milk maid. How old is your sister?"

"She's still in school." Working for Martin was the last place she wanted Nellie. She must do more to educate her sister about herbal treatments and do it soon.

"And why's she still over there at the Appelgates' every day?"

"That's none to do with you."

"Do the trustees know she's fraternizing with them so much? The place where she lived before?"

"Fraternizing? She works there, helping Helga with the little ones."

"And maybe," he went on, ignoring her response, "maybe she shouldn't be living with you either. You should know that we're all one community, all one family now."

She stiffened. Who was he to order her about? "It's none of your business where she lives or what she does."

"It might be, it just might be. And shouldn't you be home tending to your work? That's where a woman should be." Martin stood silent, one hand propped on the handle of his pitchfork and rubbed the other on his shirt. His eyes—black with hooded lids—sucked at her body as if an invisible strand connected them and drew her closer and closer.

She backed down the steps, her foot catching on the last rung and nearly tumbling her onto the floor, but she caught herself in time. The hairs on the back of her neck stood up, but when she looked back toward the loft opening, it was shadowed in darkness. "Leave me alone. Just leave me be," she shouted over her shoulder.

As soon as she was clear of the door, she took off running, soon into the woods, her feet skimming over the surface of the path, her shoes slipping now and again on moist leaves, but rather than falling, they only sped her on until her breath came in ragged spurts. She grabbed a sapling with one hand, swung herself around it, and spilled onto the ground, landing in a pile of dampened leaves. She lay back, sucking air, her heart pounding so hard she thought it would push through her chest. It wasn't only the effort of running that caused her breathlessness, but what Martin's look had stirred in her.

Lust. Pure, unadulterated lust. Nothing to do with love, or caring, or kindness.

She'd wondered if she imagined his desire when she heard he championed celibacy. But she hadn't. The man wanted to bed her.

What drew her to him? The way he moved? His body so still, contained, compacted in spite of its size. As if every movement was calculated, planned, and executed with a minimum of effort.

Off to her side a robin tried to mount his mate, but she was having none of it and scooted away, him following behind.

She lay still, listening. Had he followed her? A rustling in the forest and she struggled to rise. If he caught her here…no, it was only a deer. She caught sight of his bobbed tail bouncing away. What would she do if he did? Could she get away? Did she want to? Her face flamed as she remembered how her body had responded to his look. A tingling up her spine. And an intense longing, a longing she had never felt. Not even with Benjamin, the only man she had ever been with in that way. Damp spread over her back and still she lay there, her face flaming with the shame of it.

Inexplicably, her breasts began to leak.

— Sixteen —

t first Adelaide thought the noise came from inside their cabin. By the time she recognized the insistent clanging of the fire bell, Benjamin was scrambling for his clothes. "I'll go with you," she said, and grabbed her dress. A button caught on her tousled hair, and she jerked at it impatiently. Olivia whimpered. Adelaide rocked the cradle with her toe as she freed her hair and slipped the dress over her head.

Benjamin pulled on his boots and, without a word or a backward glance, snatched his hat off the peg by the door and let himself out of the cabin. The musky smell of smoke wafted in the door behind him. His footsteps crunched on the cinders as he hurried down the path.

Why did she feel she deserved his snub?

Nellie stumbled down the steps, and Adelaide asked her to stay with Olivia. Grabbing a water bucket, she let herself out of the cabin.

Outside people ran in several directions, some heading toward the river, others gathering treasured belongings, still others shouting for more buckets. A plume of black smoke billowed overhead, whorled around, and then shifted, sending spirals swirling back down. Choking, she shoved her way through the haze to hurry down the hill.

Silhouetted against the night sky, the hotel's skeletal frame outlined the inferno. Flames shot upward, singeing leaves that sizzled before their residue fluttered to the ground. A door fell away, its wall tumbling inward, timbers cracking and splitting as they hit the ground.

She gave her bucket to the man nearest to her and held her hand in front of her face to shield it from the heat as she joined townspeople gathered around, silent as they watched their work go up in flames.

Hand over hand, buckets of water passed up the line, the last man tossing water onto the fire but it fizzled, evaporating as quickly as it touched the flames. Others slung buckets of water onto the ground around the structure.

The wind shifted once more, and a wall of heat shoved the crowd backward. A corner support shattered to the ground, chunks splitting apart. Splinters popped off in tiny bursts and died out with a whine of spent fuel.

They were too late.

Josef shook his head and called a halt to their efforts. The men behind him—most of them she'd seen working on the building— dropped empty buckets to the ground, wiped filthy rags over sleep-deprived faces, and stood watching in silent vigil as their labor disappeared into a giant bonfire.

She'd passed the building on her way back from the woods last night and paused to settle her mind before facing her husband. Clapboards encased the first floor walls, and pillars propped up roof rafters that stretched above a full-width porch. Dormer windows on the third floor punctuated the steeply pitched roof sheathed with wood prepared for clay tiles. That roof lay in smoldering remnants near her feet.

Shouting came from the hill to her right. Reverend Truesdale, atop a mammoth black horse, carried a lantern high, his shouts aimed at the sky. As he neared, the crowd parted and he stopped, nodding to them as if receiving his due. People gathered around him as all thoughts of watching the dying fire gave way to the new attraction.

Reverend Truesdale shifted in his seat, his hand resting easily on the pommel of his saddle. His horse pawed the ground, its white blaze brilliant in the darkness.

"Ladies and gentlemen," the preacher shouted over the crackling sounds of the fading fire. "It has come to pass. Yes, verily I said unto you, yes, I did. I told you that fire will consume your work and it has. Your greed is your sin and you won't prosper from ill-gotten gains." Flares from crumbling timbers lit his satisfied smile.

Josef stepped forward. Soot streaked his face, and his burnt trouser leg showed where he'd stepped too close to the fire.

Reverend Truesdale stared down at the diminutive man beneath him.

"What cause have you to bother my people in their travail?" Josef's quiet voice belied his resolve.

"Trouble of your own making," the preacher shot back. "I told you, didn't I? Sin in this so-called nirvana. So pious, are you? But sinning in your hearts. Yes, yes, brothers and sisters," he said, turning back to the crowd, "your little village holds sinners, each and every one of you. Especially that one." He pointed to Adelaide.

"Work of the devil she is, doctoring with poison—"

"You have no cause to accuse my *Schwester*," Josef shouted at the man.

The preacher kept his eyes on her. "I told the authorities about you."

Adelaide jerked back and her shoe sank into the mud. She pulled it out with a whoosh and stammered a reply. "Told them what? I have done nothing wrong." *Other than lust after a man not my husband.*

"You'll get your reward," he said as if she hadn't spoken. "Yes you will, you'll hang, you will."

A flash of lightning illuminated the sky, and a crack of thunder followed. The horse reared, and the man yanked on the reins to finally bring him down onto all four legs, the animal still circling. "I'll be back, Bimeler," the preacher shouted over his shoulder as he clattered up the hill.

"You think he started it?" she asked Josef. "Shouldn't we do something? Report him to the authorities?"

"Only if we had just cause. And what proof there'd be just died in the fire."

"But—" she began but Josef interrupted. "He'll be his own undoing, never fear."

She couldn't imagine how. The man seemed impervious to slights. He'd come back when few Separatists showed an interest in anything more than the diversion he provided. Maybe he mistook their attention as devotion.

So he had been the one to inform the coroner about Johanna's death. To punish her for ordering him away from Jakob, she imagined. At least Simon hadn't reported her. He must not have believed his own accusation enough to go outside their community, but he could have told the preacher his suspicions. Or, more likely, the man had heard the gossip that spread through town faster than the fire they just witnessed.

"We'll start tomorrow to rebuild," one of the men told Josef as the first few drops of rain splattered the ground.

Fires weren't unknown, but this was the worst since they'd carved their village out of the forest. Food left untended to simmer on a stove until dinner time when the women returned from their jobs or the fields had caused several. Once a two-year-old had poked a stick in the fire and when it burned him, he tossed it aside. The cabin burned to the ground. The boy lived a few pain-wracked days. Whenever the memory of the boy popped unbidden into her mind, fright for Olivia washed over her. What if the meeting house caught fire? The girls in the dormitory above would never get out in time.

"How can you be so calm?" she asked Josef. "All that work and lumber and our hopes…"

He stopped to balance himself on the rough ground. "Adelaide, it's only a wooden structure. It can be rebuilt. No one's life was lost. Nothing of everlasting value was consumed. Every undertaking is an opportunity to learn a new skill or a lesson about ourselves. No effort is wasted."

"Aren't you angry?" she countered as raindrops fell around them. "At that preacher or whoever started it?"

"It may not have been anyone's fault. A spark from a chimney, lightning. And there's nothing for it to do now. You can't change the past."

"No, but you can stop it from happening again."

"Of course we will. I'll double the night watch for a while. Even if the preacher caused it, I doubt he'd do it again. He'd know he'd be suspected. And Simon'd be unlikely to allow him comfort at the inn. I heard he ordered him away. I don't think we have to worry about him anymore."

— Seventeen —

Adelaide jerked awake as the door banged shut. Benjamin's head bobbed by the window. Again, he'd ignored her. Did she deserve this treatment? Maybe.

After breakfast, she sent Nellie to Helga's with Olivia, and by the time she started dinner on the stove and readied her cabin, the sky had begun to darken. She hurried out to reach Emma's before the storm returned, but when she spied Josef's carriage approaching the destroyed hotel, she turned downhill instead.

Men, their hands encased in heavy leather gloves, tossed fragments of scorched wood into the bed of a wagon. Smoldering spires of blistered wood anchored the corners of the foundation, their blackened spikes stark reminders of the structure. The air reeked of burnt wood and water-soaked ashes as if one had stuck one's head inside a stove gone cold.

Josef stopped his carriage as she approached. Dark clouds swirled overhead, and thunder cracked in the distance. The wind picked up. She held onto her bonnet to look up at him. "Last night you said you'd double the watch. But where was he last night? Why didn't he see the fire sooner?"

He removed his hat and ran a hand through soot-streaked whiskers. He still wore the fire-damaged trousers from the night before.

"He was patrolling up north by the cemetery. I know, why would we need to patrol in such a deserted place? There's an outbuilding up there, one of the first we built. It's not used anymore, but someone reported some tramps were sleeping in it so he went up to check."

Should she ask him again about who was on watch the night Johanna died? He'd blamed her for the constable's arrival, but he seemed to have recovered his usual good sense despite the hotel's destruction.

A clap of thunder brought the downpour. She gave him a backward wave and rushed back up the hill.

Inside Emma's cabin, she shook raindrops off her bonnet and hung it over a chair post to dry. She swished her skirts about and took her seat on a stool near Emma's feet. The rain pounded the apple tree outside the window.

"You heard about that preacher? Showing up and ranting about me and how I was poisoning..." Adelaide's throat swelled, and she swallowed. "He's the one called the authorities, sent that horrible constable here. And they might be back."

"I've told you before. Don't fret about what has not happened."

"But the constable said—"

"I doubt the coroner will want to bother coming all this way from New Philly when everyone suspects Johanna's death was an accident. Isn't that why we came to America? If we hadn't believed its promise of freedom and impartiality, we never would have come to this land. Sometimes we have to trust others, even those not of our faith, to do right."

"And why is the preacher still here anyway?" Adelaide asked irritably. "Simon threw him out Sunday. Then he was pestering Jakob, and he showed up again at the fire. I think he started it."

"The fire? I can't imagine it. I suppose he just took advantage of the situation."

As suddenly as it began, the rain stopped. Adelaide opened the window to cooler air. It stirred some strands of hair loose from Emma's cap, and light shone through her hair to a pink scalp.

Adelaide fumbled in her pocket. "I must have left my casebook in my other apron. I made more notes about Johanna. I learned that Gerda was with her charges the night Johanna died."

"As I thought, she wouldn't have done it. What else have you found out?"

A cardinal perched outside on the apple tree called insistently to his mate.

"Martin Guenther," she said at last, glad that Emma couldn't see the flush that had spread up her face.

"I thought we ruled him out."

Why did she continue to suspect him? Did she want to punish him for stirring her desire?

"I said, I thought we decided he'd have no motive," Emma repeated.

Adelaide cleared her throat. "He wanted to marry her, August told me."

"Isn't Martin celibate? Well, plenty a man has been known to change his mind around a pretty lass."

She clutched her hands in her lap to keep them from shaking.

"Lust is a powerful motive." Emma shoved at wisps of white hair that skimmed her face. "And unrequited lust? Let's say it's been the cause of more than one murder."

Outside a branch scraped against the window.

"Someone's out there," Adelaide said, leaning forward to see. "Who is it?"

"No one, I guess."

"You need to calm yourself if you want to find out who killed Johanna."

"What happened to her bonnet?"

"Bonnet?"

"Johanna told her friends that Mister Welby gave it to her, but he didn't."

"Why do you care about her bonnet? Let them worry about it. You need to think about who could have killed her."

"What about Simon? He'd, um, been with her older sister, then married the next in line, and she's now to bear a child. Could he have done the same with Johanna?"

"What for? Some bizarre family tradition? Bedding all the Appelgate daughters?"

"It's his accusing me. Maybe to turn attention away from him."

Emma rubbed her distended knuckles. "That sounds pretty far-fetched to me."

"You hear about the damage to my workroom? Someone broke in and dumped out herbs and broke bottles and…" She pulled a handkerchief from her apron pocket and blew her nose. "They attacked my work. Me."

"Hush, child, yes, I heard."

"The only reason someone'd do that would be to stop me investigating."

"Presumably."

"Apparently Benjamin agrees. He's ordered me—did you hear that—ordered me to stop."

"It sounds to me like Benjamin has too little faith in your abilities."

Or fear I'd find out who did it. No, he couldn't, he wouldn't, have hurt the girl he considered a sister.

Emma directed her clouded eyes at her. "What will you do next?"

Or was she more than a sister?

Adelaide stood and moved to the table. "Why are you so intent I solve Johanna's death? Didn't you warn me about how dangerous it is to pursue this? You thought I should forget it." She busied herself laying strands of willow in straight lines.

Emma leaned back, the rocker groaning as she did. "You're right. I only wanted to protect you. But now that someone's come after you I've changed my mind. I thought at first you should stop, let everyone know you've accepted her death, and don't intend to ask any more questions."

"Would they believe me?" She brushed willow scraps into a pile, neatening the edge.

Emma snorted. "Not if they know you." She motioned Adelaide closer. "Courage," she said, "is doing what needs doing. In spite of being afraid."

"Even if I discover who could have done it, how would I know for sure? Much less prove it?"

"One step at a time."

"I need to find out who was on watch that night. Maybe he saw something."

"Don't you think he'd come forward before now?"

"I won't know that until I ask him. All I know is I have to continue."

In spite of the cost. Even to her husband.

Adelaide stood beside Emma's cabin and inhaled the sweet smells of her rain-washed town, clean enough to satisfy the most exacting Separatist *Hausfrau*. She stepped carefully over to the place under Emma's window where she'd thought she'd seen someone. Large shoe prints indented the rain-softened ground under Emma's window.

Brigit's voice interrupted her. "Come quick. It's Ilse. She's taken real sick, she is. Hurry. Hurry."

"I have to stop at home for my bag." She'd forgotten it along with her casebook in the morning's confusion.

Brigit bounced up and down on her toes. "No, no, you have to come now."

"I can't help her without knowing what she might need. What are her symptoms?"

"Her stomach hurts real bad. She's all doubled up, cramped like. Can you help her? Please."

At home Adelaide ran in, grabbed her bag, and followed Brigit down the hill toward the dairy. Through the open door, the milk maids clustered together around their worktable, butter churns and milk pots forgotten.

"This way." Brigit motioned her on, past the dairy to Martin's cabin. "He said we should move her here."

Ilse lay on a pallet along the wall, doubled up in pain.

"I'm sorry," Ilse said between gasps. "I took some of the tea you sent before but this time it didn't help."

Adelaide knelt beside her. "Don't talk. Can you lower your legs?"

Ilse winced, her gray eyes cold with fear, but she did as Adelaide asked and slid her feet along the coverlet until her heels rested at the end.

"Very good. Now just try to breathe as normally as you can." Adelaide gently raised Ilse's underdress and laid her hand on the woman's swollen abdomen. The lower right quadrant was hot.

Adelaide called to Brigit. "Go to the ice house and chip off enough to fill a bucket." To another girl who had followed them inside, she ordered, "Get some cold water and a clean cloth. Hurry. Both of you."

"I'm sorry to be a bother," Ilse said in a strained whisper.

"You're no bother." Adelaide wiped sweat from Ilse's brow with the corner of her apron.

"You've all been so good to me and I'm so grateful after—"

"Hush, now, you don't need to speak."

Adelaide turned to the sound of heavy footsteps outside. Martin filled the doorway, the light behind him putting his face in shadow. "What are you doing here?"

"She's sick. Brigit came for me."

In the aftermath of the fire, she had tried to put the encounter—and her feelings—toward Martin aside. Now here he stood, and her shivers were not all that unpleasant.

Voices outside called to Martin. He backed out as the girls returned.

When Brigit started to speak, Adelaide motioned for her to keep quiet. She slid some chips of ice into the water, dipped the cloth into chilled liquid, and swished it around. Wringing out the cloth, she warned Ilse, "This will be cold." She laid the chilled cloth on Ilse's lower right abdomen. "That should help bring the inflammation down. Keep cold compresses on it," she told Brigit and to Ilse, "I'll be back later to check on you."

Josef pulled his mare to a stop, and Adelaide told him about Ilse and what she had done for her. It wasn't the woman's first attack of appendicitis, but this one seemed more virulent than those in the past.

"That's the right treatment," he said. "Unless."

Unless it ruptured. Then nothing she or Josef or even Doctor Hertel could do would change the inevitable outcome.

She could wait no longer to ask him. She must know. "Tell me," she demanded as if she often ordered their leader about, "who was on watch the night Johanna died?"

He stared at her for a moment, then spoke. "Nathan was on first watch and August the second." His carriage clattered away before she could say anything more.

Adelaide stopped August in the garden and asked him if he'd seen anyone the night Johanna died. She assumed that Nathan had not seen his daughter out that night or he would have stopped her and certainly would have said if he'd seen anyone with her.

"No one," he said and continued into the greenhouse.

She scurried after him. "You're sure? It stormed that night."

The sun slanted through the expanse of glass, spreading the warm scent of citrus from the lemon trees inside. August busied himself loading a wheelbarrow with topsoil and when he'd filled it, he passed her going out. "I'm sure."

Why was August, usually so talkative, so terse now? He didn't even mention last night's fire, a topic on everyone's lips.

She debated asking him if he'd seen Benjamin in his shop but his unaccustomed curtness stopped her. A word to August was a word to everyone in town. Besides, she didn't want him to think she suspected her own husband. And did she really want to know?

— Eighteen —

delaide found Jakob alone in the blacksmith shop, pounding on a horseshoe he held awkwardly with foot-long tongs. When he looked up, she said, "I know about her, uh, illness."

The horseshoe clanged to the floor. Jakob stooped to pick it up.

"Stop," she said, but he'd already grabbed the hot metal with his bare hand. It banged onto the floor as he grabbed his arm.

"Stay right here. Sit down and don't touch anything," she added needlessly as Jakob sank onto a bench and let his head fall back against the wall, his left hand clutching his right wrist.

When she returned with a chunk of aloe, she found him lying on the bench, his knees bracing his upright hand. Using one elbow, he pushed himself into a sitting position, holding the injured hand well away from his body. "It's my own fault," he murmured, his face pale.

She opened the folded leaf and applied the aloe to his burn.

"I'm supposed to wear gloves," he said through clenched teeth. "But I'm so clumsy with them."

"Hold this." She lifted his uninjured hand and placed it over the wrapper, steadying her hand on top. When his face regained some of its color and his breathing slowed, she removed her own hand from his.

"How did you know?" he asked. "Did she tell you?"

Adelaide took his hand away from the burn and studied the damage. Parallel burn marks scored his palm with the horseshoe's imprint. It smelled of seared meat.

"I never talked to her about it," she said, pulling clean cloths from her bag. "She said the remedy was for one of the other girls." She wrapped a length of cloth around his palm, wove it between his thumb and forefinger, and knotted the strip on the back of his hand.

"Said she was too young, too young to bear a child."

"Jakob, you were about to tell me something the other day when Nathan called you. Something about if you'd only done something. What did you mean?"

"I guess you might as well know." He shifted around on the bench, positioning his hand on his lap. "I wouldn't leave. I wouldn't leave Zoar."

"What does that have to do with her death?"

"I told you I wanted to marry her. But she said she wanted to leave, and I refused."

"But why? Why did she want to leave? Her family's here, you're here. I don't understand."

"That man from Cleveland," he spit out. "He'd been filling her with tales of the big city. Put all kinds of ideas in her head about how she didn't have to work so hard, other ways to make money than slaving for the town. Said she didn't know how to live. Said she was too pretty to be stuck here. She kept saying if I wouldn't take her, someone else would."

"I'm sure she didn't mean it."

"You don't know her if you think that. She wanted something, she'd get it. I said maybe later when I was good enough to get work someplace else. But the fact is I like it here. Hard work, sure, but plenty of food, a warm bed, a roof to keep out the rain. She kept saying he'd take her."

"Mister Welby."

"That's why I went to see him, to tell him to leave her alone. I should have been with her instead."

"What happened?"

"He laughed at me. Called me a boy." Jakob ducked his head. "I shouldn't have hit him. I know, I know, we're pacifists, it's not our way even if he is an outsider. It's why I came here. I didn't believe in fighting." He ran a hand over the scab on his cheek.

"That was the same night she died?"

He swallowed. "Yes. I want to stay here. I don't want to give them any reason to deny me membership in the Society."

"I'm sure you'll be admitted. It's a while until your time's up in any case."

He stood. "Then I best get back to work."

She left him trying to shove his injured hand into a glove.

Could he have murdered Johanna? His lover? He wouldn't have been the first. The death of the unmarried girl expecting his child removed one impediment to his membership in the Society, which he coveted.

At the bottom of the hill she joined Mister Welby and others watching the men clean up the hotel fire. They attached one end of a rope to a blackened stake that anchored a corner and the other to the bridle of a stout workhorse. One man gave the horse a swat on his hind end, the horse took off, and the stake popped out of the ground to spew bits of sandstone into the air. The crowd hooted with approval.

"Too bad about your hotel," Mister Welby said. "Industrious as you are, it shouldn't take long to rebuild," he said, offering her his arm. She caught a whiff of musk.

Adelaide debated. Rudeness was a sin, too, wasn't it? Besides, she wanted to see if he could confirm Jakob's story about the night Johanna died. She took the proffered arm.

"I have a question to ask you," she said. "It's about Jakob Kirchner."

"Who?"

"The boy who was a friend of Johanna, the girl who died."

"So that's why he came after me. Loved her, he said. Right before he smacked me." His hand brushed his face, the faint bruise remained around his eye.

"That's what he told me. So it's true? The same night she died, he said."

"Came up to the inn, accused me of who knows what with the girl, and the next thing I know, I'm seeing stars. The innkeep and his friend, they separated us but not before I got in a lick."

"His friend?"

"That big man, keeps the cows, I think. The two of them huddled together about something—"

"Martin Guenther? The cow boss was there?"

"I don't know his name but, yes, that sounds like it. Then the boy slams in, comes for me." He chuckled. "I left him with a little reminder although I didn't mean to cut his face like that. I thought it was so sad. Him fighting for her that same night she died."

"You're sure? It stormed that night."

He nodded. "That's why the innkeep made him stay the night, that and him with too much drink in him."

"All night? Simon kept Jakob there the night through?"

"Yep. And the smell. Whew. The common room—they all slept there—still stank of beer and, ahem, sweat—pardon me, ma'am—the next morning."

So Jakob couldn't have killed Johanna. She found herself smiling. But could he have sneaked out later? Or Simon or Martin, for that matter?

Adelaide turned the corner toward the dairy and stopped. Doctor Hertel's buggy stood in front of Martin's cabin, his horse's reins tied to a rail in front.

The doctor hurried out and tried to bustle by her, but Adelaide grabbed his sleeve.

"What? What do you want?" He brushed her hand away.

"What did you tell her?"

He straightened his coat sleeve and plopped a shiny black top hat on his head.

"Did you do anything to her? Give her anything?"

"Get away from me. She didn't want me, wouldn't do what I said."

"Doctor Hertel—"

"Wouldn't even let me bleed her." He busied himself untying his horse. "You're just like Bimeler. His treatments—so-called—are no more than, than nothing. Same as yours." He stepped onto his carriage and swung his sizable body onto the seat.

She moved to the side of his horse. "I do need to ask you a question. Please."

He hooked the reins onto the carriage's frame and sighed audibly.

"Did you treat Johanna Appelgate?"

"Who?" He pulled a watch out of his waistcoat pocket and clicked it open.

"The girl who died in the river. Did you see her for her, ah, illness?"

"What illness? I never treated the girl. If I had, she'd still be alive." He snapped the watch closed and dropped it back into his pocket.

"You just used her death as an opportunity to criticize me, didn't you?"

He jerked the whip out of its upright stand and said over the horse's whinny, "It's your fault, you know, if that woman dies, she wouldn't listen to me."

Brigit hurried out of the cabin as the doctor's carriage clip-clopped away. "He said she needed hot compresses, not cold. Heat would draw out the fever, the inflammation. He wanted to purge her, too. He said she needed to clean out her body."

"My God! You didn't let him, did you?"

"No, no. Ilse said she couldn't stand it," Brigit said, her hazel eyes troubled. "It's hard for us to know what to do."

If Ilse had appendicitis, as she and Josef suspected, either treatment—heat or a purging enema—could kill her. She didn't want to frighten Brigit so she didn't explain the details to her, especially since she couldn't guarantee that Ilse would live no matter what anyone did or didn't do.

"She's still in pain although it seems to be not hurting as much. How long till she feels better?"

"It's difficult to know."

"Heat makes sense," Brigit mused, staring into the distance.

"No, it doesn't. It could release the inflammation into her body, make her much sicker. Promise me you won't use heat for her. Or let him purge her."

"She's had some broth. And kept it down."

Ilse said she felt a little better but still had pain. Adelaide knelt beside her pallet and examined the woman. "Your abdomen is a bit softer, less tender, and warm but not as hot as it was earlier. You're through the worst."

Ilse closed her eyes for a moment, and Adelaide stroked her arm without speaking. Finally Ilse opened her eyes and stared at her. "This will return, won't it? This illness. I've had it before, but one day I won't be able to recover from it. Please tell me. I want to be ready."

How anyone could prepare for death she didn't know. But she had always been honest with her patients if they asked her. She couldn't do otherwise. "That is probably true. But we never know what will happen. Or when. It could be many years."

"God's will," Ilse spit out. "I've never believed that. I've had too many trials in my life to believe that a God who loves me would harm me intentionally. You don't believe whatever happens is God's will, do you?"

"I don't know what anyone else believes, but I agree with you. I don't think God reaches down and grabs someone up to heaven—"

"Not even for our sins?"

Adelaide's mind whipped back to the previous day. Would God punish her for her sinful thoughts?

"I've already experienced hell. I don't think whatever God has in mind for me could be worse."

Adelaide straightened out her legs to release a cramp, then wiggled her feet for a moment and arranged herself cross-legged.

Ilse stared upward at the wood beams crossed under open rafters. "I need to tell you something. If I die, I don't anyone to see me." Her body had shrunk inside itself, leaving a shell of wrinkled skin hanging on a bare skeleton. But her voice was strong. "Please. Promise me you won't let anyone see me." She dug bony fingers into Adelaide's arm.

"I promise, but I doubt anything's going to happen to you for a long while."

"It's just that everyone's been so helpful here. They all think well of me."

"I can't imagine that would change."

"I don't want anyone to see my sin."

Whatever could the woman mean? That she'd had a child? No shame in that.

"Especially Martin."

Martin?

"No man would see you in any case. Only the women. Only me, if that's what you want."

She closed her eyes. "Thank you. He makes me work but, goodness knows, no more than the rest of you. And he never shirks his duties either. For all my complaints, Martin's been as fair to me as anyone. But he doesn't know the meaning of desire."

Adelaide jerked upright.

"You've never seen my back, have you?" she asked, struggling to sit up.

Adelaide slid an arm around the woman's thin shoulders. Matted hair escaped a tattered cap that tilted to the side and when Ilse's head dropped forward, it toppled onto the floor. Ilse fluttered her fingers over her shoulder, and Adelaide pulled aside her gown to see.

Healed scars criss-crossed her back. The woman had been flogged.

"You know why, don't you?" Ilse asked without looking up.

She knew. The punishment for adultery. Only women received this brutal treatment; adulterous men were exempt. Stripped to the waist, arms tied overhead, and whipped in the public square. Sometimes women died from the loss of blood or inflammation, depending on the number of lashes ordered by the court, the type of whip, or even on the viciousness of the man who administered the sentence. At the least, they were left with permanent scars like Ilse's.

Ilse lay back down with a groan. "I could have sworn a rape on him. 'Unlawful concourse with a woman not his wife.' But it wasn't true. I loved him, but Ezekiel wouldn't let me go. It was his manhood, you know." She sank deeper into the pallet. "I couldn't go to trial and lie, don't you see? And I knew it wouldn't stop my punishment."

She closed her eyes for a moment, but then they snapped open. "Do you know, they let him whip me? My very own husband. Thirty-nine stripes, that was my sentence. He was too glad for it, relished every lash, he did," she said, squinting with remembered pain. Then a small smile crossed her face. "He's in hell now, if there is a hell."

"He's dead?"

"Ferdinand shot him."

"He was your, your—"

"My lover. Ferdinand was my lover. Until they hanged him."

Adelaide felt as if she had been turned to stone. Or a pillar of salt, like Lot's wife. Is this what happens to a woman who lusts after someone not her husband?

"Don't look so stricken. It's over now."

Adelaide sat stunned, whether for Ilse's loss or her own guilt, she hardly knew.

"But," Ilse said, drawing her knees up with a wince. "I lost my babe."

Adelaide took the woman's hands in hers and bowed over them. No words of wisdom came to her.

"It's all right, Adelaide. I just wanted someone to know in case something happens, and you're so kind."

She leaned over and gave the woman a careful hug.

— Nineteen —

A banging on the door woke Adelaide, and she jumped up, drew her shawl over her shoulder, and hurried to the door just as the man raised his fist to knock again.

"I'm sorry, Missus Bechtmann, but her times 'a come." His words tumbled over each other. "It's my wife, Miss, she's, she's ill."

"Come in, Mister Bastest," Adelaide whispered.

She yanked her dress over her head, fastened a few buttons, and bent to check on Olivia. The baby had kicked off the blanket but her tiny legs lay encased in the footed leggings she'd recently finished to accommodate her growing body.

Benjamin muttered in his sleep and rolled over, his black hair mussed. She reached out to smooth it, then stopped. Instead, she scurried into her workroom to grab her medical bag. Where was her casebook?

"Mis' Bechtmann, hurry, please. The Missus, she was hurtin.'"

She pulled the bag crosswise over her chest and followed him outside. She could record events in her casebook after she returned home. Mister Bastest boosted her onto his horse and swung up in front of her.

Except for her visits to attend neighboring women in their illnesses and the trustees' occasional buying trips, Separatists never left their property. It was one of their rules, albeit never explicitly stated. It was only her work with Emma, and later on her own, that allowed her to travel to surrounding towns. When others remarked on her good fortune, she'd smile at their misconceptions. Often awakened in the middle of the night and exhausted after the birthing, she had yet to enjoy the experience.

For once, though, she was glad to be away. Away from her husband's anger, away from tales of adulterous women being flogged, and away from her community's suspicions.

Mister Bastest's horse stopped, and she jerked awake. She found Missus Bastest in a back bedroom surrounded by the women who had come to assist her.

Beads of sweat stood out on the woman's flushed face. She groaned as the pain drew into her, then lay back in relief.

One woman wiped her face with a damp cloth. "Thank goodness, you're here. She's…"

Adelaide glanced at the women around the bed, but they turned away.

"Having a difficult time, Missus."

Adelaide finished washing her hands, rolled up her sleeves, and smiled at the young mother. No matter the situation, Emma had admonished her, always be aware of the expression on your face.

"It's been since midday yesterday," her friend reported.

"I'm fine, but he's not been moving much lately," the young mother said, her words fading into another pain. When it was over, the others stepped back, and Adelaide squatted down to examine the woman. Another spasm convulsed her body, but she was far from ready to deliver her infant.

"She still has some time to go," Adelaide reported. "Let's get her up and walk her. Sometimes that helps speed him along." She added a reassuring smile.

The women helped Missus Bastest to her feet, but when she took a step, she crunched over as another spasm took her. After a moment's rest, however, she stood and the women walked her back and forth in the room, stopping intermittently to allow the pain to rise and fall, Adelaide murmuring encouraging words throughout. Finally, the pains quickened, and they returned her to bed.

She checked the woman again. "It won't be long now," she said to sighs of relief in the room.

A short time later, she ordered, "It's time."

The women knew what to do. One stood on each side of her and supported her upright in the bed. Another gripped her hand, and a fourth gathered a warmed blanket for the infant.

Adelaide knelt at the foot of the bed. "Push," she ordered.

The woman grunted, and the baby's head appeared. She gave the mother a quick smile and looked back at the infant whose head was now all the way out. Lavender-colored skin covered a face gone slack, his lips a darker hue of purple. His head was shoved back with his chin in the air, the cord a thick noose twisted around his neck.

A cry rose in her throat, but she caught herself in time. She tried to slip a finger under the cord, but it stuck fast to the infant's skin.

She propped her arms on the bed to steady her shaking hands. Whatever could she do? He would die, choked before he was even born.

The women around the bed murmured, their voices troubled.

No, no, I can't forget now. Why can't I think?

The mother's face scrunched as another pain gripped her.

Adelaide shut her eyes, relaxed her fingers, and let her face soften as Emma had taught her. She could hear Emma's voice: "Clear your mind. Take time to think through what you need to do. You can do it."

She took a cleansing breath and let it out slowly. She imagined her hands, steady, fingers deftly moving to free the child's head.

Her fear slid away.

She opened her eyes. The infant hadn't moved. She tucked a finger under the cord and felt the tension as it pulled on the placenta embedded in the mother. If it detached... no, she couldn't think about that. She inched the cord up over one tiny ear. It slid up the slimy slope of the infant's head as his shoulders came through with a whoosh.

"A boy," she told the excited mother.

As they cleaned up the mother and baby, the women chatted with Adelaide, as relieved as she was to have both well.

"At least we didn't have to call the doctor," one woman said.

Adelaide swaddled the infant and laid him in his mother's arms. "Doctor Hertel?" She'd been hoping to question them about him, but she'd been too busy until now.

"Only doctor around," the woman said. "But we don't have him unless it doesn't go well."

Adelaide coaxed the newborn to his mother's breast where he rooted for a moment, found her nipple, and grabbed on. "He attend many births around here?"

The women glanced at each other. "One baby he'd delivered," one said, "came out with her limbs dislocated."

"I wouldn't call him for my animals," said another to murmured agreement.

"What about when, uh, a woman didn't want to birth another? He have any help for that?"

They all talked at once.

"Lord, no," one said.

"It was God's plan," said another, rolling her eyes.

And finally, "Women deserved the pain, according to him."

So he wouldn't have helped Johanna rid herself of the babe. Reluctant to give him up as a suspect, though, she asked, "We were looking for him Thursday last. Any of you know where he was?"

"I don't like him much either, but he couldn't have done better by Father," said a woman entering the room with a cup of broth for the new mother. "Sat up with him all night and into midday till he died, that he did."

"When was that?"

"Why, just a week ago it was, Thursday last," the woman said. "The night of the storm."

The night Johanna died.

Mister Bastest rushed in and fell to his knees beside his wife and baby.

"Josiah," the new mother said. "Josiah Bastest. That's his name." She nodded at her son, who sucked contentedly.

"Thank you, Missus Bechtmann, I surely do thank you," the new father told Adelaide. His face reminded her of Benjamin's at his first sight of Olivia, eyes wide with awe.

Shortly thereafter the women left, and Adelaide settled the mother, who soon fell asleep, the baby cradled in her arms.

Adelaide spread a folded quilt on the floor beside the dozing mother. So Doctor Hertel could not have killed Johanna. She lowered herself and tried to find a comfortable position on the

improvised bed. She jerked upright. But he could have given her
something that made her ill. Still, that didn't explain how she came
to be in the river.

It seemed only a moment later that Baby Josiah made his presence known. At least his cry hadn't been hurt by his ordeal, she
thought, as the room lightened with the day.

After assuring herself that mother and baby were adjusting to
each other and showed no untoward symptoms, she left the new
mother with several tablets of *secale cornutum*, a homeopathic
remedy that Josef recommended as a preventive to blood loss, especially for those mothers not living nearby. Adelaide grabbed a piece
of cheese and some bread from the family's breakfast table, and she
and the father headed out.

At the edge of town they passed the sheriff's office. Outside two
men hammered a platform in place.

"For a hanging," Mister Bastest explained. "Or a flogging."

She turned away so as not to see.

"I hear you're having an inquest 'bout a girl's dying. You better
hope they don't find anyone responsible."

Adelaide clung to his waist as the thumping continued.

"They take 'em right off to jail, yep, they do. I've seen 'um. Tied
up, loaded on a cart, and paraded through town. If that's what the
jury finds." He turned around and glanced at her. "They don't even
have to have no evidence. Just a suspicion. 'Course later they got to
prove it but by that time everone believes 'um guilty."

She shoved his words away, but the pounding lingered in her
head long after they'd left the town.

The new father kept up a stream of talk that flowed around her
until they came to a halt at the path that paralleled the river. "You
can make it the rest of the way, can't you, Mis' Bechtmann? I best

be back with the Missus," he added as Adelaide slid off the horse. "I do thank you, ma'am, for safe delivered me a son." He pressed American dollars and cents—one, eighteen—into her hand and when she nodded, he turned quickly, dug his heels into the horse, and trotted away.

Glad that the grateful father had gifted her with money the Society could always use, she started off. A canopy of branches filled out with new leaves hung over the path, and the sun, fully risen now, pressed moist heat down on her. A large boulder beckoned, but she knew if she sat down it would be all the more difficult to get back up. A faint rumbling in the distance hinted at a another storm.

A new babe safe delivered.

Johanna, though, would never birth her child.

Thunder rumbled closer now and, in the increasing gloom, the thought that she had struggled to keep at bay spilled out: Benjamin could have been the father of Johanna's unborn child. She swatted at her face. *No, I can't think that.* She clapped her hands over her ears to silence the notion, but her thoughts jumbled ahead.

Desire. She knew desire. Desire that comes without warning, screeching its way into your mind, your body, filling you up, consuming everything within its path—your life, your thoughts, your body. Is this the devil? The one the preacher warned about? The devil that steals your soul?

The river rose, sloshing water onto the bank, and the wind caught her skirts and tangled them around her legs. How could she chastise her husband if he desired another when her own thoughts were unclean?

Wind whipped under her apron and flapped it over her head. She shoved it down and faced into the wind, the air cool against her warming cheeks. Maybe the burden of goodness is being tempted but turning away. Not as the preacher said, that we should deny temptation but rather admit to it, examine it, and let it go. Sinful her thoughts may be, but she needn't act on them. It's actions that cause others harm, not thoughts.

The wind tossed branches above her and scrabbled leaves along the ground as the river picked up speed, dragging decay and debris away in its wake. With a glance at the darkening sky, she broke into a run. The bridge to town wasn't far ahead.

— Twenty —

Benjamin rubbed linseed oil across the top of the chest of drawers, but he couldn't stop thinking about Adelaide. She had been called away during the night and had not returned before he slipped out early to work.

She tried his patience but, goodness knows, he loved her. And he knew she loved him. She always gave herself to him willingly, eagerly, wanting only him. Her distress when she'd learned about Martin trying to separate husbands from wives told him that.

A disturbance outside distracted him. If he were to finish Mister Welby's order by the next morning, he had no time to see what minor event called the people hurrying past his door. Any change in the dull routine of their days brought everyone running, welcome relief from their unending chores. He still had another cabinet and a side chair to oil by evening so that he could leave them to dry overnight before the boat returned the next day for the man and his furniture.

Satisfied with the oiling, he turned the chest around and in a corner near the bottom, he added his signature mark—a tiny Z for Zoar and the year, '33. The year Johanna died. He shoved the completed chest aside.

What would he say to Adelaide when he saw her? He'd already asked—admit it, ordered—her to stop speaking about Johanna. That probably made her more determined. He knew that much about his wife. But he thought that after the damage in her work-room and the constable's inquiry, she would have been frightened into keeping quiet. But, no, not her.

She'd been seen with Jakob, undoubtedly questioning him about Johanna, she'd pestered Josef about the night watchman, someone told him, and even quizzed Martin, according to August. And that was only what he'd heard.

The heavy limp of their leader sounded on the cinder road outside. "Where's Adelaide?" Josef asked.

Benjamin stood upright and wiped his face with the back of his hand. "In Bolivar. A woman was—" He stopped when he saw Josef slump against the doorframe, his walking stick clattering to the ground.

"What's wrong?" Benjamin asked, picking up Josef's stick.

"It's the constable. He's back."

"To investigate a drowning? You said it was an accident."

"Of course it was, but the coroner's coming from New Philly to hold an inquest."

"What do you mean? What's an inquest?"

"It's like court. A jury decides if there's a cause to suspect a crime."

He felt his knees buckle. "A crime?"

"People who know anything about the death testify—"

Benjamin grabbed the smaller man by the front of his smock and shook him. "You have to stop them! You can't let them talk to Adelaide. You know her. You know what she'll say. And it's her they'll blame."

Josef's head slammed against the door frame, left eye bulging.

"Oh, Josef, I'm so sorry." Benjamin fell to his knees.

Josef righted himself, then rubbed the back of his head. "That's all right, son." He laid a hand on Benjamin's shoulder. "I know. You're afraid as we all are. I'm going to see if I can't make them see some sense. Lewis is our legal authority, which I tried to tell the constable. Maybe the coroner will listen to reason. But if I'm unsuccessful," he said, helping Benjamin to his feet, "you'd best prepare Adelaide. He gave me a list of witnesses, and her name is on it."

On the road near home Adelaide heard August calling to her as he scurried out the garden gate toward her. She dropped her medicine bag on the ground and wiped sweat from her face with her kerchief. The air hung heavy under an overcast sky.

"He's back. I told you, didn't I? I told you he'd be back." August bent over to catch his breath.

"Who?"

"The constable. I told you, didn't I?" A bee circled his nose, and he swiped at it with his glove. "You best go, maybe up to the inn, it's out of the way, maybe he won't find you there. Or maybe into the woods. Or take the canal boat aways, no matter what the rule is. Just get away, please."

His words hammered her head, and she reared back.

"Did you hear me?" came his voice from a distance. "Adelaide. Someone help." She heard his shout, and her mouth worked, but no words came out. His face drifted into view.

"Thank God," he said. "I tried to find something to rouse you." He waved an arm toward her bag beneath her body.

She tugged it out and pushed herself to a sitting position.

August patted her back, his face creased with frown lines.

"I'm just tired, that's all. But what was it you said?" She leaned against him, and he wrapped an arm around her shoulder to help her stand.

Tousled hair flew about as August shook his head. "Not now, I can't tell you."

"August, please, what's happening? I'm fine." She shrugged off his arm. "The constable returned. Why?"

His reticence didn't last. "He's recruiting a jury. They're going to hold an inquest. An inquest, Adelaide." His voice took on the excitement of a preacher. "To find out what happened to Johanna. Why did you have to go telling everyone that someone killed her? Whyever did you do that?"

She grabbed his hand to steady herself. "Stop it. This is for the best. Now it will be official. We'll know what happened."

"No, we won't. They'll think it's you. Simon's already on the jury. Martin, too, I heard. There'll be twelve of them. Men only, he said."

Simon who thought she had killed Johanna. And Martin. She tried to recall his face, but his image had faded.

Benjamin hurried to join the crowd as a horse and buggy approached from the south. A man in a black coat and top hat sat aboard the driving bench, a brown leather case propped on his lap. The driver steadied the reins on the two geldings who pranced about as if in a parade, and townspeople jostled each other for a glimpse of this new attraction.

The carriage stopped at the meeting house. The man stepped down, brushed dust off his coat, and removed his top hat. "I am Coroner Masterson," he said, with a nod to the crowd. "I'm here to investigate the death of," he consulted the sheet of paper, "Johanna Appelgate."

A flash of lightning lit the sky.

Josef stepped forward. "Gentlemen," he said, his back erect, eyes straight ahead. "I'm Josef Bimeler, the agent-general of this community. What need have you to investigate this sad accident?"

"To arrest the guilty one," Constable Helling shot back.

Benjamin jerked as if the man had struck him. Dear God, what had she done? Brought the law here. To their community. And to his family.

A few drops of rain splattered the ground, but no one moved.

"We have our own law here." Josef's tone held an edge to it.

"This is state business," the constable said. "Not your little kingdom."

"We're here to investigate a death," the coroner said. "No decision about the outcome has been made. That will wait until after the inquest."

"This man is Lewis Birk." Josef shoved the stoop-shouldered man forward. "He's our justice of the peace."

"*Was sagen er?*" Lewis asked.

The constable sniffed. "He doesn't even speak English. That's what wrong with these foreigners."

"This death was no more than an accidental drowning," Josef said. "If someone thinks we need an investigation, Herr Birk will conduct it. There's no need for all of you."

Coroner Masterson consulted his papers. "It says here that Zoar is in an unincorporated part of Tuscarawas County. That makes a County judge the ruling official for your town."

A Zoar man spoke up. "We're voting for incorporation next Tuesday."

"No," Josef said to the man, "that corporation is for our doing business."

"That won't apply here," the coroner said.

"Wait a moment," Josef said. "Lewis is authorized by the state of Ohio to serve as the justice of the peace in this jurisdiction."

"So he's adjudicated cases here?" the coroner asked.

"No need," said the man who had spoken before. "There's been no crime in Zoar."

"So you're telling me," Coroner Masterson continued, "that your Mister Birk here, although he's been duly appointed, has never heard a case? Not even a civil case?"

Josef answered. "As my friend said, there's never been a transgression against a person or property in our Society."

"It doesn't matter in any case. I have to determine if there's been a crime involved in this death and who is accused of it. If the jury's verdict is such, then the felon is apprehended and brought to the justice of the peace for examination. However, since your Mister Birk has never tried a case—and I assume that means that he has never examined a felon—I would recommend that the case be referred to a County judge."

"You can't—" Josef began, but the coroner raised his hand.

"Sir, we don't even know if a crime has been committed here. You, yourself, said it was an accident, and that most probably is what happened. So don't trouble yourself until we know more."

Josef opened his mouth to speak again, but the coroner continued. "Constable Helling tells me he has a jury of twelve men, and we're going to exhume the body. I need the father for identification."

"I can speak for him," Benjamin said. At last something he could do to help.

"You a relative?"

"I lived with the family."

A man's voice behind him murmured, "And with her killer."

Benjamin jerked his head around, but the men all stared straight ahead.

"I'm Johanna's father. I'll go," Nathan said.

"I'll go with you," Benjamin told Nathan as the rain picked up.

"Will you lead the way, sir?" the coroner asked Nathan, his voice softened. Benjamin and the other men gathered shovels and followed behind.

What grief must it bring a man to see his own child, buried a week, dug up? He'd seen a deer once dead in the woods but it had been ravaged by vultures, the stench of rotting flesh lingering in his nostrils for weeks.

Benjamin stumbled on the path, made slippery by the rain. Whatever could he do to stop this? Nothing. This was worse than the outcome he'd feared—that they'd be banished from Zoar. Much worse. Adelaide could be hung, Olivia would be motherless, and him, he'd be alone. Again. All he'd worked for, planned for, dreamed of, gone. In a moment of reckless words.

Mayhap this was his fault. For basking in Johanna's worship. Now God would punish him. Take away his wife. Even if she made a mistake, she didn't deserve whatever punishment they ordered.

They crested the hill, and the cemetery spread out before them. The coroner hesitated at the clearing, then clutched his top hat and lowered his head into the wind as the rainstorm began in earnest. He followed behind the officials to Johanna's gravesite. Tiny sprouts of grass peppered the mound. Nathan stepped back and stared off toward the woods, rain pelting his face. Or was it tears?

— Twenty-one —

"Dug up?" Adelaide said, jerking Olivia away from the breast. "For-ever why?" she asked Helga.

Olivia let out a howl.

Adelaide repositioned her while her mind raced with thoughts. The coroner was to hold an inquest. Exhausted from birthing the Bastest babe, scant sleep, the long trip back to Zoar, and now this.

Helga reached an arm around her shoulder. "Hush, now, Adelaide. The authorities must do their job. You mustn't fret. Isn't this what you wanted? To find out how Johanna died?"

How could Helga bear it? Her treasured daughter brought out of her grave. And for the men to see with only Adelaide's shawl to cover her nakedness.

"Now maybe we can know with sureness what happened," Helga said. "Even Nathan can't fault the law, and I think he'll be as relieved as I am to know. No one should lose a child and not know why."

Her mind jumped to the sight of Johanna's body after a week in the ground. What if it were Olivia? She couldn't abide the thought.

"Doctor Hertel told them he could—"

Dear God, they were going to cut her open.

"I have to go," she said, thrusting Olivia at a startled Helga. *I have to be there! I have to stop him!*

"You're too late," Josef told her a few minutes later. The meeting house door slammed behind her, cold water splashing along the floor. "They've already gone to dig her up."

"You couldn't stop them?"

"Wouldn't listen to me, no they wouldn't."

She turned to Lewis. "You're our justice. Couldn't you do something?"

"There's nothing anyone can do now." Lewis shrugged as rain pounded the roof.

"Yes there is." She started out the door, but Josef grabbed her arm. "You can't go. No women allowed."

She jerked away and, before he could follow, she sprinted out, oblivious to the rain that pummeled her face. She had to keep Doctor Hertel from cutting her open. And learning about her unborn babe. For Helga's and Nathan's sake, surely, and because it would implicate whoever fathered her child.

Benjamin heard the commotion ahead and as he rounded the corner, there she stood under a weeping willow, oblivious to the rain. Hands on her hips, chin jutted. What had she done now?

"We've finished our examination, Missus Bechtmann," Coroner Masterson said, shaking water off his hat. "We're on our way back."

"You've, uh, examined her already? Up there?" she asked, hair plastered around her face. "Where's the doctor?"

"We don't need him." A shudder passed through the coroner's body.

"I thought he was going to—"

"Ahem. No. I saw no need. But I do need your testimony at the inquest since you found the body. Constable," he said and the man stepped forward. "This is a summons, commanding you to appear and to testify at the inquest into Johanna Appelgate's death," the coroner continued as the constable held out a paper.

He willed her to not argue with the man. Just this once.

"I don't know how she died," she said, ignoring the constable's outstretched hand.

"You found the body. You must testify to what you saw."

"When I found her you mean?"

"Yes. The inquest is Monday next," the coroner said.

At last she took the paper, stuffed it inside her kerchief crossed on her bosom and clasped her arms to herself with a shiver.

"It's at your meeting house."

She nodded, turned on her heel and bounced away, the men all watching. Her wet clothing clung to her body as she moved.

He felt his jaw tighten. Did she have to attract the men like that? She doesn't do it on purpose. Besides, she's not even aware of how the swing of her hips and the toss of her head suggests the treasure—and the pleasure—her body inspires.

— Twenty-two —

Adelaide read the summons again.

You are hereby commanded to appear before me and the jury in Zoar, Ohio, at nine o'clock in the morning on thirteen May in the year of our Lord eighteen hundred thirty three, and there to give testimony and the truth to say, of and concerning the death of one Johanna Appelgate. Signed: Milton Masterson, Coroner, Tuscarawas County, State of Ohio.

Now she had no choice. She was compelled to tell the truth. But what was the truth?

She should rise and kindle the fire. The rain had stopped but left the air cooler. Instead she drew a knitted afghan around her shoulders and leaned back in her rocker.

Johanna did not drown. That she could report with confidence. If she testified she believed that Johanna had been poisoned, she would implicate herself. Besides, she had no proof, however much she believed it, that someone had stolen poisonous herbs from her workroom. But if she stayed silent, she would be lying. By omission. She groaned. Whatever was she going to do?

Benjamin came through the door. Tired lines creased his face, and mud caked his hands and clothing. He poured water into a basin, grabbed the bar of soap, and scrubbed his hands and arms with a vengeance.

Nellie busied herself setting the table. A pot of cottage cheese, a loaf of bread, and a bowl of cold sauerkraut stood ready for their evening meal.

During supper, Nellie ignored Olivia's happy chirps and only toyed with her food. Her sister had not mentioned the coroner's arrival nor the inquest scheduled for Monday. Adelaide must talk with her about it, though, no matter how much she wanted to avoid the subject. She couldn't let her sister worry any more than she was.

Benjamin ate quickly, focused on his plate. When he finished, he rose, tossed his napkin onto the table and, mumbling that he still had Mister Welby's order to finish before the next day, went out the door.

Adelaide left Nellie to clear up and headed out. She could not allow a lie, however much it was a lie of omission, to remain unsaid.

Not to her leader.

Josef left his supper table, wiping his mouth as he followed her outside. "I haven't told you everything," she began.

He propped himself on his walking stick and turned his bulging eye toward her.

"It's about Johanna. I know patient confidentiality continues after death but I—"

"You know something about how she died and you're just now telling me?"

"Calm down, Josef, I couldn't violate her privacy, but now I think I must." She told him that Johanna was to bear a child.

He dropped onto the bench beside his cabin. "You examined her?"

"I saw the signs after she died." Please don't ask me to speak of them to you, she begged silently.

"Harrumph." He toed the rough ground beneath his feet.

He was embarrassed as well.

"I don't how much I should tell at the inquest. You know I'm to be a witness, don't you?"

"Witness? You could be found culpable." He shifted so he could look at her directly.

She'd brought this anguish to him, no matter she blamed Simon and the preacher. Her questioning had kept up the talk.

"Do you know what could happen then?" He went on without waiting for her answer. "You, or whoever, would be carted off to jail right from the inquest. No return home. No time to see your baby, your sister, or your husband. Just loaded into a cart and hauled—"

"Stop." She covered her ears to shut out his words. "You're frightening me."

"You should be frightened for yourself and for all of us. Consider this: How would a verdict of murder against one of our own change our community? Once evil enters, trust vanishes. Our refuge against the world is irretrievably lost. We're just one more place that harbors the wicked." He banged his staff on the ground. "And our freedom is gone!"

"Freedom? We haven't any freedom. Not here in Zoar. Our rules are just like those back home. Can't be changed no matter what. We don't have to think about what to do, just follow the rules."

His look told her how much her words had surprised him. Never before had she raised her voice to their leader. She straightened her skirts and continued. "I know what you'll say," she continued, "that rules make for an orderly society. But at what cost? I'll tell you what cost—our freedom. The very reason we came here."

"What would we do without rules?"

"You mean something bad could happen, like a murder?" She'd spoken without thought, and now it was too late to retract her words. Not that she wanted to. She spoke the truth. Rules, no matter how stringent, no matter how rigorously enforced, could not prevent evil if someone willed it.

He studied her, his head cocked to the side, his bulging eye turned away. "But we are free, free from the tyranny of the state."

"That we've exchanged for our own form of tyranny."

"But it's for our own good. Besides, most people don't want that much freedom. They want security, they want rules to follow."

"Or," she said, "they're afraid to be free."

He stared to the north where the main road climbed beyond Zoar, stretched three miles to the town of Bolivar, and on another sixteen to the city of Canton. She quelled an urge to apologize for her outburst. But then he pulled himself up by his staff, gave her a brief nod, and returned inside.

Adelaide remained sitting and let her pride wash over her. She had stood up to the man they all submitted to without question or doubt. A tiny part of her also knew that she was as smart as he was, a finding she would keep to herself, hold close, like the treasure it was.

— Twenty-three —

Sleep didn't come easily to Adelaide that night. The air held the promise of more rain that never came, leaving only a heaviness that seemed to wear on them all. Olivia had been cranky and nothing Nellie tried distracted her. Adelaide even had to coax her to the breast. Finally the baby had fallen into a fitful sleep, but Adelaide remained awake, alert to her infant's uneasy breathing, which she prayed didn't portend illness.

Benjamin had stayed late at the shop, and when he'd returned he'd gone straight to bed. Maybe if he had argued with her, screamed at her even, they would at least be talking. When he lay down beside her, she longed to reach over and take him in her arms but the angry set of his shoulder kept her still. She listened until his breathing evened out and watched the moon rise in the sky as her mind returned again and again to the inquest on Monday. The next moment, it seemed, Nellie was shaking her awake.

There was nothing for it but to keep busy. Monday would come soon enough. Down in the cellar she scooped potatoes, carrots, and onions onto her apron and leaned forward to reach the dried apples. The vegetables tumbled out of her apron. She grabbed at them, but only managed to spill the rest onto the cellar floor. She sank to her knees, her world tumbling down around her. She sucked in the stench of sauerkraut in the barrel beside her as if to punish herself with its acrid odor.

Once again she'd failed. She'd failed her mother and, God knows, she failed her sister. And she'd failed Johanna.

She thought the tears might finally come. The tears she'd held in for so many years. But they didn't. Just the familiar gnawing, knowing pain of sadness so deep that weeping couldn't touch it.

Cold seeped through her skirts. She couldn't remain here forever, that much soaked into her dampened brain.

A pale sun appeared as she emerged into daylight. She stood in its watery warmth, resolve clear in her mind. She would redeem herself and reclaim her right to care for her community.

In short order she scrubbed her vegetables, tossed them into boiling water along with a few pieces of dried beef, left the mixture to simmer on the stove, and made her way outside. At least she could finish cleaning out the perennial beds in the garden. That should keep her body, if not her mind, occupied.

No one was about when she walked up the path to the green-house. In spite of the glass that enveloped the two-story building, graying clouds had returned and obscured the light, shadowing the interior. Adelaide stepped through the door and into the darkened quiet.

A swish of air and something smacked her in the face.

She staggered backward, arms flailing. Her feet slipped out from under her on the slick ground and out of the corner of her eye she saw a smattering of tools scattered about on the floor. Why would they be there and not in their hooks on the wall, she wondered, even as she felt herself falling face first toward the knife-like spikes of an upturned pitchfork. Her instincts took over, and she flung her body to the side. A sharp pain stabbed into her arm as her face smacked into a puddle. She spit out mud to the side and tried to jerk her arm loose, groaning as it remained impaled on the pitchfork.

Wind rattled through the greenhouse, and the door slammed behind her.

Carefully she reached across her body, tightening her jaw as the pitchfork dug deeper into her arm. She wove her fingers between the prongs at its base and jerked upward to fling it aside. Her cry pierced the air as the pitchfork landed with a clatter next to a rake. When she opened her eyes, she saw that she had stepped on the rake's teeth, which popped up the handle to smack her in the face. This was all her fault. If she hadn't been distracted... She clutched her arm and lay still, waiting for the pain to ease.

Finally, she steadied her arm and drew her body up into a sitting position. A wave of nausea swept over her. After a moment it subsided and she examined the gash that had torn through her sleeve. She hooked a finger into the torn fabric to see into the wound. A puncture dotted her arm, dribbling blood.

She struggled to stand and bile rose in her throat as she steadied herself against the wall. After her stomach settled, she opened her eyes and shuddered at the sight. If she hadn't twisted to the side, the prongs of the pitchfork would have stabbed her in the face. In the eye, possibly.

Fear gave way to anger. Who had done this? Left tools strewn about for her to fall on? When she found them, they'd have to answer to her. And their community.

Pain washed over her again, and she leaned against the wall for a moment. The blood-stained pitchfork lay aside as if resting, its work completed. She pushed herself away from the wall, cradled her arm to her body, and picked up the pitchfork by its handle. A scrap of blue fabric clung to one of the mud-covered prongs. Mud? No one would put a garden tool away without cleaning it, leaving a precious implement to rust.

"What's going on?" said August, hurrying in the door. "You're hurt."

"You left this on the floor. Muddy. And I fell on—"

"I would never do that, Adelaide. Everything was put away when I left last night." He picked up the rake and hung it where it belonged, its pole tucked between two nails embedded in the wood, the toothed crossbar toward the wall. "How'd this happen?"

She couldn't speak; the gnawing pain spread down her arm. "I have to get home. I have to take care of this."

"Let me go with you." He wrapped a sinewy arm around her waist.

Outside, she began to shake. He insisted she sit a few moments on a bench. He talked soothingly to her as if she were a recalcitrant plant that needed his encouragement, and after a few moments she felt steady enough to continue.

Had she deserved this? For disobeying her elders? For a forbidden lust? For violating her marriage vows, albeit in her mind? For her failures?

Back at the cabin, Adelaide allowed August to help her inside. He insisted on drawing water from the cistern outside and setting it to warm on the stove. Nellie rushed in behind them, and Adelaide directed her to gather clean cloths, soap, and her medical bag from the workroom. Then she shooed August away, who looked relieved to be asked to leave.

She winced as her sister helped pull her arm out of her sleeve before draping a shawl over her shoulders for modesty if not for comfort, and they stared at the injury.

"Ohh." Nellie backed up.

"Sit down," Adelaide ordered. Nellie would never become a healer if the sight of blood turned her as pale as she was now.

Nellie looked out the window. "Matron's coming."

"Oh, no, send her away."

Gerda entered without knocking. "What happened to you?"

"Just a little accident," Adelaide said. "I'm handling it."

She closed her eyes, took a breath and as she expelled it, forced her mind to distance itself from the immediate situation—a strategy Emma had taught her when she had faced her first serious injury, a man whose hand had been nearly severed at the saw mill. Her head cleared and her mind dispassionate, she studied the wound.

"Shouldn't you be at Helga's?" Gerda asked Nellie as the water in the kettle began to boil.

"I needed her here," Adelaide said, her eyes on her injury.

"Back home in Germany, hands were never idle. There was always some work to be done."

Nellie rolled her eyes at Adelaide. Good. Maybe her sister no longer feared the woman.

"Being careless, I suppose," Gerda said, watching Nellie scoop leaves into a teapot.

"What are you doing here?" Adelaide asked.

"Just doing my Christian duty," Gerda said, undeterred.

Adelaide dipped a clean cloth in water, rubbed it on the bar of lye soap, and began to clean the wound, rubbing soap into and around the puncture until she could stand the stinging pain no longer. She took a moment to breathe normally again. She rummaged in her medical bag for her tweezers, rubbed the ends of them into the soap until they were well coated, wiped the excess on a clean cloth, and clenched her teeth. She wouldn't let Gerda see her cry.

"That's what you young folks do, hurrying to do who knows what." Gerda clicked her tongue. "I try to teach them."

Nellie placed a cup of tea in front of Adelaide and snuck her a sideways smile.

Adelaide nodded and turned to her injury, digging out each piece of embedded dirt and tiny kernels of sand and depositing them on a linen square until the wound was clean, at least what she could see. She shoved the soap and cloths aside and leaned over her tea cup, waiting for its steamy aroma to revive her.

"You can't do your work right if you rush it," Gerda went on.

Adelaide took a sip of tea, found it too hot, and returned to her task. She dug a jar of salve out of her bag, coated the wound with a generous amount, and extracted a linen pouch. "I need your help," she told Nellie. "After I get the bandage on, you need to tie it in place. Can you do that?"

Nellie, some color returned to her face, nodded. Adelaide pulled a clean white cloth square out of the pouch. "There's a roll of cloth you can use," she said with a nod toward her bag.

Nellie tied strips of fabric around Adelaide's dressing as Gerda continued her complaints. "Why you need a workroom in your cabin is beyond me. Emma never needed that," she added, sniffing. "And the way you spoil that baby, just like Helga did and you know what happened to her daughters—"

"Stop." Adelaide demanded. She didn't care that she had just offended an elder. Another sin on her conscience made worse because she didn't regret it. "It's none of your business how we care for Olivia."

"It will be when she comes to the dormitory. That's what I came to tell you. It's been decided that we're going to take the children as soon as they're weaned, not wait until they're three years. Spoiled by then, they are."

No. Not her baby. Not Olivia. She clutched her arm to her side.

"Well, one of us has work to do," Gerda said and left.

Nellie gathered the soiled cloths and hugged them to her chest. "You don't think she means that, do you? That they'll take Olivia when she's weaned?"

"I'm sure they won't." She couldn't let Nellie see her worry. "Give her no mind. But I'm surprised you stayed when you saw her coming."

"I couldn't leave you," Nellie said, giving her shoulder a hug.

Adelaide squealed.

"I shouldn't have touched you."

Adelaide took her sister's hand in hers. "I'm glad you did."

She knew she should talk to Nellie about the upcoming inquest, reassure her that no danger would come to her, that she would only be telling the court about finding Johanna's body.

Nellie, though, seemed to have forgotten about it, at least for now, and she was reluctant to remind her.

"How did this happen?" Nellie asked, frown lines crimping her forehead. "You're not usually careless."

"I wasn't. Someone left a rake out, and I stepped on it and fell on the pitchfork."

"You should be all right, though. It's probably not as bad as I thought."

Nellie sounded so hopeful, she didn't want to disappoint her. Besides, she'd cleaned it so thoroughly that she doubted inflammation would set in. Adelaide glanced around her chair. "You don't see my casebook anywhere, do you?"

"Your casebook?"

"Where I keep all my records. Of treatments. Plants." She fumbled in her pockets. "I thought it was in this apron."

The door slammed open. "*Liebchen!*" Benjamin cried, sliding onto one knee in front of her. "What happened? Oh, *meine Liebchen.*" He rose up and folded her into his arms.

She squawked. "My arm, Benjamin."

"I didn't think. Bad?"

"Not too much. I'll be fine." But worry clogged her mind. Had the pain distracted her, lulling her into a false sense of security because she didn't want to dig at the wound anymore?

He pushed himself upright and frowned. "What were you doing?"

"I just walked into the greenhouse and stepped on a rake. It was an accident. It can happen anytime," she added to make certain he understood that she was just going about her daily work, not investigating.

"Are you sure? Maybe someone wanted to keep you from testifying on Monday."

Adelaide closed her eyes. Thankful that he'd set aside his anger since she'd been hurt, she didn't want to begin the argument again and certainly not now with pain clouding her mind. When she opened her eyes, his face had softened.

"You know I," his voice choked. "I only want to keep you safe."

Adelaide started to rise but a wave of pain washed over her, pinning her to the chair.

"My *Liebchen*, what can I get you?"

"Rest. That's all I need."

"I better get back then. We're finally loading Welby's furniture, and I want to see that the men are careful with everything."

"So he's pleased with his order?"

Benjamin ducked his head. "He couldn't stop talking about the excellent work we'd done. I think we can count on more orders from him."

She squeezed her husband's hand. "Now off with you. Nellie will take care of everything. Go, go," she demanded when he didn't move.

With another long look at her, he left, and she allowed her head to drop against the back of the chair, sinking into the pain. Breathe deeply. That's what she taught her mothers during birthing. Breathe in the good air, she told them, and out with the bad, releasing the pain.

Nellie fussed over her, bringing more tea, fashioning a sling to hold her arm steady. Watching her young sister handle her arm, Adelaide revised her opinion of her sister's potential as a healer. She had paled at the sight of her blood, but it wasn't uncommon for even experienced healers to quake when a loved one is harmed. Yes, she thought, watching Nellie prepare their dinner, she'll soon be able to be my helper and, letting her mind drift far into the future, take my place someday. With that, she rested.

— Twenty-four —

Benjamin tossed the night through until finally he rose, grabbed his shoes and a lantern, and tiptoed out. The door to his shop creaked on its hinges. Mister Welby's order had been loaded on the canal boat, and the man had given Josef extra payment "for the fine job," he'd said.

Benjamin shoved away his pride, and began to clean up the shop that had been left as it was the day before. He stacked scraps of wood into a pile for firewood, and the longer pieces he propped along the wall to use for another project. His tools all needed cleaning. He laid them out on his bench, grabbed a clean rag, and began with the plane, dragging the rag along the cutting surface.

Adelaide. How could he live without her? Yesterday she'd been hurt, and his heart ached as if it had been his wound. If such a minor injury pained him, whatever would he do if he lost her forever? He couldn't think of that. He must stop her from saying anything that could implicate her, cause the court to charge her. But, if he knew anything about his wife, it was that she'd offer more than she needed to. She was determined that the cause of Johanna's death be found.

By the time daylight seeped through the window, he'd finished sweeping sawdust into a pile, propped his broom against the wall, and let himself out.

Back at the cabin, Nellie told him Adelaide had gone to hunt for wildflowers. He followed the road out of town and into the woods. He heard her before he saw her, low humming came from ahead.

Humming?

She knelt in a bed of hyacinths, her back to him. Auburn hair escaped her cap to curl around the base of her neck, and damp stained the back of her dress. She dropped a blossom into her basket, and a sweet aroma surrounded her.

Her contentment galled him. However could she be so cheerful? With effort, he tamped down his irritation. If he expected her to take his advice now, after being so dismissive of her concerns these past few days, he couldn't let his annoyance show.

He stepped forward and a twig snapped beneath his foot.

She jumped up and flowers spilled out of her basket. "It's you," she said, steadying her injured arm. Light played over her face, but he couldn't tell what she was thinking.

"I needed to see you." Why did his collar suddenly seem too tight? "To talk to you about Monday."

"I have to tell the truth," she said simply.

"Truth? What truth? That you treated her? Is that what you'll say?"

Her hands tightened on the basket handle. "If I have to."

"So now you'll say it when all along you've denied it. Even to me." *Especially to me.*

"But it didn't kill her." She scooped up blossoms off the ground.

"I've talked to Emma, Josef, too. They both said what I gave her wouldn't have killed her."

Jealousy swept through him. He had only wanted her to say it, to admit what she'd done, but she refused, and all the while she'd been telling others.

"You knew all along?" she asked, reading his face. "So why have you pestered me to tell you, to violate my conscience? Just to satisfy your urge to know?"

"Why couldn't you have told me? I'm your husband. Can't you trust me?"

"Do you think I did it? Harmed Johanna? You do, don't you? I see it in your face."

"Adelaide, stop. Johanna told me. She told me you gave her a remedy."

"And did she tell you what it was for?"

"Please, Adelaide, I'm frightened for you and I want to help."

"Help? And just how do you think you can do that? All you've told me is to not talk to anyone, not ask questions—"

"And look what that's done. Brought the law here, invaded us with their accusations, their suspicions, their power. They could take you away. You might be..." He couldn't say it out loud. Not to her. Not now. "Yesterday, I, I realized... I can't lose you."

He shouldn't feel this way about her. He'd been told often enough that they were all brothers and sisters, one no different from another, all one family as if one person was interchangeable with another. But he didn't believe it. Not about her he didn't.

Maybe he should send her away. Or should he gather his family and they all leave? No, that's just what he'd feared from the start. But if we don't leave and she's found guilty...

"Benjamin." She took a step toward him, her face softened. "I have to do what I think is right. Not you, not Josef, not anyone, can decide that for me. I could not live with myself if I keep silent."

She loved her truth more than she loved him.

"But you can mind your words. Not tell any more than you're asked. Don't say you gave her anything? Can't you?" He felt as if she was slipping away from him. "You don't have to say that. You've said your patients' treatments are confidential, that you can't tell anyone. Don't tell them that. Please, Adelaide, I'm begging you."

"I know you think you know what I should do, but you can't. This is my decision. And it's mine to bear whatever the outcome." Her voice wavered at the last, and she swiped a gloved hand across her face before continuing. "I don't know what you think I did, but it was nothing wrong." She turned back to her work.

He'd vowed once to protect her, cherish her. But he could do neither.

August ducked his head when he saw Adelaide inside the greenhouse. He stared down at the pot of budding zinnia seedlings in his hands as if seeing them for the first time.

Adelaide dropped her basket of hyacinths on a low shelf. "Did you see my casebook? I've looked all around in here but..." She stopped when noticed his strange expression, almost as if he was embarrassed. "What's wrong?"

"I wanted to tell you, I really did."

"You found it?"

"No, it's just that—"

"You left the tools out?"

"No, no, I wouldn't. It's not that."

"Tell me," she demanded.

He placed the pot on the shelf by the door and turned to her. "I lied to you," he said in one swish of breath.

"What about?"

"All the planting, so weary I was." He rubbed at the dirt staining his calloused hands.

"What is it?" She stamped her foot in frustration, wincing as the movement jarred her arm.

He motioned for her to join him on the bench, shoved a pot aside, and brushed off the seat. Adelaide caught a whiff of geranium.

"He should have wakened me. I'd have gone out even in the rain. I've done it before. Even Benjamin has, I'll wager."

"What in the world are you talking about? Rain? Waking up? Just say what you mean."

He raised a hand against her onslaught. "The night Johanna died I was supposed to take second watch at two A.M.—"

"I know, you told me. Josef told me."

"But Martin, he didn't wake me. I slept right through the storm and didn't wake until daybreak. When I heard about the downpour during the night, I thought that he had gone to bed knowing that fire was no danger then. That's what I lied to you about."

"You didn't lie."

"Yes, Adelaide, I did. I implied the lie when I said I hadn't seen anyone the night Johanna died. Don't you see? It's the intent. I intended to deceive you. That's the same as if I'd lied directly."

Why couldn't he just be quiet about lies?

"But, uh—"

"There's more?"

Stray whiskers bobbed on his sun-browned neck. "I didn't want to tell you, but I think you should know. It's just that some are saying you're the cause of the law here."

"I didn't bring them here. That preacher did."

"Yes, but your questioning alerted him."

"But it's Simon accusing me. I had to find out what happened, who did it."

"Everyone thinks it's likely you gave Johanna a remedy, no matter you won't tell. Whether it killed her or not, they don't know. But then you found her body."

"What does that have to do with it?"

"I'm just saying that it's suspicious, that's all. You're too much involved."

"You don't understand. I want to tell what I know so they can find out what happened to Johanna. She didn't drown, that I know. And I think I know how, but I have no idea who did it."

"Didn't I tell you to leave? Didn't I? I told you about jail. For a woman. And what if, what if, they flog you?"

She sank back down onto the bench and cradled her arm, which had begun to throb.

"Or worse? Adelaide, we need you here in Zoar. I need you, but now you have to go to court—"

"I couldn't just ignore what I knew. What if the person kills again? Then what? How do you think I'd feel if that happened?"

"If only you hadn't talked about it so openly. That's what's got the men riled up. Not proper for a woman to talk about."

"So that's it. Women are relegated to the home, doing women's work." Her voice sped up as her anger grew. "After we helped clear the land, raise the buildings, and dig the canal, we must return home. Like good little children. Well, not me," she said, standing. "What are they going to do—burn me at the stake?"

He scrambled to his feet. "Adelaide, calm down. Of course not. But they've been telling Benjamin how he can't be on the standing committee if he can't control his wife." He raised his hands in frustration. "I don't know what to tell them."

"Tell them I'm a person, not a child. That I make my own decisions," she said, forgetting her injured arm as she slammed her hands onto her hips. She grimaced, but continued. "Just like they do. And if they don't, I'll get the women to vote them out of office. That's what you tell them."

Outside, Adelaide forced her thoughts away from the men's grumbling. A few doors away voices raised in hymns. Sunday Meeting had begun. But she had no intention of facing her neighbors this day. She had to find her casebook. Had she dropped it when she fell or had she left it somewhere else? The music stilled, and the slow cadence of Josef's voice drifted through the window.

She turned the corner and saw Martin's cabin up ahead. She should check on Ilse, but she hesitated. Even though all desire for him had vanished, the thought of seeing him still unnerved her. Would her body betray her? Would desire, no matter how unwanted, return in his presence?

Nonetheless, she shoved through the door.

"I'm much mended," Ilse said and struggled to sit up. "They brought me some bread in milk. It was ever so tasty."

"No more pain?" Adelaide knelt by her side.

"Not so's you'd notice. But weak as a baby, I am."

"That will take time."

"Tell that to himself."

"Martin?"

"He keeps asking how much longer I intend to lie about, doing nothing."

"You're recuperating, that's what you're doing."

"Umm."

"Ilse, you must rest until you're well and truly recovered. You will, won't you? No matter what he says."

"Whatever you say, Adelaide," she said and a small smile lit the woman's pale face.

If only she could be certain that Ilse would follow her advice, she thought, as she let herself out the door. Probably she should talk to Martin herself, insist he allow her the rest she needed. But Ilse was improving. She should be well soon. No need for Adelaide to face him again.

Josef pulled up his mare to rein her in when Benjamin flagged him down.

"What would happen," Benjamin said, then waited until the last few stragglers from Sunday Meeting passed by, "if Adelaide didn't appear in court tomorrow?"

Josef fixed his bulging eye on Benjamin's face. "She isn't thinking she can avoid being there, is she?"

"No, no. I'm that worried, though."

Josef leaned back on the bench and stared off into the distance. "I've tried so hard, we all have, to keep us free from the sins of the world. But maybe that was not to be. After all, we have to live on this plane for now."

Benjamin stifled his impatience. The last words he wanted now were his leader's philosophy.

"But, I suppose," Josef went on. "The coroner would issue a warrant for her arrest, and the constable would come for her."

Constable Helling. He'd studied Adelaide with unsettling attention.

"She thinking about running?" Josef asked.

"No, and I doubt I could get her to. She's that intent on speaking."

"Well, even if she did, she'd be on foot, and they'd soon catch up with her."

"Then what would happen?"

"They'd take her straight to the jail. Have you ever seen the jail in New Philadelphia? Debtors, thieves, murderers, even. No, of course you haven't. It's no place for a woman. Nor anyone else, for that matter."

"How long would they keep her?"

"I imagine until the jury rules. I suspect her fleeing would signal her guilt. Why else disappear before the inquest is even held? Her running away would most certainly bear on their ruling."

"What would happen then?"

"We don't know that they'll rule Johanna's death anything but an accident."

"Is that what you think will happen?"

"It's what I hope the outcome will be," he said by way of an answer.

— Twenty-five —

Adelaide told Emma about her injury and her lost casebook. "Do you think someone could have set up the accident on purpose to steal my casebook, thinking they could grab it while I was distracted? I might have seen someone leave as I was falling, but it may have been just the wind that blew the door shut. If I hadn't turned at the last moment…" She ran a hand over her face to clear it. "I'd have landed face down on the pitchfork."

"Don't think about that. It didn't happen." Emma set aside the basket in her hands. "I can't imagine anyone would have thought of such an elaborate scheme to hurt you. If that's what they wanted, it was a pretty inefficient way of doing it."

"They vandalized my workroom last Tuesday. Since that didn't stop my questioning, maybe they thought to attack me outright."

"That doesn't make sense, Adelaide. How would anyone be certain you'd be the next person through the door?"

"Maybe he was there lying in wait for me, picking his weapon, and when I was hit accidentally, he escaped."

"I think you're letting the upcoming inquest cloud your thinking. Most likely someone left without returning the tools to their proper place and intended to return later." She shifted on her seat and continued. "I heard you went to Bolivar. How did it go for the woman?"

Adelaide brightened. "Safe delivered of a boy."

"And?"

She told Emma about the cord around the baby's neck and how she'd slipped her finger under it to release the baby's head.

"You've done well, my child. You knew more than you thought you did."

"Ah." Something shifted in Adelaide's mind. Her worry about not being capable seemed foolish. She had delivered Missus Bastest's infant despite the complication. She had known exactly what to do in an emergency. Whyever was she fussing that she wasn't good enough? She had just proved otherwise.

Emma broke into her thoughts. "What do you intend to say at the inquest on Monday?"

"I have to tell the truth."

"Ah. There's truth and then there's truth."

"What are you saying? Truth is an absolute. Isn't that what you taught me?"

"I also told you that life is not always so certain. Sometimes there are mitigating factors, such as when telling the truth will harm someone else. Then, if you can possibly avoid it, I would advise you to keep quiet. I'm not talking about lying. No, you should never do that, but ofttimes, you can simply keep your peace."

"But isn't that lying if only by omission?"

"Yes, Adelaide, now we're talking about intent."

Intent. That word again.

"That's another factor. If you intend to imply a lie by avoiding answering then, yes, you are lying, albeit I'm not so sure that's as serious a sin as lying directly." Emma leaned back in her rocker and closed her eyes for a moment. "I think now you're talking about theological issues that I'm not equipped to answer."

"But what would you do?"

"It matters not a whit what I would do, child. As Josef says, we each are responsible for our own conscience."

A thought still tickled her mind. What was it? Something August had said reminded her, but what was it? "If I only had my casebook."

"Maybe you left it somewhere."

"I'm trying to remember when I last used it. I had it here on Monday when we talked and then at the town meeting that night." Where had she been? Ilse's, for one. Had she written anything in her book about Ilse's condition? No, she hadn't had a chance. She couldn't find it before she went to Bolivar. Then she'd come home and found the coroner in town.

Shame flooded her body as realization dawned. The last time she'd had it was when she went to see Martin.

"I said, what use could anyone else have for it?" Emma asked.

"Pardon?"

"Your casebook. No one would know what your notations mean so why would anyone want it?"

Had she dropped it in his barn? Or lost it in the woods? Or on the way home? She'd stopped to see the hotel. Only a few hours before it went up in flames. Did she lose it there?

A jolt of fear returned. Without her book, its records of her patients and treatments and her herb-planting information, what would keep her safe from mistakes?

"Maybe a way to discredit you, do you think?" Emma said.

"As if I haven't been already."

"Stop that, child, I've told you before. A healer needs to keep affirmative thoughts."

"How? How can I do that when—"

"As you've done in the past."

"Not so's you could tell."

Emma's rocker banged forward. "I have spoken to you about that. Admittedly, recent happenings are worse than usual, all the more reason to keep your thinking clear. How long has it been since you've been alone in contemplation?"

"I was afraid someone would see me."

"I explained that you need the time apart, that no one should stop you."

"Still, with all the talk…"

"I told you all the more reason you must." She shoved one toe against her footstool and rocked.

"Yes, ma'am," Adelaide said, smiling in spite of herself.

"Harrumph. What use would anyone have for your *Kasusbuch*? Don't you think if anyone finds it, they'll return it?"

"I made notes about Johanna's death."

"You think they could make sense of it? I mean, how specific were you?"

"I listed each person I suspected. I used initials like I do with my treatment records, but it wouldn't have been difficult for someone to figure out who the people were."

"More importantly, what did you write about them?"

Adelaide adjusted her arm on her lap. "Too much, I'm afraid. Why they might have wanted her dead, how they could have done it—supposing she was poisoned by something, where they each were as nearly as I'd been able to tell."

"And your conclusions? Did you identify any one person you thought more likely than the others?"

"I don't know who it is. That's so frustrating. You told me to concentrate on Jakob, but he spent the night at the inn. Simon was there, too, as far as I can determine. Martin as well. Doctor Hertel, I learned in Bolivar, was there tending a dying man. I don't know where Brigit was that night, although I can't see her hurting her sister in spite of wanting Jakob."

"It has to be someone who had a reason to want her dead."

Benjamin. *Maybe I shouldn't have been so insistent, so forthright with the constable.* No, it's for the best. Maybe the coroner can find out how Johanna died. *I'm certain Benjamin had nothing to do with it.*

"If only I had my book."

"You'd best find it. More rain tonight."

"Your arthritis telling you that?"

Emma ran one hand lightly over the opposite fingers. "Find your casebook before water ruins it."

Adelaide saw the commotion below her on the road. People hurried toward Martin's cabin. She grabbed her skirts and ran, catching up with Brigit.

"Something's happened at Martin's," Brigit said, her voice excited. "Herr Bimeler and that doctor are fighting."

Adelaide heard the raised voices as she turned the corner. Martin's cabin sat a few feet ahead. She pushed through the crowd gathered in front and rushed inside.

"If you'd done what I told you in the first place instead of trying all your supposed treatments," Doctor Hertel shrieked at Josef, "she'd be alive."

Adelaide knelt beside Ilse, who lay on her pallet, her eyes open. On one arm an inch-long cut scored the skin, a dribble of blood drying below it, the metallic smell of blood lingering in the air. She reached up and closed Ilse's eyes, and said, if not exactly a prayer, a hope that she had found the peace that had evaded her in this life. "What happened?"

"She got sick again," Gerda said, "and I just did what he told me to."

"He told her," Josef said, pointing to the doctor, "to use hot compresses. And then, then, he bled her. You killed her, you imbecile!"

"What do you know about medicine?" the doctor scoffed. "That homeopathy, bah. It's not real medicine. Old wives' tales, that's what that is."

"He's a real doctor," Gerda said with a sniff.

Doctor Hertel nodded his appreciation and turned to others who had entered the cabin. "Unlike your leader here. He never went to medical school. He ever tell you what's in his medicines? No? Well, I'll tell you—nothing."

"Nothing?" murmured one man.

"Absolutely nothing. Sure, he starts out with something but then he dilutes it down and dilutes it and dilutes it until there's nothing left. Then he gives it to you, saying it's a cure." He stabbed a finger toward Adelaide. "About as much a cure as that woman's plants. Why you people let them go on treating you, I don't know. If I were your doctor—"

"Out!" Josef yelled. "Out of my town!"

"You can't throw me out. This isn't your precious Germany; this is America. We're free here. Free to come and go as we please." His voice faded on his last words as three men, including Martin, came toward him. They grabbed him, pulled him aside, and dragged the struggling man toward the door, but he turned back over his shoulder to say, "I'll be back, Bimeler. You can't stop me." His last words were lost in the scuffle, but a smack on his horse's hind end sent the doctor, sprawled on the seat of his buggy, surging away.

Adelaide sank down beside Ilse. *I did not do my duty by her.* She should have explained about heat and purging to her as well. Brigit knew not to allow the doctor to treat her, but Gerda would do whatever the man ordered. *I was too quick to accept Ilse's assurance that she was recovering.* All to avoid Martin.

She had been wrong. Thoughts can cause sin.

— Twenty-six —

The sun splashed over her hands clutched in her lap, but still they felt cold. Benjamin sat beside her, his back straight and his jaw clenched. He'd accompanied her to the meeting house and, defying tradition—albeit the Society had no precedent for where to sit during an inquest—joined her on the women's side.

People crowded into the room, whispers of anticipation growing louder as excitement became palpable. Ignoring the swell of voices around her, Adelaide tried to concentrate on what she would say, but Simon's accusation from a week ago still hung in the air.

Tell the truth, Emma had said, but she had also cautioned Adelaide not to volunteer anything that she was not asked. Would she be able to answer the coroner's questions without implicating herself? Or her husband?

She dropped her head on her chest, closed her eyes, and drew into herself until the din of voices around her faded. A shiver of pride jolted her. Pride? How could she be proud of causing her community to question itself? All could be lost. Her town, her baby, her life, even. Whatever was the matter with her? She should be afraid, ashamed of bringing the law to their community, but instead she sat up straighter. She'd stood up for what was right. No matter the cost to herself. Regardless of the outcome, she'd remember this moment.

She came back with a start as the door opened. Murmuring quieted as twelve men proceeded to the front and arranged themselves on two benches aligned along the wall to Adelaide's right. Coroner Masterson followed and settled into Josef's chair behind the desk at the front. A man joined him, spread open a leather folder, and took out several sheets of paper. Constable Helling stood to the side, eyes surveying the room.

The coroner banged a gavel on the desk and called the proceedings to order. He introduced himself again and turned to the man seated next to him. "This is John Dickson. He's a clerk for Tuscarawas County," he said as the clerk opened an ink pot and laid a quill pen beside it. "He will record today's proceedings, including the testimony of witnesses who will be asked to read the account and sign it if they agree it is accurate.

"We're here today to examine the death of one Johanna Appelgate, a resident of the unincorporated town of Zoar in the County of Tuscarawas in the State of Ohio." He turned to the men in the jury seated to his left. "Please stand," he instructed, "and raise your right hand."

He read from a document the clerk handed him: "Do you solemnly swear or affirm, as the case may be, that you will diligently inquire into and true presentment make, according to the best of your understanding, how, in what manner and by whom the deceased person, who lies dead in the Zoar cemetery, came to her death, as the case may be, and deliver to me a true inquest thereof, according to such evidence as shall be laid before you? You may answer I do."

"I do," said the chorus of men.

"You may be seated."

He consulted his file. "Nathan Appelgate," he called.

Nathan rose and made his way to the front, shoulders bent, his massive arms at his side.

"State your name, sir."

"Nathan Appelgate."

"Raise your right hand. Do you swear to tell the truth, so help you God?"

Nathan looked to Josef.

"Is there a problem, Mister Appelgate?"

"It's our belief, sir," Josef said, standing, "that swearing an oath is wrong."

"So you're telling me that no one in this room will swear to tell the truth?"

"We speak the truth at all times, sir," Josef said.

Coroner Masterson conferred with his clerk, who found a paper in his folder and handed it to the coroner.

"Mister Appelgate, my clerk tells me that you are similar to the Quakers in that belief, and we've made accommodation for them. He assures me that we can do the same for you. Anyone who objects to swearing an oath can simply affirm the truth of what you'll say. Will you do that, sir?"

Nathan glanced at Josef, who nodded.

"Please repeat after me," the coroner continued. "I, Nathan Appelgate, do declare in the presence of Almighty God the witness of the truth of what I say."

Nathan repeated the statement.

"You may be seated." He motioned to a chair beside him that faced the room.

"You are the father of Johanna Appelgate, aged sixteen February last. Is that correct?"

"Yes, sir," Nathan answered.

"You accompanied me, Constable Helling, and these men of the jury Friday last to the cemetery where your daughter's body was disinterred."

Nathan nodded.

"You must speak up, sir, for the clerk to record your words."

"Yes."

"And did you identify said body as that of your daughter, Johanna?"

Nathan swiped a calloused hand over his face as if to erase the vision of Johanna's dead body. "Yes, sir."

"I understand your daughter lived above the dairy. Did you have occasion to speak with her the day of her death?"

"No."

"Do you know any reason she might have been near the river on that night?"

"No, sir."

"The court thanks you for your help, sir, and offers condolence for your loss."

Nathan sat there a moment as if he didn't know what to do until the coroner said, "You may leave, sir."

"Adelaide Bechtmann," Coroner Masterson called, his eyes skimming the audience.

Her pride slipped away as quickly as it had come. Shame flushed her body now. Shame at bringing the law to their town. Shame at thinking her husband disloyal as surely as she herself had been.

Helga reached from the row behind to pat her on the arm. She gripped her skirts in her hands and stepped in front of Benjamin, who turned to the side to let her pass.

After asking her to state her name, the coroner read the affirmation to her, and she dutifully repeated it. He motioned her to the chair Nathan had vacated. Martin glared at her from his seat on the aisle a few rows from the front.

Adelaide averted her eyes to examine a timber along the ceiling. She had never noticed that about midway it bent to the right.

"Missus Bechtmann," the coroner said. "Did you hear me?"

"Yes, sir." *I must keep my mind on what he asks.*

"I understand that you found the body of Johanna Appelgate. Would you explain how that occurred?"

"I found her in the river."

"Go on."

"She was face down in the water, caught under a willow tree that had fallen in the storm. I pulled her out, but it was too late." Someone hiccupped in the back, and Adelaide looked up to see Jakob drop his head to his chest, his shoulders shaking.

"The tree knocked her down into the water?" the coroner asked.

"I wouldn't know that, sir. I wasn't there."

"Ah," he said. "You're the village midwife, is that correct?"

"Yes, sir."

"And you're also some kind of healer, they've told me." He glanced toward the jury where Simon gave him a nod.

What had Simon told him about her? That she had killed Johanna? "I'm an herbalist. I give my patients healing herbs."

He consulted his notes. "I've heard that you said it wasn't an accident. You think someone drowned her?"

"No, sir."

"No? But I thought you said someone killed her. Explain yourself, Missus Bechtmann."

"She was dead when she went in the water."

Murmurs rippled through the crowd.

"How do you know that?"

She nodded an apology to Helga and turned back to the coroner. "A drowning person breathes in water that fills the lungs instead of air. Without air, one cannot breathe. When a drowning victim is rescued, the water he inhaled comes out through his mouth. If little or no water emerges, then the person did not drown. When I lifted Johanna up, no water came out of her mouth. So she did not drown."

"Let me understand this. You think the girl died before she went into the water?"

"I'm certain of it."

Chattering filled the room.

He banged his gavel for quiet. "If she didn't drown, how do you think she died?"

Adelaide stared down at her hands. *If I say she was poisoned, I implicate myself. If I keep silent, I'm lying, if only by omission.* She raised her head. "I think she was poisoned."

The coroner gaveled for silence. "I will empty the room if you don't quiet down." He cleared his throat and turned back to Adelaide. "Why do you think she was poisoned? I saw the body. I've seen poisoning victims. One, I recall, his skin turned bright red. Mad, too, they said he was before he died. His wife killed him with jimson weed berries she made into tea. There wasn't any evidence of poisoning on Miss Applegate as far as I could see. In fact," he said, coughing, "we, ah, couldn't tell much."

The body had begun its deterioration! Grave wax, the soapy substance that forms first, probably covered her exposed body.

Insects? No, not since she was beneath ground. Adelaide swallowed and deliberately pushed the image away. "Nonetheless, I think someone poisoned her. And then when she was dead, he threw her in the river."

Shuffling at the back drew their attention. Jakob stumbled out the door, letting it bang behind him.

"What poison could have killed her, Missus Bechtmann?"

This is a trap. If she explained what medicines could kill, she will have told him that she knew how to kill her. If she says that someone had been into her stores, he'll think she's just trying to cover up for herself.

Only the sound of the clerk's scratching pen broke the silence.

"Any number of substances can be poison, sir."

"But you, you're a midwife and herbalist, you say. You give plants for healing, but many of those can kill, too, can't they?" he asked, his tone mildly inquisitive.

"Many can be poisonous if taken in sufficient amounts."

"What are those? Missus Bechtmann, are you being deliberately obtuse? You are not on trial here. This is only an inquiry into her death, and it behooves this court to have all the facts to consider. Now, from your knowledge of plants, tell this court what you think poisoned Johanna Appelgate."

"Several groups of plants are especially toxic. The glyco-sides—foxglove, lily of the valley, and oleander. Or the alkaloids. Deadly nightshade, henbane, jimson weed—as you mentioned—mandrake, monkshood, and, oh yes, hemlock."

"Thank you, Missus Bechtmann."

Adelaide thought she was finished but as she started to rise, he asked, "Did you treat Johanna Appelgate for any ills or give her any medicines?"

Here it was. The question she had been dreading. Her eyes sought Benjamin's, and she saw the pleading in them. If only she were anywhere else but here.

"Yes," she said at last.

A ripple of gasps spread through the assembly.

There she'd done it. Now they'd all believe Simon was correct about her. She felt Simon's eyes on her, and it took all of her effort not to look at him. Proud, he was, but she wouldn't give him the satisfaction of seeing her cowed by him. She lifted her head and stared straight ahead. "She came to me for help with a woman's ailment, and I gave her a remedy. The day before her death."

"And what was that remedy, Missus Bechtmann?"

"A combination of blue cohosh, pennyroyal, and tansy commonly used for women's problems."

"Ah, yes." He cleared his throat. "To the best of your knowledge, did she take your remedy?"

Should she admit that Jakob said she had? No, she had no direct knowledge that what he said was true. "I did not see her use them. And she said they were for another girl."

"So you cannot say if she took your, ah, remedy or if it had anything to do with her death."

"I can say that the amount I gave her would not have been fatal."

"Ahh." He stared down the papers in front of him for a moment. "Do you have any evidence to support your claim that she was poisoned?"

"No, sir."

"And do you have any idea who might have wanted her dead?"

A memory from a month ago came back to her. Johanna dawdling at the door to the cabinet shop, face aglow, and her own overwhelming urge to grab the girl away from her husband, a man with too much sympathy for her. But even if he'd sinned with her—God help her for even thinking that—he would never have harmed her. *I wouldn't even be thinking this if I hadn't seen them talking the night she died, and that's all it was. Talk.*

"All I know for certain is that she was dead first and then put in the water. Whatever killed her, I do not know."

The coroner nodded to her. "You are dismissed."

She left without looking at Martin, but she could feel his eyes on her as she made her way back to her seat.

"Ilse Forster," Coroner Masterson called. The clerk leaned over and whispered to the coroner who then spoke. "I understand Missus Forster died recently, but that Martin Guenther can speak to the deceased's work."

Martin rose from his seat, pulled his loose-fitting jacket together, and strode heavy-footed to the front. August had been wrong. Martin wasn't a juror but, just as troublesome for her, he was about to testify.

After requesting that Martin state his name and eliciting his promise to tell the truth, the coroner asked him, "What is your position in the community?"

"Cow herd boss," he said, head erect. "I'm in charge of feeding, birthing, and caring for our more than one hundred milk cows."

"You also supervise the work of the girls who work in the dairy, don't you?"

"Ilse Forster was the dairy mother, but I had to oversee her work."

"Why was that?"

"Not consistent enough, she wasn't. These girls need a firm hand with all the work they have to do, and she didn't always make them keep at it."

"So you had to watch out that they did."

"Yes, sir."

"So you knew the deceased, Johanna Appelgate?"

"Yes, sir, she was one of the girls worked for me."

"Do you know any reason she would be out that night?"

"None, sir."

Martin was dismissed.

"Call Doctor Hertel," the coroner said, and Constable Helling strode through the room to the back and opened the door.

From his seat on the front row Josef, along with everyone else, turned to see the man, who only the day before he had thrown out of Zoar, striding toward the front. Josef started to rise, but the coroner motioned him back down.

Unlike the Separatists, Doctor Hertel was willing to swear to tell the truth. "So help me God," he added with a lift of his chin.

"You sir, are a trained medical man, is that correct?" the coroner asked.

The doctor stroked his graying goatee. "I am, sir, unlike—"

"No need to get ahead of ourselves. Did you know the deceased, Johanna Appelgate?"

"Well, no." He coughed into linen handkerchief and returned it to his pocket.

"You never treated her for any illness or condition?"

"No, sir."

The coroner shuffled through the papers his clerk had spread on the desk until he found the one he wanted. "The girl was found in the Tuscarawas River on Friday week last. You knew about that, didn't you?"

The doctor glanced at Simon, who remained impassive. "I heard, yes, sir."

"There has been testimony that she might have been poisoned. Do you know anything about that?"

"All I know is that if that man," he pointed to Josef, "or that woman," he said, a pudgy finger outstretched toward Adelaide, "gave her anything, that's what killed her."

Josef leapt to his feet. "He knows nothing about what we do," he shouted. "A woman died yesterday because he—"

"Mister Bimeler, I must ask you to be seated. You are not the witness. If you have something to say about the matter before this court, you will have ample opportunity." He turned back to the doctor. "Do you, sir, have any direct knowledge that either Mister Bimeler or Missus Bechtmann gave Johanna Appelgate poison?"

"Not directly I—"

Coroner Masterson raised his hand. "We have heard testimony that the deceased may have taken a mixture of herbs." He paused to consult the clerk's list. "Blue cohosh, pennyroyal, and tansy. If she had, could it have killed her? To the best of your medical knowledge."

"Ahem." The doctor tugged his waistcoat down over his abdomen. "I, myself, don't use any of those old-fashioned plant remedies."

"But, as far as you know, could the mixture Missus Bechtmann gave the deceased be fatal?"

"That'd be unlikely," he admitted. "But if you'd allowed me to dissect—"

"Please, sir, the girl's family is in the room," the coroner said and swiped a hand in front of his face. "One more question, Doctor. If the girl had been poisoned, would you have had any way to detect that? Even had I given permission for you to examine her, ah, more extensively?"

The doctor shuffled in his seat. "Well, I don't know, do I? Depends on what it was."

"That will be all."

As he stood Doctor Hertel looked aside to Simon in the jury. Simon lifted his shoulders in a slight shrug.

We wouldn't even be here debating how Johanna died if it weren't for the two of them colluding to discredit her and Josef, she thought. What did the doctor want with her community? Our business, apparently. He didn't know Josef then. He had flaws, he readily confessed, but change his mind or admit he was wrong? Never.

The man huffed his way to the back where he took a seat.

The coroner turned to Josef. "Do you, sir, have any direct knowledge pertaining to the death of Johanna Appelgate?"

Josef stood and balanced himself on the back of the bench. "No, but, as the agent-general in charge of this Society, I would like to speak to the court."

Coroner Masterson sighed but nodded his acquiescence, and Josef duly promised to be truthful.

"What do you have to say pertaining to the matter of Johanna Appelgate's death?" the coroner asked him.

Josef leaned his elbows on the chair arms and lifted his body to the side, wincing as he arranged his lame leg. "First," he said, "we are pacifists. We don't believe in killing even in the name of war or, more correctly, especially in the name of war. Secondly, no one would have any reason to want our Johanna dead. Her death was simply a sad accident."

Josef returned to his seat, and the coroner asked, "Does anyone else here have any information concerning Johanna Appelgate's death?" Greeted by low murmurs but no other response, the coroner turned to his clerk. "Do you have the testimony of the witnesses prepared for signing?"

"Yes, sir." He laid out several sheets of paper on the desk and wiped his pen on a cloth.

Coroner Masterson laid them aside and turned to the jury. He read from a document: "You have heard the testimony offered here, and it is now my charge to you to sequester yourselves and return when you all and together agree on the cause and manner in the death of Johanna Appelgate. You must decide if Johanna Appelgate died of felony, mischance or accident, and if of felony, who were the principals or accessories, in what manner, by what means and with what instruments, with all the circumstances which may come to your knowledge, and if by mischance or accident, whether by the act of man and whether by hurt, fall, stroke, drowning or otherwise. Also to inquire whether she was killed in the same place where the body was found, and if elsewhere, by whom and how the body was brought there, and all other circumstances relating to the said death.

"Do you understand your charge?"

The men mumbled their assent.

"You may now retire."

The men filed out, faces solemn. Passing her, Simon shot her a glance, and she returned the stare.

The coroner called the witnesses to the front to read and sign their statements. Then they waited.

Outside a light mist turned to drizzle, gently at first, until it built to a crescendo of fury that hammered the roof, pounding a staccato on its tiles. Rivulets of sweat trickled down between Adelaide's breasts. She gripped the bench and willed herself still. Imprisoned in the room where she had found comfort, if not her deity, she could not now escape, run away from her fears. Even if she desired it, the elders would stop her, demand that she remain until the verdict released her.

If it did.

Martin shifted his gaze to her. She stared back. It was as if the air had cleared and made him visible, real. His black hair, longer now, flopped over his eyes, but it couldn't conceal the man beneath. A man who, no matter how much he avowed celibacy, was no more holy than any other human. His behavior was dishonest, certainly, but the only person he deceived was himself.

Whatever could be taking so long? Was Simon trying to convince the others that Johanna died by her hand? But these men knew her. She'd delivered their babies and tended their children. Other than Simon's accusation, they had no cause to blame her. Nor did they have any evidence. Which they didn't need to bring her to trial, according to Mister Bastest. Surely they will not find cause to accuse her. Her thoughts, however rational, failed to assure her.

The rain stopped, but still the jury had not returned. Coroner Masterson sent his constable out to see to the their deliberations. "They say they need more time," Constable Helling reported a few minutes later.

"Then I will temporarily dismiss this court. We will reconvene when the jury has reached a verdict. In the meantime, no one is to leave the town limits of this village." He banged the gavel, gathered his papers, and rose from the desk. Constable Helling followed him out.

Word spread rapidly that the jury had returned, and soon the townspeople left their work and crowded back into the room, grown warmer after the rain. Adelaide and Benjamin sat side by side on the same bench they had occupied earlier in the day.

Noise hushed as the jury filed back in. Not one of the men looked at Adelaide. The coroner, his clerk, and the constable resumed their places.

"Gentlemen," Coroner Masterson asked, "have you reached a verdict?"

Simon stood. "We have, sir."

"What find you?"

Simon cleared his throat. "We find that the deceased, Johanna Appelgate, died by accidental—"

A moan rose from the back, and the coroner banged his gavel on the desk as someone led Jakob away.

"Accidental drowning," Simon finished.

Relief flooded Adelaide such as that she had experienced when Olivia had finally slipped free of her body. Elation, yes, but worry still. The same as when she took Olivia's tiny body in her arms and didn't know what to do next.

The coroner's voice broke into her reverie. "Do you all and together agree on the cause and manner in the death of Johanna Appelgate?"

"Yes," the men said collectively.

Coroner Masterson addressed the assembly. "I hereby declare that the aforenamed deceased, Johanna Appelgate, died by accident. The cause of death was drowning." He banged his gavel and, as the clerk gathered their papers, he came around the desk to speak to Josef. Both men nodded and shook hands before the coroner and his staff departed.

— Twenty-seven —

Election day dawned bright and crisp, a day on the cusp between spring and summer. Now that the inquest was behind them, Adelaide's neighbors had gone back to work with some regret, she thought, as she watched out the door. Even Josef's mare shuffled more slowly as she hauled their leader toward the meeting house where voting was due to commence.

Dresses, aprons, pants, shirts, kerchiefs, and bedclothes lay crumpled in a basket, her flatirons cold on the shelf. She should have dampened the clothes last night, but fatigue and disinterest discouraged her.

She sighed. It was official: she wasn't believed. But she wasn't going to jail. Or hang. So why didn't she feel free?

No one knew the truth! No matter what she found out now about Johanna's killing, no one could be brought to justice. Once the coroner ruled Johanna's death an accident, Josef explained, then no accusation for murder could be entered. Ever.

All her efforts to discover how Johanna died had come to naught.

She slammed one iron and then the other onto the stovetop,

dumped the basket's contents onto a chair, and spread a cloth over the table. At least ironing would keep her hands busy.

Someone knew how Johanna died and how she came to be in the river. But who? She knew something, but what? She couldn't remember. Did it have to do with Johanna's death? Even that she couldn't be certain.

Her thoughts circled around and around until finally she gave up. The answer would come, she often found, when she was ready for it.

She spit on her finger and touched it to an iron's flat bottom with a satisfying hiss.

And now her neighbors thought she had been wrong. Would they trust themselves to her care? At the least, uncertainty would taint her work. A look, a nod, or a glance between them would trigger her insecurity. Then she'd make a mistake.

She couldn't let it be. She had to find out what happened to Johanna to prove, for herself, that she wasn't to blame. Her life as a healer was at stake.

It wasn't until late in the afternoon that Adelaide finally had time to go to the meeting house. Simon stood outside greeting one and all with enthusiasm and good cheer. He even gave her a quick smile as she ducked inside, his allegation that she had killed Johanna forgotten now that the inquest was over. She doubted he would have the grace to apologize to her. Whether he was still determined to keep her from attending Maria, she didn't know and she didn't intend to ask him. With fortune, he would be away when Maria's time came.

Gerda was in charge, as usual, Josef overseeing. He gave her a nod but no smile. Would he ever forgive her for causing the authorities to invade their Society? Maybe now that they were gone, the community would return to work and soon the inquest would only be a memory. She had only done what was right. Wasn't that what he admonished them time and time again? To search one's soul and to follow one's conscience?

"Move along," Gerda ordered.

By this time tomorrow they would know who had been elected trustee. In spite of Simon insisting that Josef poorly managed the Society's money or even hoarded it, Simon's words probably appealed to only a few discontented folks. Besides, she didn't think Simon was all that much liked. When it came right down to it, people vote for those they like. Nathan, both well-known and well-liked, would surely be reelected trustee.

But, unless she acted, they still wouldn't know who killed Johanna no matter how many days elapsed.

"Pay attention," Gerda said and handed her a ballot. "Shouldn't be voting if you can't listen," she murmured under her breath.

Adelaide ignored the jibe. The woman couldn't keep her or anyone else from voting. It was a core principle: equality for everyone.

She studied the ballot. It listed three entries: yes or no on the Articles of Incorporation; select one of the two candidates for trustee; and, check the box that indicated she agreed with the slate nominated for the standing committee.

She voted yes for the Articles, and named Nathan as her choice for trustee. She pondered the list of five men running for the standing committee. No women? What would happen if she crossed out a man's name and wrote in a woman's? Nothing. They might all be equal, but the difference didn't extend to serving as one of their leaders. Shrugging, she dropped her ballot in the wooden chest.

The day had turned warm, but a light breeze kept the heat at bay. Standing in line, she'd thought of what to do next. She needed just a bit more information, and only one person could provide it.

A few moments later she entered the horse barn to see Jakob shoeing a horse in her stall. She waited until he looked up and started to speak until he put a finger to his lips. He let the horse's hoof down gently, then inched himself around the wall, and slipped through the door. He shut it quickly and slid the bar into place as hooves crashed into door.

"She'll calm down soon," he said as he pulled a worn handkerchief out of the pocket of his pants and wiped his face and neck.

"How's your burn?"

He opened his hand to her. Tiny blisters sprinkled the two lines on his palm. "It's better." He flexed his fingers, then waved away the musty odor of horse flesh. "You came to see me?"

"I want to ask you something."

The horse kicked the door again, but she had lost enthusiasm for it.

"There's something I can't figure out," she said after they had settled themselves on a bench outside.

He pulled at his wisp of a beard. "Do we have to talk about this?"

"Yes, Jakob, we do." Adelaide used her most formidable tone, the one recalcitrant patients required. "You and Johanna had some plan to be together." She waited as he seemed to consider her implied question.

"It wasn't easy. Not with Martin working her all the time."

"So how did you do it?"

"Once we figured it out, no one was the wiser." He pointed toward the main road through town. "You can't see it from here, but the window in the blacksmith shop, well, from there you can see the dairy. The girls sleep upstairs and the window on the gable end faces the window of the shop. If either of us thought we could sneak out that night, we closed the shutters on the window. If the other one could meet also, that person closed the shutters. Clever, wasn't it?"

"I wouldn't have thought of that."

"Neither did anyone else."

"But how did you manage with Nathan there?"

"I'd be sure to work late after he left." He gave her a rueful smile. "Of course that wasn't difficult since I took so long with my work anyway."

"Then what? You must have had a place to meet." A private place, Adelaide thought to herself as a blush spread up her neck.

He smiled, blue eyes dancing. "You know that outbuilding near the cemetery?"

"Where the night watchman was when the hotel fire started?"

"It's so far out and no one uses it anymore. No one ever thought to look for us there."

"Did you plan to meet that night?"

"No, I wanted to have it out with Welby." He slapped his knees with his kerchief. "Get him to stay away from her before he convinced her to leave. I knew it was him. I knew that's who she meant when she said someone would take her away if I didn't. There wasn't much time before he left, and I was afraid she'd go with him. Maybe if I hadn't been so stubborn, I could have kept her safe."

"Stop, Jakob. You didn't harm her. It's not your fault."

"Yes, but still—"

"Stop blaming yourself for something you didn't do. Please. You have to for your own sake." When he looked unconvinced, Adelaide

went on. "You have your whole life ahead of you and nothing you
or I or anyone else can do or could have changed what happened.
You must get on with living. Because there are lots of us who care
about you."

Suddenly she realized that was true. He irritated her with his
unruly grieving, unused as she was to such outbursts, but the young
man had just lost his beloved and his unborn child. She smiled her
understanding.

"Thank you, Adelaide. I'm trying. I'm back working and..."
He looked as if he might say more but instead he stood and gave
Adelaide a hand up.

She left him at the corner, intending to head back home, but
changed her mind. Someone must have lured Johanna out that
night, someone who knew about their signal. Who else knew about
their rendezvous? One of the other dairy maids? Any one of them
could have told someone else.

The blacksmith shop was only a short walk away and as soon as
it came into view she could see that its window faced Main Street in
sight of the dairy's high gable window. Almost anyone could have
learned about how the lovers planned to meet, gone to the shop,
closed the shutters, and then waited for Johanna.

One mystery solved.

Adelaide continued up the road to the dairy. Beyond it the cow
barn doors remained closed so the cattle must still be out to pasture.
Shadows spreading across the opening told her that it wouldn't be
long before Martin and his boys would return with them for the
evening milking. That also meant the dairy maids would be called
back to work. She hurried her steps.

Inside the dairy was empty. Pungent rounds of cheese sat aging
on shelves to one side, but the kettle used to make more was empty,

as were the butter churns. A corn broom stood upright by the door, the floor swept clean.

Adelaide started up the stairs to the loft above, but when she was about half way up a soft giggle stopped her.

"Hush," a girlish voice whispered.

"It's me, Adelaide," she called up the steps. Brigit and another dairy maid poked their heads out of the opening.

"Hurry," Brigit ordered with a look toward the pasture. "Before he returns. She gave Adelaide a hand up and pulled her into the loft. "We found it," Brigit said, waving a richly-colored bonnet in the air and promptly plopping it onto her head. Crimson, plum and lush green ribbons shone with iridescence. The other dairy maid—the one who'd been churning butter the last time Adelaide saw her—scrunched back in the corner as if guilty to be found there.

"Look at this," Brigit said, knotting the gold-tasseled ties under her chin. "Wait till Mister Welby sees me. He'll forget Johanna." She twirled herself around so they could see it from all sides. Adelaide didn't tell her that her admirer had already left town.

"Where did you find it?" Adelaide asked her.

"I didn't steal it if that's what you're thinking." She ripped the bonnet off her head and sent her cap flying. She retrieved her cap and set it atop thick, tawny hair loosed from its pins. Adelaide continued to stare at Brigit until she said, "Oh, all right. It was here, under her pillow, and that's the truth."

"So she didn't wear it the night she, uh, died?"

"What?" Brigit looked at her friend. "Did she?"

"You know she did," the girl whispered, her head sunk into her shoulders.

"Oh, all right. She did, but after it was just here and that's the truth," Brigit said again.

"Someone brought it back here after she died?" Adelaide didn't remember seeing it near the riverbank where she'd found Johanna's body.

"I told you. It was just here." Brigit stamped across the floor and said, "We'll just see what Mister Welby thinks of me now." With that she levered herself out the opening and disappeared down the steps, the bonnet still clutched in her hand.

The other girl pushed herself up and brushed dust and straw off her skirt. She smiled shyly at Adelaide. "I'm Melanie," she said, dipping her head. Straw-filled pallets marched in rows across the floor, their coverlets tucked neatly around them except for one at the end that had been stripped bare. "That was Johanna's," the girl said softly. "But the bonnet," she smiled, "was really their mother's brought from Germany. Too fancy for Zoar, Frau Appelgate said."

"So the man from Cleveland didn't give it to Johanna?"

"That's just the tale she told Brigit. It made her frightful mad. I tried to tell Brigit that, but she believed Johanna."

"You miss her, don't you?"

"Whenever she was around, she made everything a game. Even work was more fun with her about."

"I heard she didn't want to work too much."

"Oh, she was all right. She grumbled about getting up in the dark, but she worked once she got started. Did you know she could sing? She had a beautiful voice, and she knew all these songs from Germany." Melanie giggled, her cheeks flaming. "Some of them weren't very nice."

"That made it all the more fun, didn't it?"

"You understand? You're not so old after all."

Adelaide sighed. She supposed that at twenty-six, she seemed old to Melanie who was maybe fourteen, if that. She pulled a couple of stools over near the window and motioned for Melanie to join her. While the girl was arranging her skirt, Adelaide rotated the shutters.

Melanie giggled.

"So you knew about the signal? Between Johanna and Jakob."

"It was so romantic, don't you think?" The girl leaned back against the wall. "I hope when I meet someone, he's just like Jakob."

"Who else knew?"

The girl jerked upright. "Why everyone. We all knew about it."

"I mean besides you girls. Did Herr Guenther know?"

"Oh, no, we wouldn't tell him. He wouldn't have allowed it."

"I want you to try to remember the night Johanna died."

Melanie nodded, her mouth turned down.

"Think carefully now. Did Jakob signal for Johanna that night? And did she go to meet him?"

"Yesss. But he wouldn't have hurt her, he loved her. Besides, she drowned."

"And all of you girls were here all night? Brigit, too?"

"'A course. Where would we go?"

With that, she had learned all she could from the dairy maid. Back on the road, she pondered what had happened after Johanna left for her supposed rendezvous with Jakob. Had she made it to the outbuilding or had someone stopped her, convinced her to go elsewhere, and then killed her before dumping her body in the river? But who?

The cows in the distance headed toward the barn, their brownish-red bodies swaying as they walked. Martin wouldn't be far behind. Adelaide quickened her pace. She didn't need his challenging her about why she'd been in the dairy long after the morning's milk had been distributed. Since voting continued at the meeting house and she didn't want anyone asking where she was going, she headed toward the path that led to the river. Farther along it wound its way past the lake and then uphill and away from prying eyes.

Before she could make good her escape, Brigit shouted from behind her. "It's for real, this time. It's Maria's time."

Adelaide's throat clenched. No, she couldn't let her fear overtake her. This was Maria. Helga's daughter. And she couldn't let Helga lose another. Not if she could help it. "You're sure?"

Gulping air, Brigit nodded. Johanna's bonnet flopped on her back, the ties caught in her collar.

Adelaide gathered her skirts to run toward home and her medical bag.

"Terrible pain she's in. Not like last time. She says she wants to push but I told her not yet, not till you tell her to. That's right, isn't it?"

At home, she ran into her workroom and stopped to think about what she'd need. Several clean pads of cloth. She'd told Maria to have some ready, but she might need more if Maria's bleeding became excessive. She spilled some cranesbill geranium into a tin cup and slammed the lid tight. It might help stop the bleeding, but she hoped it wouldn't come to that. Emma had told her that if a mother starts to bleed, sometimes nothing will stop it.

Should she take laudanum? Commonly used for pain by medical men, it slowed the birth process, which inevitably led to a lengthy, difficult birth. She could imagine how Doctor Hertel would handle an hysterical mother in the throes of childbirth.

Maria's fright about dying worried her. At the least she probably would tighten up internally, the exact opposite of how she needed to use her body to aid in the birth. In the end, she added the laudanum. She might need it to calm her if nothing else.

"Hurry," Brigit called to her, bouncing on her toes. "Isn't this exciting?" she asked when they were back on the road heading toward the inn. "I can't wait. My first niece or nephew. And don't worry about Simon. He's in town with the voting and I talked Emmett—he's Simon's apprentice—into waiting to go for the doctor until you tell him to."

Before they had stepped off the bridge and onto the path uphill to the inn, they heard Maria's screams. "My God! Who's with her?" Adelaide's bag flapped on her back as she picked up speed.

"The girls were when I left, but they were scared. They didn't know what to do."

"Aren't there any other women coming?"

"She said Simon wouldn't let her have them. He said only the doctor."

They passed Emmett sitting on the steps, his face pained. "Shouldn't I go for the doctor now? She sounds fearful bad sick."

"Let me see how she is and we'll let you know." They let themselves in and she sent Brigit for a basin of water and soap while she ran up the steps to Maria's room.

Another scream rose into a crescendo of pain. Maria's back arched off the bed, her chin stretched upward, blue neck veins distended. Adelaide let the scream finish and then grabbed both of her hands as Maria's head dropped back onto the pillow.

"Maria. Open your eyes. Listen to me."

Maria squinted through lowered lids.

"Wide. Open them wide."

She peeked a look at Adelaide. "I didn't know it'd be this bad. I just catch my breath and then it comes again."

"I'm going to remind you how to breathe," she said, washing her hands in the basin Brigit brought. "Close your eyes, no, not squeeze them, gently let your eyelids rest together as if they're sleeping. Good. Take a deep breath and let it out. No, slowly. A slow breath in and a slow breath out."

"But," Maria said, her back beginning its arch.

"Out. Breathe out," Adelaide demanded and Maria's breath took over the scream. "Oh," she said when it was over, "that was better. I'm sorry. I know it's wrong what he's doing but I'm to blame, I know I am, maybe if I could help more—" The last word dragged itself into another pain.

When it was over, Adelaide asked, "What's wrong? You said that before."

"Something to do with currency, I think. Maybe," she added after a moment.

"To pay Doctor Hertel?"

Brigit stepped in. "For certain, that's what you mean," but Maria shook her head.

"I'm going to examine you now," Adelaide said. "I'll be quick." Before Maria could object, Adelaide raised her gown to her waist, lowered her britches, and slipped her hand into the woman's birth canal. She smiled as she pulled her hand out. "It won't be much longer now," she told Maria already in the throes of another pain.

"What are you doing here?" Simon stood in the doorway, eyebrows knitted into a scowl. "Where's Emmett? Why didn't you send for the doctor?"

Maria's face contorted into a grimace as Adelaide reminded her, "Breathe out, breathe out, let all the pain out with your breath."

"I asked you a question," Simon said, advancing toward the bed, but when he saw Maria's gown bunched around her waist and her britches lying to the side, he scooted backward and bumped into Brigit.

"Out!" Adelaide commanded. "If you want a healthy baby, you keep away from her." She had had enough of Simon's accusations and the doctor's abuse. It was time to demand her right to be with any woman who wanted her in her hour of travail. No man, even the child's father, was going to keep her away.

Simon backed out, and Brigit's eyes widened at Adelaide's boldness.

Adelaide ignored her to check on Maria's progress. She stood back and asked Brigit to help her pile pillows behind her sister's back. She examined her once more, then smiled. "It's time."

Brigit squealed.

"Hold onto her hands," she told Brigit as she moved to the foot of the bed and bent over to reach between Maria's outstretched legs. "Push, my friend, push with all your might."

Maria groaned with the effort.

"Almost," Adelaide told her. "He or she has lots of hair." Another push and the head emerged in a swish of fluid. Adelaide grabbed a cloth, wiped the baby's face and mouth but the infant made no sound. *Please, God, let it be alive.* "Push again." She maneuvered the infant's shoulders through the widened birth canal and pulled its body and legs free. Only the cord remained attached to Maria.

Adelaide laid the baby across her arm and smacked its bottom. A lusty cry and she let out her breath. She lifted the infant up so Maria could see. "A girl. You have a perfect baby girl," she told the weary mother.

"She's beautiful," Brigit said.

Adelaide laid the baby on the cloth between Maria's legs, tied and cut the cord, and cleansed the infant, swaddling her in the blanket Maria had knitted for her. When she placed the baby in her mother's arms and watched Maria cuddling her newborn, a sense of wellbeing washed over her. This is where she should be, the work she was called to do.

While Brigit cooed over the infant, who had latched onto to her mother's nipple with relish, Adelaide told Maria to push once more to expel the afterbirth. She cleaned up Maria and bound her with cloths.

Outside the room, Adelaide sent Simon in to see his baby and met Emmett outdoors. "I hid in the bushes so's Herr Huttmann couldn't find me. She's aright now, isn't she? Her sickness all over?"

Adelaide ruffled the boy's hair. "She's fine, and they have a beautiful baby girl."

He frowned. "I think *Herr* wanted a boy."

"Well, he wasn't in charge, was he?"

"I suppose not," Emmett said, ducking his head. She had come too close to talking about forbidden subjects for the fifteen-year-old.

Her body ached with exhaustion but she would finish her earlier errand, no matter how weary she was.

Twenty-eight

At the top of the hill bordering the cemetery, she paused. The sun was setting behind the trees just as it had the evening they buried Johanna. She'd been troubled then; she was troubled now. Someone had killed Johanna and dumped her in the river. But who? This was the land she knew, people she knew. How could a Separatist be a murderer?

To her right stood the outbuilding—little more than a shack—where Jakob and Johanna had met. Splintered graying logs left gaps between them, and a makeshift door sagged on rusty hinges.

The night watchman. That's what she'd been trying to remember.

Adelaide pulled at the door but it listed at an angle and wouldn't move more than a few inches. She tugged harder and the door gave way, a bird flying at her in its haste to escape. Cobwebs dangled from the door frame, and she shoved them aside.

Josef had said he thought that Nathan and August were on watch the night Johanna died, and she realized how he could have been confused. When August admitted he hadn't served his watch that night, he'd given her the answer.

Dusty light spread across the dirt floor and revealed a worn coverlet, woven in Zoar blue, bunched on top of a pile of straw in the corner, stubble poking up through moth-eaten holes. Adelaide pulled a cobweb away from her mouth. She tugged the coverlet off the straw, releasing a flurry of insects that she waved away. She kicked at the straw and sneezed as dust rose in the air.

The door slammed behind her.

"Who's there?" she yelled, jumping to the door. She pushed but it wouldn't move. "Whoever's out there, you'd better open this door. This minute."

Were some youngsters, freed from their chores, having fun at her expense?

Her stomach grumbled. She hadn't eaten since dinner at noon, and it was long past suppertime. *When I don't come home, someone will come to look for me. But up here?*

She squinted at the wood. Scratches? Slumping against the wall, she realized what had happened. She had wondered why Johanna's fingers had splinters in them. Whoever poisoned her had left her to die in here. Alone. Trying to scratch her way out.

Footsteps sounded outside.

"I'm in here!" She pounded on the door with her fists, slowing as the person walked away. Why? Why would anyone leave her here? She sank to the floor. Abandoned again. Strange. She couldn't remember her father's face. Only his back as he trudged up the hill out of town. He never looked back.

This won't do, she admonished herself.

The only reason someone would try to keep her here was if he murdered Johanna and thought he'd left incriminating evidence behind.

With the scant light seeping through the cracks, she knelt to see if she could find anything to implicate Johanna's killer. She shook handfuls of straw but only dust fell away.

She sat back against the wall, her hands beside her. What did she feel? Strands of something. Hair? No, too coarse. She lifted them to a crack in the wall. Golden, shimmering strands glinted in the light. Adelaide fingered them, releasing the silky threads that had been twisted together in a manner similar to the way ropes were made. But this cord wasn't strong enough to hold anything more than a wisp of fabric. What was it? A part of clothing? Or a blanket? It felt like silk, but the Separatists never used anything this fine. Johanna's bonnet. Part of the tassel from her bonnet.

Somehow in her struggle to get out, she'd torn the tassels. When the killer returned for her body, he remembered the bonnet but missed the remnants. But what did that mean? That Johanna wore the bonnet that night? She'd learned that much from Brigit and Melanie. So Johanna's killer had returned it.

In the waning light, Adelaide continued to search the ground, spreading pieces of straw apart to see if she could find any other signs of her killer's presence. "Ah ha," she cried, a scrap of paper in her hand. She unfolded it to feel dried residue inside. She rubbed the powder between her fingers. Dust. She sniffed her hand. Deadly nightshade. Belladonna.

Dizziness threatened to topple her, but she held onto the floor until it passed.

That's what had been taken from her stores. Small doses calmed fluttery hearts and stomach spasms and, in dire cases, alleviated desperate pain. But too much, as everyone knew, could be fatal.

A hiss of wind and an acrid smell.

Fire!

She stumbled to her feet as smoke curled around the edges of the door. She pushed at it but snatched her hand away from the heat. Smoke burst through a crack in the wall and scorched her throat. Fear roared in her ears. If she didn't escape right now she'd be caught inside as surely as if in a cage.

The coverlet. She dropped to her knees, eyes burning, and crawled over to it to drag it behind her to the door. She threw the coverlet over the door, momentarily confining the smoke, but it quickly saturated the material and ignited bits of straw that still clung to the cloth. Even so she shoved against the covered door with as much force as she could muster. It didn't move. Flames licked the door frame.

Choking, she hurried to the back of the cabin as far away from the flames as she could and shoved her mouth and nose into a crack and sucked in. Cool air filled her lungs, but she knew it offered only a few moments reprieve. What would she do when fire devoured the cabin? It would ignite the straw, the walls, the roof.

She'd burn to death before anyone found her.

— Twenty-nine —

Flames burst above the trees and Benjamin spurted ahead, his lantern swinging precariously near the brush beside the path. Brigit told him that she saw Adelaide heading up the hill toward the cemetery, and when fire erupted there, his only thought was to go after her. He shouted to Nathan to form a fire brigade, but Nathan only shook his head. The shack stood atop a steep embankment. They could no more quench this fire than they could the hotel fire, and then water was closer at hand.

If only she'd stopped questioning Johanna's death. Why had she kept on this disastrous quest to find someone to blame? There wasn't even a murder, they'd learned at the inquest, only a sad accident. Officially, in any case.

The blaze lit the hillside, the cemetery rising beyond it. Where Johanna lay in her watery grave. He'd turned away when they'd opened the coffin, fearful of the sight of her body after a week in the ground, then ashamed of his cowardice. And because he hadn't been able to save her.

The wind brought a rush of heat down on him, smoke burning his throat. Was Adelaide inside, struggling to free herself? Was she even conscious?

A crow shot out of a tree and swooped by his head. He swatted the bird away and quickened his steps, his breath coming in bursts of effort.

She insisted she had not harmed Johanna, but he hadn't believed her. If she was convinced someone murdered Johanna, why didn't he trust her judgment? He'd been blind to her reasoning, consumed by his own guilt. But she would never have put herself nor her family in jeopardy if she wasn't convinced she was right. He'd been so worried that she'd anger the trustees and they'd be banished that he failed to listen to her. He could have helped her, protected her, but instead he'd argued with her, ordered her to stop, and ignored the nagging suspicion that she might anger a killer.

Now maybe she had. And he couldn't let her live. How simple to start a fire in the tinderbox of a shack. Not suspicious, just unfortunate.

If she survives, he promised silently, he'd never again question her judgment. But if she dies? He'd rather die with her than face his guilt.

— Thirty —

A delaide pulled her skirts up over her head, forming a tent around her face and gasped outside air as fast as she could. Breathe normally, she told herself, purposely blowing out through her mouth. A giggle bubbled up unbidden. She could faint if she inhaled too rapidly.

Behind her the door smashed inward, igniting the coverlet. Adelaide watched mesmerized as strands of yarn, woven so carefully by Weaver Hamlin, curled into themselves, leaving wisps of blackened wool in their wake. A rush of heat hit her, bringing her attention back to the present. She raised an arm to shield her face. Beyond the wall of flames the outdoors loomed tantalizingly close. What if she tried to run through the blaze?

Her mind filled with the image from long ago of the little boy, so badly burned, he'd screamed when Emma and she tried to change his dressings. His mother begged them to leave him be, and they complied, watching helplessly as inflammation began its inevitable march through his tiny body.

No, her clothes would catch fire, her hair too. She'd rather die now than go through what she'd seen happen to that child.

The heat pressed her back against the wall. Someone surely saw the flames by now. But what could they do? Fire-quenching water lay far in the distance.

The rest of the front wall crashed to the ground with a roar, sending flaming fragments into the air. *I have to move! Do something!*

Behind her a spark ignited her skirt, and she beat at it until the flame was out. She shoved her shoulder into the opening and felt the logs give, their supports weakened by time and neglect. She took another breath in the now-widened space, turned her body sideways, and pushed again. Her upper torso was out. Balanced over the log, she drew in smoke-tainted air. To her, though, it felt like pure oxygen.

Crackling sounded behind her, and heat spread under her skirt and up her legs. She clutched the log she lay across and pulled, but her hips and tangled skirts kept her pinned in the crack. She jerked again and her skirt caught on the rough wood. Compressed between the logs she had no way to remove her clothing. She wiggled her body onto the spike near her hipbone and felt it dig into her flesh. Willing herself to remain impaled on it, she gathered her strength and twisted toward the opposite side. The fabric gave way, ripping skin off as surely as if a plow had gouged a furrow along her hip.

Her skirts torn away, Adelaide wiggled her body through the opening and dropped onto the grass. Behind her a roar sent the cabin into a spasm that shook the ground beneath her. She scooted away as the remaining walls fell. She watched the fire devour the building's remains while she hugged her knees to her chest.

Shouting roused her. A lantern bobbed down the hill, Benjamin in the lamplight. She pulled herself up and gathered the remnants of her torn skirts to her waist. She tried to call out, but smoke clogged her throat. She knew Benjamin would be frantic, thinking she'd been caught in the fire.

She turned to a rustling to her right. Someone was running down toward the river. She now knew who it was. The person who had started the fire. And murdered Johanna.

What should she do? Wait for her rescuers and relieve Benjamin's worry? Or follow a murderer?

For Adelaide it was no choice at all.

Thirty-one

A delaide rushed headlong down the path, her feet remembering the way long after darkness in the forest had closed off any remaining light. An overhanging branch snagged her already-torn skirt and, for the first time since her ordeal began, she felt tears choking her throat as she struggled in vain to free herself. Finally, she ripped her skirt to the hem and gathered the remains of it into one hand as she ran, her feet a quiet whisper on the leaf-dampened path.

At the bottom of the hill, she veered onto the path that led around the lake to the river until she reached a stand of trees and bent to gather her breath. What would she do if she caught him?

Keeping to the shadows, she crept closer.

Martin sat in the moonlight, head held high, eyes shadowed in darkness. Wind swooped from behind her and rustled the leaves above. He turned at the sound. "I told you to stay home, didn't I? I warned you. But no, you couldn't stop," he said as if he could see her.

She slid partway behind a tree.

"Think you know everything, do you? Hah! You know nothing. She sinned, that's what I know. Just like you." He smiled. A bizarre smile, to be sure, twisted to the side as if he was unused to feeling his face contorted so.

She backed up, her feet catching on a stone in the path.

He smiled the crooked smile again. "Sin. I told you. I told them all. Sin is man's downfall. But, no, she wouldn't listen. I did try to help. Offered to save her from her shame." He shook his head as if he couldn't help what he had done. "She tried to destroy her issue. That was too much to abide. I had no choice."

Whatever had caused her to think she could accost him by herself? She should creep back up the way she'd come and go for help.

"You gave her the poison. Tried to kill her sin." He held her casebook aloft. "They accuse me, they'll accuse you, too." His laugh echoed over the water. "Want me to destroy it? Your precious book? It condemns you, too. Right here on the page. Says you killed her."

"I did not!" Adelaide rushed forward, her fear forgotten. She'd teach him. He wouldn't get away with it! No matter that he wouldn't hang. If she could just have the satisfaction of watching his fall, his holier-than-thou image shattered. That would be reward enough.

Martin pivoted, side-stepping her approach, but she was moving too fast to stop. His palm caught her in mid-step. Her head snapped back, her cheek stinging as she tumbled backward and her petticoat caught on the stump. Her feet slid out, and she landed with a slam on the ground.

She scrambled to her feet and lunged at him, but he caught her shoulder and twisted her around to face him, her head bouncing about as if tied to a string. He smashed a fist into her jaw. Adelaide slumped to the ground, dizzying thoughts jumbling in her head.

Voices came from far away. Her would-be rescuers. While they doused a fire and searched for her uphill, she'd die down here as the ghost of her once-sheltering tree stood by.

His hands reached under her, and he picked her up in much the same way she'd plucked Johanna from the water. He slung her under his arm, and her head bounced as he started downhill. She flailed her arms about, but he only sniffed at her useless efforts.

The sound of rushing water came closer. *No! Not that!*

She battered him with her fists but, with her arms pinned to her side, her jabs did little. She swung her legs around but they dangled too far out of reach.

Did she deserve this? This nightmare death she'd always dreaded? Because she'd desired him? No, she'd never acted on her thoughts, sinning only in her mind.

Her casebook slid to the ground, and he shifted her to one arm to grab it. His breath smelled stale, with undigested meat.

A few more steps and they'd be at the river.

What will he tell the others? That she drowned? That he tried to save her?

My baby! Olivia. They'll take her away. Put her in the dormitory. No! That's not going to happen!

She wiggled to the side, reached up between his legs, and squeezed. He dropped her with a wail and clutched his hands to his crotch. She scrambled out of the way but his hand snaked out, and he yanked her back by her petticoat, his breath coming in gasps.

She had only a few more seconds before his pain would subside enough to release his other hand. She twisted to the side. Her petticoat tore away, and she rolled downhill, her arms drawn in automatically to cover her face, as her body gathered speed and raced toward the churning waters. She grabbed at tufts of grass, but they slipped out of her grasp. Her hand splashed in the water, and she dug her fingers into mud on the bank as the rest of her body tumbled behind her into the water. She held on as the river tried to drag her under. At last her feet touched the bottom. She rammed her shoes into the mud and, bracing herself, she pushed upright and slogged through the water and up onto the bank.

Martin rushed toward her, his face a contorted mask, her casebook grasped in one hand. She darted away but her shoes slipped on the grass and she fell forward, grabbing the tree stump as her feet slid out from under her. He pivoted on his heel and lunged for her. She threw herself aside, and he hit the stump and sprawled to its side.

She reached for her casebook, but he rose up in one sweep, grabbed her by the hair, and dumped her on the ground, her casebook falling out of her reach. She scrambled away on her belly, but he grabbed her petticoat and dragged her back. He planted one foot on her back and with an easy overhead swing, flung the book toward the river. It tumbled over and over itself until it slipped into the water with barely a sound.

"No." She thought she'd screamed, but her voice was a strangled squeak, her face smashed into the ground.

With a growl like a wounded animal, he dug both hands into her sides and lifted her up, her arms and legs flapping about uselessly. He flung her onto the ground on her back and a sound like a bone cracking jarred her elbow. Pain shot into her shoulder, and she rolled away from it, but he caught her arms and pinned her to the ground. She squeezed her eyes against the onslaught. She needed to stop struggling. It made the pain worse, and she was no match for his strength.

A rumble, almost a laugh, came from deep in his throat as he knelt and dropped one knee onto her chest. Her breath whooshed out in a gasp, and she struggled to suck in air.

The moon lit his face, tantalizingly close, pin pricks of black centered his eyes, and his mouth twisted into that taunting grin again.

Anger pounded her temples and coursed through her body. Anger at herself. She'd brought this on. Brought the law to town. Freed him from retribution, but that hadn't been enough for her. She had to come after him. Risked everything in her pursuit to right a wrong, regardless that she couldn't bring Johanna's killer to justice. Now she'd pay for her obstinacy. Pay with her life.

Olivia. Nellie. Benjamin. They didn't deserve this.

She wasn't to blame. He was! Burning, scalding rage raced through her. He killed Johanna. She'd had nothing to do with it. And now he'd never be punished, never forced to admit his guilt.

She shoved her arms against the ground and managed to raise herself a scant few inches before he slapped her, the sound echoing in the clearing.

Her ears were ringing. She had to think. What could she do?

She felt him scrabbling at her neck. Creases dug deep furrows in his forehead where beads of sweat stood out.

She'd come this far, fought so hard. She couldn't give up now.

His hair flopped forward, and she saw her chance. She grabbed a chunk of hair and jerked his head down. Salty sweat dripped on her face, but she ignored it. She stretched up and clamped her mouth onto his nose, her teeth sinking into flesh.

He screamed and clawed at her face but she held tight, blood dripping into her mouth. She stilled the gag that threatened as he thrashed about. He was up on his knees now, intent only on freeing his nose. Her head bobbed as he tried to jerk away.

She felt the crunch of bone in her mouth and let go.

He slammed her head into the ground with one hand and grabbed his face with the other. He rolled away and curled into a ball, his face cuddled in his arms.

She clutched her arm to her side and backed away. With her good arm she pushed herself into a sitting position and spit out blood.

Martin still clasped his face in his arms.

She scooted back until she reached the tree stump. She pushed against it and levered herself upright. A rush of dizziness swept over her, and she closed her eyes until her head settled.

"You want your precious book, do you?" Martin stumbled toward her, blood gushing from his face. "I'll take you to it." He lowered his head and barreled into her, taking her with him toward the river.

She clawed at him with one arm, but he only growled and shoved her backwards, her feet slipping in front of her. Suddenly she toppled over and felt herself spinning in the air until she slammed into the river on her back. Water closed over her head, and she sank, feet and arms churning as she tumbled over and over.

Quiet enveloped her in a watery cocoon. She watched her hands float above her as if an invisible puppeteer pulled them to him. Then her feet floated up, too, guided by their unseen master. What is it like to drown, she wondered, her thoughts as languid as the water swirling around her. Giddiness bubbled up inside her, a feeling almost pleasurable. A peaceful death, that's what drowning is. Trusting only what she could see and feel, she doubted heaven existed. Nonetheless, she uttered a prayer, hoping God would forgive her doubts. And her guilt.

Her heart pounded in her ears, and her lungs burned in her chest. She should do something, but she couldn't remember what.

Her back hit bottom. She flayed her arms about uselessly until her body turned itself over, and her face slapped the muddy river floor, waking her from her reverie. She shoved against the mud with more strength than she knew she had. Her face broke the surface and she gulped air. An overhanging branch dangled nearby. She reached for it but a wave slapped her back under water again. Another push upward and she grabbed the limb coming up.

Martin shoved through the murky water toward her. She yanked on the limb and pulled her feet out of the mud with a sucking sound. He reached for her but stepped instead into a sink hole and stumbled. Just when it seemed that he'd regained his footing, an undertow pulled him backward. Arms outstretched, he grabbed at the water, but his feet slipped over a drop in the riverbed.

She swung her feet wide over the roiling water and screamed for him to grab on, but the noise of the water cloaked her words. A wave washed over his face, and he sputtered, arms akimbo.

The branch above her sagged, cracking with her weight. "Hurry," she screamed at him even as she knew the limb wouldn't hold them both. Her arm ached, but still she clung on.

He gave her one last lopsided smile, spread his arms wide, and lay back. The water closed over his head as if he'd been no more than a stone dropped into the river. She kept swinging her legs until her arm gave way and she dropped into the water, clutching the tree. For a moment she watched the water rise and swell, splash over rocks, and continue its march downstream. Finally she steadied herself, took exploratory steps back through the water, and dropped face down on the bank.

Voices sounded nearby. She tried to raise her head, but it was too much effort.

— Thirty-two —

Adelaide felt herself being lifted and Benjamin's voice murmuring *"Liebchen, Liebchen."* His face nestled into her neck as he carried her, stumbling with the weight of her wet body.

"I can walk," she mumbled into his collar.

"No, not till we're home. I'm not letting go of you."

She gave herself up to the bumpy movements, lulled by the voices around her.

At home, Benjamin sat her in a chair, covered her with a warmed coverlet, and ordered Nellie to make tea. He bent to unbutton her water-logged shoes.

She started to talk, to tell him what she knew, but she could only shake. When Benjamin wrapped his arms around her, she began to cry—deep, draining, sobs neglected for too many years. Loss, grief, and longing melded into one, and she felt as if a river of emotion swelled inside, reached a crest, and then spilled away. At last she slumped forward and uttered a sigh.

Benjamin's worried face greeted her. Benjamin, who'd never coveted another. Had she sinned against him, if only in her thoughts? No, she'd already absolved herself of her temptations long before she knew Martin murdered Johanna. Cleansed, now, even in her heart.

He started to help her out of her wet clothes, but she groaned when he grabbed her arm.

"*Liebchen*, you're hurt."

"Just sore." She sent him to check on Olivia, then managed to change into dry undergarments, gritting her teeth as she pulled her arm out of the remnants of her sleeve. Burn her clothing. That's what she'd do with it even as the stench of river and death lingered in her nostrils. She crawled into bed, her body sinking into the mattress with grateful relief.

The next moment she was in the river, Olivia bobbing in front of her, just out of reach, her impotent churning only pushing her baby farther from her. She tried to scream, but no sound came out. Olivia's head dipped beneath a wave and, at the fright on her little face, Adelaide's heart constricted. She splashed harder but the more she struggled, the farther Olivia drifted away, almost as if she were inadvertently backing away from her mother.

"Wake up." Benjamin shook her.

She squinted into the sunlight, and then pushed him back so she could see his face, his eyes soft and glazed with unshed tears. With one finger she outlined the muscle on his forearm, ruffling dark hairs on his skin that stood up to her touch. She took one of his hands in hers and brought it to her mouth, stroking its rough calluses on her lips.

He moaned.

She grabbed him to her with such force that he toppled on top of her, their rope bed groaning under the weight, and bruises screaming for her to let go. But she prolonged the moment until she heard rustling from the side of the cabin. "Nellie," she whispered in Benjamin's ear. He straightened and looked down at her with such longing, and she felt a yearning for him in a way she never had before. But weariness suddenly overwhelmed her, and she sighed.

"You rest," he said, brushing her face with his whiskers. He tucked the coverlet under her chin. She wanted to be up and clean herself. Her hair, her body, every bit of her smelled rank with river water and fear.

She must have slept. The smell of coffee woke her. She slung a shawl over her underclothes and struggled to the table.

Nellie and Benjamin stood to the side, both grinning with pride at their efforts. A woven cloth graced her place at the table. On it a soft-boiled egg nestled in one of her mother's egg cups beside a bowl of warmed rhubarb liberally sprinkled with sugar and cinnamon, its crusty burnt edges attesting to the cooks' inexperience. A slice of dark bread topped with creamy cottage cheese lay on a plate, and a tiny cup of lily-of-the valley blooms sat beside it.

Tears filled her eyes as Adelaide realized how near she'd come to losing her life, this life with people she loved and who loved her, with work that gave her another kind of joy, despite her doubts, and her home where she found pleasure in the everyday tasks, even as they sometimes wearied her.

After she had eaten—Benjamin insisted on doing the clearing up—she bathed and dressed. Benjamin poured her the last of the coffee, and she had just been about to ask him what he'd heard about the night before when a knock on the door interrupted her.

Josef stood in the doorway. "I didn't know if you'd feel up to, uh, talking yet," he said, rolling his fingers along the edge of his hat, its straw bending as he did.

"Come in, come in. I want to tell you everything."

He settled himself awkwardly at the table, propping his walking stick alongside.

Benjamin started more coffee as she began her tale of the previous night's events. When she finished, Josef blew on his coffee. "You were right all along."

"Not that I take any pleasure in that."

She looked out the window where in the distance Gerda was admonishing a cringing child about something. She would not give Olivia to that woman, no matter the rule.

Benjamin interrupted her thoughts. "But how did you know it was Martin? How did you know what happened?"

"It wasn't that difficult once I knew about her bonnet—Martin was the only one who could have returned it to the dairy loft without anyone noticing—and then I remembered about the night watchman."

"I'm sorry I didn't tell you sooner." Josef cleared his throat. "And I was wrong."

She took a moment to ponder his admission, then said, "When you told me Nathan had been on watch, I knew that couldn't be right. Whoever was on watch that Sunday night—the one following Johanna's murder—was also night watchman the night she died. Nathan's week had begun the first night of the week—on Monday— and August had reinforced that when he had said his second week ended on Sunday night."

"I had it wrong," Josef said, studying her with interest.

"Besides, August told me that Martin hadn't awakened him the night Johanna died, and on Sunday night I heard Martin say he was going to start his watch."

"But why?" Benjamin asked. "What reason did he have to want Johanna dead?"

"Ahem," Josef said. "I suppose he thought she'd sinned." He shot a glance at Adelaide.

"I know about that," Benjamin said to their startled looks. "She told me, well, hinted."

"I thought you should know what people think," Josef said and gave Benjamin a keep-this-to-yourself look.

Benjamin nodded.

"It's simple," Josef said and turned to Adelaide. "Martin drowned, and you jumped in to try to save him. That's it. All think well of you for that."

She smiled ruefully. "For the wrong reason, though. No one knows he murdered Johanna then? And that he tried to kill me?"

He shook his head.

"So his reputation is intact."

"Adelaide," he warned. "It's not up to you to judge. He's before a higher power now."

"But don't you think someone ought to know? The Appelgates?"

"What good would that do? Their daughter's dead and knowing who killed her would only distress them all the more."

"But they'll go on thinking—"

"That she drowned and that it was an accident. There's no need for them or anyone else to know otherwise. Agreed?" he asked, directing a look at each of them.

"I did try to save him," she said.

"Even though you knew he murdered Johanna?" Benjamin asked.

"I'm not surprised," Josef said. "You always do what you know to be right."

She inclined her head at the compliment.

He went on. "There is one thing, though. Brigit brought me this." He pulled a folded square of paper out of his pants pocket and handed it to Adelaide.

Inside lay several dried nightshade leaves.

"She found it in Martin's cabin."

Adelaide scrunched the paper into a wad, bits of leaves scattering on the table.

"I want to thank you, Adelaide, for pursuing this in spite of my reservations—"

"And mine," added Benjamin. He lay a roughened hand over her smaller one.

"So we three are the only ones who know," she mused. "Oh, the election. Was Benjamin elected?"

"He was, and Nathan will be trustee for another three years. The Articles of Incorporation were passed with only two dissenting votes, and presumably Martin and Simon cast those. Simon's admitted as much. He told some of the men that Martin had planned to run for trustee next year. Their goal, it seems, was to replace the current trustees with their cronies."

"And ultimately you," Adelaide added.

"It seems that may have been their intent. Simon, at least, is still determined to do away with our communal way of life. He says we're behind the times here in America." He stomped his walking stick on the floor. "But that's not going to happen. Not as long as I'm alive."

"Marriage still intact?" she asked with a smile for Benjamin.

"Yes. The only way they could have managed that would be to have the Articles fail and then bring amendments forward. Those would have to be voted on and, if passed, the amended document voted on again. That, too, won't happen in my lifetime. How else are we to continue?" he asked rhetorically. "In any case, Simon is lying low up at the inn and about time. Maybe now he can begin to make some money."

"Oh." She jumped up. "I should be up there checking on Maria. See to her and her baby—"

"She's taken care of," Josef said. "Helga took some women up there this morning and one of them plans to stay with her through the night. And I hear the babe has a lusty cry."

"She said something about Simon, Maria did. She thought he was doing something he shouldn't."

"He'd been talking to Martin about you," Benjamin said to Josef.

"I'll keep a watch on him," Josef said, leaning on the table for support.

"Let me know what you find out," Adelaide said.

Josef tilted his head to the side as if thinking about what she'd asked. Had she convinced him that she had more than medical skills, that she could think, solve problems, help him?

Finally he nodded, and Adelaide stifled her pleasure.

Later, she made her way outside. All around her apple trees had blossomed into bloom, filling the air with their scent, and spreading petals on the ground. She bent to gather a handful and buried her face in their faint fragrance. Finally, she tossed them aside and started down the road to the river.

She stood beside the remains of her tree, its stump the only reminder of her shelter, and stared at the water tumbling easily over itself. She imagined that at any moment Martin would reappear, trudging out of the water, her casebook in hand, with the smile that she'd seen only at the end.

He had been willing to give up his vow of celibacy to save Johanna from the shame. And she would have turned him down, probably laughed at him. After offering to sacrifice his salvation for her, that would be all it took to trigger his rage.

She ran her hands over the boulder. This spot, so long her refuge, was only a place, a place where she had been able to draw into herself. She thought she needed to be here to find illumination or consolation. But she had learned that it wasn't the place, but her own thoughts that soothed her, that made clear what she needed to do. The power wasn't at this place, or anywhere else, for that matter. It was inside her. And she could reach within whenever she needed to.

She fingered a tiny green sprout that had broken through the jagged edge of the tree stump, and turned toward home.

— Author's Note —

Our grandmother taught my sister and me to revere the village our ancestor, Joseph Bimeler, led, but it took many long years for me to recognize how singular the place and its people were. This is the first book in a series of fictitious mysteries that I've set amidst the lives of these unique people.

Escaping religious persecution in their native Germany, the Society of Separatists founded the village of Zoar, named for the place where Lot found sanctuary just as they did in Northern Ohio in 1817. The Society prospered until 1898, when it was disbanded. Today, the village thrives with a plethora of museums, shops, and homes, providing living history events for schoolchildren and visitors alike.

As he did in reality, Joseph Bimeler plays a central role in my story. Much has been written about this distant grandfather of mine, so his actions are as true to life as possible. In fact, his Sunday discourse in this story includes his actual words as transcribed by a Separatist at the time. His wife, Dorothea, and his son, Peter, are mentioned, but little is known about them. All other characters are figments of my imagination. Unlike in my fiction, though, no murder ever occurred in historic Zoar.

With appreciation for the fine work by Edgar Nixon in his 1933 Ohio State University dissertation, *The Society of Separatists of Zoar*, and to Kathleen Fernandez for her knowledge and her book, *A Singular People: Images of Zoar*, I have attempted to create a work that is historically accurate. Any mistakes, however, are mine alone.

Bringing my ancestors' lives to the page in a series of fictitious mysteries has been my passion and my pleasure.

—*Eleanor Sullivan*

CPSIA information can be obtained at www.ICGtesting.com
Printed in the USA
LVOW091722280911

248288LV00002B/31/P